Mary

by
Rhonda Kulczyk

Mary
Copyright © 2018 by Rhonda Kulczyk. All rights reserved.

Published by *Freedom Series.*
P.O. Box 3211
Boone, NC 28607
rhondakulczyk.com

Published in the United States of America
ISBN: 978-0-9988327-7-7

Foreword

My favorite Christmas song for as long as I can remember has been "Mary, Did You Know?" The lyrics of that song are so beautiful. Every time I hear them, I get goosebumps. Every single time. "When you kiss your little baby, you kiss the face of God." Wow!

And then a few years back, a man named David Blust got up and spoke about Mary in our church, and I'll never forget what he said that morning.

He spoke about Mary and how when most people thought of Mary, they thought of what a blessing it had to have been to be chosen to be the mother of Jesus. And it was. But rarely do we think of everything she most likely had to endure and overcome when she accepted her role as the mother of Jesus.

God must have chosen her because she was faithful. He must have chosen her because she was pure. And yet she spent the rest of her life with people doubting her faithfulness, her purity. I left church that morning with a new awareness and a new appreciation for Mary.

And I knew that day I would write a book about her.

I don't pretend to be some great historian or Bible expert. I don't have a PhD or a doctorate in anything. I'm just a small-town girl who loves Jesus and is so thankful for His birth, His life, His death, and His resurrection. I hope you enjoy my imagined story of Mary.

Merry Christmas,
Rhonda Kulczyk

Nazareth was a lovely little town snuggled in the hills overlooking the broad and fertile valley of lower Galilee. It consisted primarily of small white stone houses. A synagogue rested on its highest knoll, and a marketplace stood at the entrance to the village. We were farmers, although there were also some skilled craftsmen among us whose shops were found in the marketplace—a potter, a weaver, a dyer, a blacksmith, and a carpenter, to name a few.

Nazareth was my home. I was born here. And with just over three hundred residents living here, it would have been impossible not to notice him.

I forced my gaze away from his as I followed my parents across the packed dirt floor, quickly taking my place on the stone bench next to my mother. I could feel his eyes studying me. Had he also felt the connection when our eyes met ever so briefly as I entered the synagogue?

I refused to look his way and instead focused on the aged rabbi as he opened the Torah and began reading. For several minutes, I concentrated on the words spoken by the rabbi. But no matter how I resisted, my eyes found his a second time.

His name was Joseph. And seated next to him were his younger brother Cleophas and their father Jacob. His mother had passed away several years ago. I had learned this information from Zillah, my closest friend.

I startled when my mother's calloused hand covered mine. A quick glance at her face was a reminder to pay attention and focus on the mundane voice echoing throughout the synagogue.

The Lord spoke to Moses, saying, Speak to the children of Israel, and let them turn back and encamp in front of Pi hahiroth, between Migdol and the sea; in front of Baal Zephon, you shall encamp opposite it, by the sea. And Pharaoh will say about the children of Israel, They are trapped in the land. The desert has closed in upon them. And I will harden Pharaoh's heart, and he will pursue them, and I will be glorified through Pharaoh and through his entire force, and the Egyptians will know that I am the Lord…

Zillah appeared at my side as soon as I cleared the door of the synagogue. She nodded her head toward the hillside in front of us. I obediently looked to my father. When he nodded his consent, I took off after Zillah, my leather sandals slowing me down. But I knew better than to take them off with the entire assembly of people gathered outside. It took several minutes before we reached the top, both of us gasping for breath.

"Did you see him?" Zillah finally managed to rasp as we both dropped to the dusty ground beneath my favorite Sycamore tree.

I purposefully delayed my answer, pretending to study the branches high above. I had been sitting beneath this very tree since before I could walk. At over 175 feet tall, it was by far the tallest tree on this hill. I reached out and picked up one of the leaves that had just recently fallen from one of its branches. For years I had measured my hands by the size of this tree's leaves. I could still hear my father's words.

When your hand is the size of this leaf, dear daughter, your betrothal will soon follow. My hand was nearly the size of the leaf beneath it, and I felt my face flush red.

"So you did see him," Zillah nudged my arm playfully. "Isn't he hand-some?" She lay beneath the tree with a contented sigh.

Again I refused to answer. How could I? I was all but betrothed to Zillah's older brother, Yosef. "How old do you think he is?" I finally asked a question of my own.

"My father says he's twenty-one." Zillah rolled over onto her side, her eyes vibrant and alive for the first time in months. "I think I'm in love."

"Like you are in love with Micah? Or wait, is it Calev?" I dodged the small pebble she flicked my way.

"Not all of us have the advantage of knowing who we are going to mar-ry from the day we are born, Mary."

Zillah was right about this. I had always known that Yosef and I would someday marry. There was a certain comfort in knowing he would be my husband. I was almost certain our formal betrothal would be announced soon. As was custom, after a year, we would then celebrate with a ceremony where we would pledge our lives to one another. "He is three years older than Yosef. I'm surprised he doesn't already have a wife."

"He's been waiting for me," Zillah replied dreamily.

Hearing voices nearby, we both sat up as Yosef and his friend Calev came up over the hill. "I should have known this is where you would be," Yosef directed my way.

I studied Yosef more intently than I ever had before. For years we had been mere friends. Now, there was a certain awkwardness between us that had never been there before. He had grown especially handsome in the last several months.

"Your father asked that I find you," he said. "Your mother needs help with the supper preparations."

I stood to my feet, gently brushing loose twigs and dirt from my tunic. My mother would not be pleased. She had only just finished making my linen tunic mere days ago. Long after I had retired to bed, I could still hear her soft, melodious humming as she had intricately woven each design into the linen material. I would take it off behind our home and shake every last piece of dirt from it. I rushed past Yosef, his voice calling from behind me.

"Wait, Mary. I'll walk with you."

"No need." I knew if he walked me home, I'd never have a chance to shake the dirt free from my outer garment. I heard him protest but hurried on. Halfway down the hill, I looked back. He hadn't followed but stood watching me from the top, disappointment marring his features. I stumbled but was able to right myself. I hurried by each home before finally coming to my own, where I watchfully moved around the house to the back and into the shadows.

Removing my tunic, I shook it as hard as possible, watching the dust fly from the material just as I had hoped. Of course, this wasn't the first time I had tried this simple technique.

I froze as I heard a chuckle only steps away from where I now stood. The tunic slipped from my hands and flew through the air, landing with almost expert design at this young man's feet. I forced my gaze up and froze a second time as I stared into *his* dark brown eyes. Another chuckle escaped his lips as he reached down to pick up my tunic.

"You seem to have dropped something," he voiced with humor. He was now standing in front of me, my tunic dangling from his large, tanned hand.

I yanked the tunic out of his hand and rushed into the house without any reply. It was then that I realized my mistake, for both my father and my mother stared at me from across the room. *Could I have made any more of a dramatic entrance?*

"Mary, why are you not wearing your outer garment?" The voice belonged to my father.

I looked at the tunic clutched in my right hand, and all rational words fled. *Why indeed was my tunic still in my hand and not covering my body?*

My face flushed ten shades of red, which I quickly realized only made me look guiltier. I groaned with the realization that *Joseph* had in a matter of minutes seen more of my skin than Yosef had in all the years I had grown up with him.

"Are you hurt, Mary?" My father walked toward me, his eyes now filled with alarm.

"No, I'm not hurt." I forced myself to look up into my father's concerned eyes. "I managed to cover my new garment in dust while visiting with Zillah beneath the Sycamore tree. And I had hoped to shake the dust free before I entered the house, only I saw someone coming and realized I needed to cover myself quickly, but I was running out of time, so I hurried into the house to escape being seen by the passerby."

I saw the twinkle in my father's eyes even though he did his best to hide it from me.

"Well, let's hope the passerby wasn't our dear rabbi," my mother voiced as she took the dirty tunic from my hand and set it over in the washing pile. "I had hoped you'd get several more days of wear from this before I needed to wash it, but no matter. We'll have it clean again soon. You'll have to wear your old one if you plan to go out again today."

"Yes, Mother. Is there anything I can help you with?" I threw out the question hoping to move our conversation in a different direction, but my father was much too clever for that.

"Did you recognize the passerby?" My father was standing over by the window and had gently pushed aside the curtain to peer outside.

How I hated to answer his question, but I knew better than to lie. Lying not only hurt me but it hurt those I loved, and perhaps more importantly, it hurt the One who mattered more to me than all else. My heavenly Father. "Yes. It was the new boy. I believe his name is Joseph."

"Ah, yes." The curtain dropped back into place. "I spoke with him after the meeting. He seems very kind. I don't believe he'll spread any rumors, even if he did see my daughter's *bare* arms." My father turned toward me, a smile displayed on his lips. "Although, daughter, this should be an opportunity to learn from. What if it had been someone else? In order for me to protect you, I need you to follow the rules of our culture. Which one did you break today?"

I joined my mother, taking from her hands two flat stones. Methodically I began grinding the corn in the wooden bowl into powder. "I took off my outer garment before I entered the confines of my home."

I watched my father return to his chair by the window and lift the scroll from the ledge where he had set it when I so rudely burst into the house not long before. He glanced over at me before he resumed his reading, his kind eyes letting me know he loved me unconditionally. I felt my eyes well up with tears, and I blinked rapidly trying to rid myself of them. It was of no use, for my mother took notice. I felt her gentle hand upon my shoulder, proving to me her love was just as steadfast.

I stepped from the house the next morning, the water pitcher held snug on my shoulder. As was routine, I made my way toward Nazareth's only spring, located at the edge of town. The spring had long been a source of concern as the village was hindered by its poor water supply. The water was clean but simply could not sustain further growth.

I waved to Abana, my neighbor, who was outside with her small daughter, shaking dust from their sleeping mats. "What a good helper you are, Lillian!" I stooped down, careful to keep the pitcher steady on my arm. "If you're a good helper this week, I'll take you with me to the race on the hill." This earned me a wide smile from the blond-haired child.

"May I, Mother?" Lillian quickly turned toward her mother in eager expectation.

"If you are a good helper, like Mary is to her mother, then yes, you may go to the race on Friday afternoon."

I stood to my feet once again, remembering just how well I had listened to my mother yesterday, which was why I was now covered in my old, frayed tunic instead of my beautiful new one. I said my farewells and continued on my way to the spring. Looking up, I took note of the farming terraces dotting the hillside above. There was also a tall watchtower where the men took turns keeping watch during the dark hours in order to prevent thieves from stealing our grapes, olives, or grains. The village depended on the land's produce to pay taxes. We lived off of what was left.

My steps slowed as I neared the edge of town. I was tempted to turn around and return home without our daily supply of water, but after yesterday's catastrophe I couldn't quite bring myself to do so. I'm not sure how long I stood there debating if I could make myself invisible, but *his* voice startled me once again from my reverie.

"I'm sure she doesn't bite." He was standing right behind me, and the words he'd just whispered sent a tingle down my back.

If only he knew. Dinah, daughter of Alad, did indeed bite. For some reason, she had made it her mission in life to tear me to shreds with her words. And to make matters worse, she had such a *nice* way of doing so. In fact, to the general public she seemed to be complimenting me when she was, in fact, dishonoring my father, my mother, and myself. The most irritating fact was that I didn't know why she disliked me so. I had never intentionally said or done anything to deserve her hatred.

"You're next." Joseph threw out his arm and bowed in dramatic display. I would have smiled if Dinah wasn't swaying toward us. She had a voluptuous figure and often used it to garner the attention of the men. She barely glanced my way, her eyes centered on Joseph alone.

You are invisible…you are invisible… I silently whispered as I moved stealthily away from her advance and toward the cistern. "It truly is a shame, Mary, that your parents cannot afford an outer garment better than the one you have on. My goodness, your tunic is so worn, I can almost see through it."

I had been hoping she would be so enthralled with the new man in town that she would simply ignore me for once. I should have known better. Of course she would use me as her pawn to procure Joseph's attention. And now that she had humiliated me, I knew what was coming next.

"I have several extra tunics, Mary, if you'd like to borrow one," Dinah offered, although her tantalizing eyes never left Joseph's face.

I was now at the well, my hands busy with the tethered rope as I brought up the bucket made of sheepskin. I could hear water splashing over the sides and silently thanked God for the water he had provided me with today. My prayer was interrupted by Joseph's sincere words.

"Actually, Mary has a beautiful tunic which regrettably met an unfortunate mishap yesterday." My eyes connected with his, and I realized with satisfaction he was not the least bit affected by the beautiful attention-seeking woman at his side. And perhaps even more gratifying was that he knew Dinah was insulting me.

Dinah's eyes blinked rapidly as she fought hard to find something else to say. "My, but this pitcher is growing heavy…"

I barely managed to contain my smile as I watched Joseph step back out of her way. "Excuse me for standing in your way. Please, continue on." The look on Dinah's face was absolute shock. I had never before seen her speechless. She studied Joseph a few seconds longer before turning away and swaying her hips toward home.

I filled my pitcher to the brim with water. Carefully placing the pitcher on my shoulder once again, I began to stand to my feet. Out of nowhere, I felt his hand on my elbow. He removed his hand once I was steady on my feet.

I nodded my thanks and turned to leave, but had only taken three steps when I remembered our incident yesterday and my need to apologize. I turned back toward him. In just a matter of seconds, he had drawn the bucket full of water to the top of the well and was now spilling its contents into the large sheepskin he had at his side. It was the duty of the women to get the family supply of water each day. It was then that I realized there was no woman in his family's home, his mother having passed away.

"I'm sorry." The words were said before I knew what I was saying.

Joseph lifted his head. "Sorry for what?" He stared at me with his intense eyes. Eyes that spoke even when he wasn't speaking. How could that be?

"I want to apologize for my unseemly behavior yesterday afternoon. It was never my intention for you to…to…" I felt the heat spreading over my cheeks and down my neck.

"To see your inner tunic?" His mischievous eyes bated me.

"You see, I had…"

"Grown hot and simply could not wait a few seconds longer until you were in the safety of your home."

"You're putting words in my mouth, sir." I couldn't help but smile at his contagious laughter. Even his brown eyes danced with humor.

"But that wasn't what you were apologizing for, was it?"

How could he read me so proficiently after only a few moments together? "I am sorry about the loss of your mother." I forced the words out, even though my mind told me not to. The sparkle in his eyes dimmed and the smile left his face. I knew then that his mother was as dear to him as mine was to me, and he missed her terribly.

I knew not what else to say, so I turned and made my way toward home.

My forehead was beaded with perspiration when I at last crested the hill with Lillian on my hip. I gently placed her on her feet. At four years old, the climb was short but steep, and she had quickly grown tired.

"Are you racing today, Mary?"

"I'd better! Once I'm betrothed, I can no longer partake in these silly activities." Lillian's giggle brought a smile to my own lips. We made our way toward the crowd of young people. I searched for Yosef but could not find him. This wasn't the first time he had been missing from such a function. It seemed he missed more than he attended as of late. I noticed Zillah waving for us to join her.

"Is Yosef still in the fields?" I couldn't help inquiring. He usually loved attending the races as much as I did.

"Yosef? He's not here? He left the house before I did."

I did my best to put all thoughts of Yosef aside. There were many reasons he might not have joined us on the hill, although I could not think of any at the moment.

Calev raised a hand, and a hush fell over the crowd. "If you plan to race, please make your way to me. We will divide into teams before long."

I left Lillian in Zillah's capable hands and joined the group of racers. We were quickly divided into two teams, starting with the youngest to the oldest. We tried to keep it fair by racing each participant with someone of their own age and gender. This was an easy enough task with the younger children, but not many females desired to race at my age. So I was usually paired with a male, which made the opponent's loss even harder to swallow. I had always loved to run, and I was quick on my feet. We formed two lines, beginning with the youngest and ending with the oldest.

It was then that I noticed Joseph. He was leaning against *my* tree. Even though I was surrounded by people, I knew his eyes were only on me. Not once had I felt self-conscious about running in front of anyone until this moment. The screaming voices brought me back to reality. The race had begun. We cheered for one another until our voices grew hoarse.

"We're behind several paces, Mary. If we've ever needed your speed, it's now." The voice behind me belonged to Calev. I nodded my head in acknowledgement, as I gently slipped my bare feet from the confines of my sandals.

This was perhaps the only time I approved of wearing a girdle. The wide belt came in very useful in tying my inner and outer tunics up above my knees. It was impossible to run at full speed if my legs were hindered by my garments. I quickly made use of the girdle as the runner ahead of me was already making his way back. Double-checking the knot, I bent in as modest a position as possible, my right leg slightly ahead of my left. The runner's hand tagged mine, and I bolted from my spot.

It only took four strides to overtake the boy on my left. I rounded the marked tree and made my way back toward the finish line. Knowing *he* was watching made me push harder than I ever had before. I was several paces ahead of my competition when I tagged Calev's outstretched hand. I sank to my knees in exhaustion, a feeling of lightheadedness overtaking me. I fought hard against the darkness, only to succumb to it completely.

A soothing masculine voice was the first thing I heard when I awoke. It was the strangest feeling, not knowing where I was or in whose arms I was laying. I desperately tried to open my eyes, but my eyelids simply refused to obey my command.

"Please, stand back. She needs room to breathe." It was the soothing voice again.

As my consciousness improved, so did my senses. The strong arms holding me felt warm and secure. They also felt delightful. *Delightful?* My eyelids immediately opened, and I was staring into *his* comforting eyes.

"What happened?" It took me a moment to realize the raspy sounding voice was my own.

"I'm not quite sure." One of Joseph's eyebrows rose a notch.

How was it even possible this one tiny movement could improve his good looks even more?

"One second, you were running like the wind; the next, you were lying on the ground."

I felt someone pulling on my outer tunic. Looking down, I saw a frightened Lillian staring back at me. "Where's Zillah?" I asked.

"She went to get your father."

I closed my eyes in despair. How much more embarrassment could I bring my poor family? My parents had been barren for over fifteen years. Fifteen years! And then God had blessed their barrenness with me.

What were You thinking, Father God?

When I opened my eyes again, there was a crinkle in Joseph's eyes—much like my father's when he found humor with me.

"You can put me down now. I believe I'm stable enough to stand on my own."

Joseph gently placed me on my feet, the crowd beginning to disperse now that they knew I was alive and well. He kept both hands on each side of my arms until he was sure I was steady on my feet. Dropping his hands to his sides, he took a step back, only to quickly step forward again.

"Mary," his tender voice whispered. "Something has just come to my attention." He shrugged off his cloak and, in one swift movement, his cloak surrounded me. At first I tried to resist, but then I saw my parents rushing toward me, their faces displaying deep worry.

Joseph relayed to them what had happened. After I assured them I was fine, they led me away from the hillside and back toward the safety of our home. It wasn't until later in the evening that I realized I was still wearing *his* cloak. Odd how warm it made me feel, and not just in a physical sense. I reluctantly took it off and was in the process of hanging it on the hook by the door when I heard my mother gasp.

"What is it?" I examined myself carefully but could not for the life of me see anything out of the ordinary.

"You're bleeding, Mary."

I pulled my tunic around and gasped in horror. There was blood! And not just a speck or a spot. It could not even be considered a smudge. Rather, it was a splotch. A huge red splotch. This was my moment of celebration. For I was now fully considered a woman in every sense of the word. My menstruation had finally begun.

But the only thing I could think of was *his* words to me before he had covered me with *his* cloak. *Something has just come to my attention.* I quickly snatched his cloak off the hook and, with horror, noticed a small smudge of my blood there as well.

"Don't worry, daughter. I will wash your inner and outer tunic this evening while you rest." My mother finally noticed the cloak in my trembling hands. "Is that Joseph's?"

I was at a loss for words and could only nod my head yes. She gently took it from my arms. "I will wash this as well, and your father can return it to him in the morning after it has had time to dry."

A few hours later, I carried my mat to the rooftop. My parents seemed to understand my need for solitude. In fact, they had encouraged it. I lay out under the stars, my father's cloak covering me. We often slept here on the rooftop during the heat of summer, and it was one of my favorite things to do. Summer was over and had been for several weeks. The nights had a defining chill I wasn't accustomed to, but I did not care.

I rolled over onto my side, my mind racing. My mother had tried to waylay my fears, but I still had so many questions.

I had finally entered the *betulah* phase of womanhood, the phase between puberty and giving birth. It was during this phase that some man would offer my father a contract of marriage. The most important part of the contract was the bride price, which was the price the young man was willing to pay to marry me. My father was not a wealthy man, and I was his only child. My bride price would secure a stable future for both my mother and father.

For the next several days, I would be relieved of many of my normal duties. My mother would get our daily supply of water. My main duty was to think and rest. After menstruation, I would be allowed to bathe from head to toe in the *mikveh* just outside of the village. It was a pool of clean water designed in a unique way. The pool of water allowed enough headroom so that the woman could completely immerse her body in the water. My mother had told me the washing of the body in this way was a tangible way for a woman to renew herself mentally, emotionally, as well as physically.

My mind was so engrossed in these matters that it took time to register the familiar voices inside the house. I sat up on my mat when I recognized the voices belonging to Zillah and Yosef. Standing to my feet, I silently moved toward the stairs leading down from the roof. I sat down on the first step, inclining my head to the side so I could to hear what was being said.

"She's in good health," I heard my mother say.

"In good health? Healthy people don't pass out in the middle of the day. It wasn't even hot outside." This was Yosef. I was relieved to hear the concern in his voice.

"She just needs a good night's sleep," my father said next. "Thank you, Zillah, for returning Mary's sandals. We must have forgotten them on the hill in all the confusion."

"I don't believe it's wise for Mary to continue racing. I've told her so on many occasions, but she seems resistant to listen to me."

Resistant?

I remembered our discussion a few weeks back. Yosef had expressed to me that he thought I was too old to race, but I had thought he was teasing. If he had asked me with kindness, I would have been happy to comply.

"Mary is hardly resistant." My father's defending words warmed my heart. "Now, I will admit my daughter has an adventurous spirit, which has at times brought about unintended mishap." I could hear the humor in my father's voice, and it brought a smile to my face.

"It's time for her to marry and settle down," Yosef responded, no humor evident his voice. "I will speak to my father, and we will draw up a contract."

I stood to my feet and crept back to my mat. Yosef's words should have reassured me of his commitment, but they did not. Two words continued to replay in my mind. *Settle down, settle down, settle down.* Was he suggesting he was not content with who I was now? Did I need to become less *adventurous* in order to make him pleased with me?

For the first time ever, I questioned my ability to make Yosef happy. It was a long time before I fell asleep, and it wasn't due to the cool temperature outside.

My father's words could not have described me more accurately. *Adventurous.* After three days of being confined behind closed doors, I felt an intense need to go outside, if only to stare up into the great sky above. I felt like a caged animal awaiting its escape. The end of the week could not come soon enough.

I had not attended the meeting at the synagogue the day before, and I missed seeing all the familiar faces of the village. My father said he'd done his best to answer the concerned questions over my well-being. After my fainting spell on Friday evening and then missing the meeting just two days after, I could see how I would be an interesting topic of conversation.

We had just finished our evening devotions when my father stood to his feet and gathered both his and my cloak in his arms. I eyed him with uncertainty, but felt instant relief when he smiled and draped my cloak over me. "We should be fine, don't you think, daughter, to take a quick stroll to the vineyards and back again?"

I threw my arms around him and kissed him on both cheeks. He knew my heart so well.

"Heli," my mother admonished kindly. "You do spoil this dear daughter of ours."

"Yes, well, I will have to part with her someday, so I aim to take advantage of this time when I am the only man in her life." My parents shared a meaningful smile before my father linked his arm through my own, and we made our way outdoors.

"Thank you, Father," I whispered as I leaned in against him. The night was still and although there was a full moon in the sky above us, the sky had blackened considerably with dark clouds. I could smell the scent of rain.

My father was staring at the dark clouds as well. "Our walk may be cut short, but we'll at least get in a few paces to calm this restless daughter of mine."

We soon left the village and made our way along the worn path toward the vineyards. Several minutes passed in comfortable silence. I considered my compassionate father beside me, recognizing how I had taken him for granted. My upcoming betrothal made me entirely aware of what his absence from my life would feel like. I let my hand fall from his arm and gently intertwined my fingers with his weathered ones.

"Father?"

"Yes, daughter?"

"How did you know mother was the one you were supposed to spend your life with?"

"I knew it…here." He patted his heart with his free hand. "But before I knew, I prayed for God's wisdom. Finding the right partner is perhaps the most important decision you'll ever make. It affects the rest of your life."

"I thought I knew but lately I've felt…unsure." We had stopped walking, and I wasn't sure who had turned toward who first. "Do you think Yosef is right for me, Father?" I searched his eyes for assurance but didn't find it. Instead I read uncertainty, the same as me.

He cupped both my cheeks in his warm hands. "Daughter, I do not have that assurance, but do know I am diligently seeking our Father for His guidance…for His wisdom. And I will not give you to any man until I have attained it."

A warm tear fell on my cheek and then another. My father took the edge of his cloak and gently wiped away my tears. "You will not leave my house until I am certain the man wishing to marry you will offer you the same protection I have offered you these many years."

A rain drop fell. And then another. We turned and hastily made our way toward home.

I slept peacefully that night, dreaming of the delicate purple flowers that grew among the rocks where I used to play as a small child. I'd jump from rock to rock holding tightly to my father's hand, knowing he'd catch me if ever I should stumble.

I followed my mother up the winding path toward the *mikveh*, where a hollow space had been formed inside a cave. Several cisterns had been cut into the soft limestone of the hillside so fresh rainwater could collect and drain into the deep basin. I listened carefully as my mother explained the ritual of our Jewish rite for purification. She then left, and I stood silently watching her until she walked out of sight.

Gently laying out my clean undergarments and outer tunic I then cautiously undressed and deposited my soiled garments in a pile. There was a small pool at the entrance of the cave where I washed my hands and then my feet. Finally, I entered the main pool. The chill took my breath away. I did not look forward to the more frigid temperatures in the cooler months to come.

I closed my eyes and counted to three before submerging my entire body beneath the surface of the water. Full immersion into the water was necessary to become pure again. Since I wasn't married yet, the practice of purification was primarily to initiate the tradition of our people. After marriage, the ritual would become necessary before my husband and I could resume marital relations. I felt my face warm at the thought.

My body shivering uncontrollably, I pushed to the surface. During the summer months, the water would be much warmer and surely a more enjoyable experience. I walked up the stone steps of the pool and wrapped the linen cloth around my trembling body. Once dry, I quickly dressed and left the cave.

The bright sun beckoned me further up the mountain. I knew I should return home, but I instead began to ascend further up the trail. My wet, tangled hair was in desperate need of a comb, but I couldn't resist. The climb was exhilarating and quickly warmed my cold body.

Oop, oop, oop. I stopped in my tracks to study the bird directly in front of me foraging in the dirt for something to eat. It was a Hoopoe. I knew by its distinctively tapered bill. Even as a small child, I had been entranced by the movement of their wings. Where the wings of most birds opened and closed fully, the movements of the Hoopoe's wings strongly resembled those of a butterfly. They opened and closed partially with a short sequence of beats. Sensing my presence, the bird made a *charrrr* sound and immediately took flight.

I continued up the hill. When I reached the top, I closed my eyes, lifting my face towards the bright sun. How I loved the Creator of heaven and of earth. *I love You, Father,* my heart cried out. I lifted my hands towards the heavens and began to spin in circles, laughter bursting forth.

This time, I shouted the words. "I love You, Creator of heaven and earth!" I heard the words echo off the rocks below. Eventually I grew unsteady on my feet and was forced to sit down.

I sat for some time in silence until suddenly I felt the presence of another and turned to find *him* watching me from the tree line. I felt my cheeks redden in embarrassment. How long had Joseph been standing there?

How childish he must think I am.

When I had built up the courage to look again, he was making his way toward me. I quickly turned my head away, and began studying the valley below. I didn't want to face him. Couldn't he just leave and pretend he had never seen me?

He sat down beside me and didn't say anything for several long, excruciating minutes. Finally, unable to bear the torture any longer, I turned toward him. He managed to conceal his smile, but the amusement in his eyes was impossible to hide.

"I'm glad to see you're feeling so much better, Mary."

"I am…feeling better. Thank you, Joseph."

A few more minutes of awkward silence passed by. I wanted to thank him for the use of his cloak several days earlier, but it brought up such painfully mortifying details that I could not bring myself to utter the words. It was best left unsaid.

"I love this view," he quietly said. "You can see for many miles in three different directions." I knew he was looking at me, but I couldn't face him quite yet. He lifted his tan hand and signaled toward the south. "Over there is the Jezreel Valley. So many significant battles were fought there, one of them Gideon's defeat of the Midianites." He pointed again in another direction. "And over there, to the west, is Mount Carmel where Elijah defeated the prophets of Baal."

He was looking at me again, and finally I brought my timid eyes up to meet his. I instantly forgot my humiliation and was instead struck by the zeal in his eyes. "I would have loved to have been a spectator that day when Elijah proved that God, and not Baal, was the one true God," he said.

"I love that story too." My voice was tinged with excitement. "The prophets of Baal called upon the name of their god for hours without any results."

"They even cut themselves with their swords, believing their blood would spur Baal to move on their behalf." Joseph's eyes searched my own.

"And then before Elijah prayed, he made a trench around the altar and had it filled with water until not only the trench was full, but the altar was soaked with water as well." My voice shook with emotion.

"With one prayer, the fire of the Lord fell and consumed the burnt offering and the stones and dust as well. The fire even evaporated all the water that was in the trench." A raindrop fell on Joseph's cheek, and we both looked up at the sky. Dark clouds hovered over us. Joseph stood to his feet and reached down for my hand.

I hesitated only briefly before I slid my small hand in his strong warm one. He gently pulled me to my feet, and we hurried toward the trees where we'd begin to descend the hill. Suddenly, I remembered my soiled clothes and veered off course for a moment to retrieve them. He stood waiting for me by the worn path, gesturing for me to pass in front of him. We were halfway down the hill when he spoke from behind me.

"Ironic, isn't it? After God proved He was the one and only God, He then sent a heavy rain." As if to emphasize Joseph's words, a flash of lightening moved across the sky, followed by a loud crack of thunder. And then sheets of rain fell from the heavens.

We were both soaked through by the time we came to the village. "I've been purified twice today." *Had I just said the words aloud?* The gleam in his eyes was proof that I had. I hurried in front of him, hoping now that we had reached the safety of the village, he would head to his own home. He didn't. He walked me to my door and then stood there in silence, waiting for me to go inside.

I looked up and found him studying me. The rain on my face, the wind on my skin, they were chilling and sent a shiver down my spine. He reached his hand forward as if to wipe away the moisture on my cheek. The door opened. There stood my father. And directly behind him stood Yosef.

I stood, my eyes downcast, staring at my muddy sandals. I was unable to think of anything to say. My father reached out, grasping my cold hand in his warm one and pulling me into our home. "You're nearly chilled through, Mary." He gently removed my wet cloak, and a few seconds later, I felt him drape his own cloak around me.

"Where have you been, Mary?"

The voice belonged to Yosef. I lifted my gaze to meet his. His eyebrows were creased in frustration. Suddenly remembering Joseph, I turned toward the doorway, but he was gone and the door was closed.

"I was…" I felt too embarrassed to say the words aloud, and I knew he would take my embarrassment as guilt. Thankfully my mother filled in the rest.

"Mary was bathing at the *mikveh.*"

Realization registered in Yosef's eyes. For a brief moment he seemed pleased, but then his eyes once again filled with irritation. "But that doesn't explain Joseph's presence."

"The sun was shining so beautifully, so when I was done bathing, I took the path to the top of the hill. Joseph happened upon me as I was getting ready to leave, and it began raining halfway down."

"Well, that explains your soaked garments and muddy sandals," my mother said. "Supper is now ready. Shall we eat?"

We gathered in a circle on the ground, my father blessing our meal. I didn't realize how hungry I was until my mother handed me a bowl of lentil stew. I reached for a piece of bread from the platter sitting in the middle. The bread was still warm. I dipped it into the stew before taking a bite.

I realized that I would now be able to return to my normal duties. I looked forward to collecting our daily water in the morning. Perhaps I'd see Joseph again.

My cheeks instantly reddened with color, and my eyes found Yosef's. He had not taken his eyes off of me since I'd arrived. There was a possessiveness about him that had never been there before, and it frightened me.

"Yosef, with the help of his father, has prepared a contract, Mary. After supper, he wishes to present it to us." My father waited for me to look up at him. "Are you compliant, Mary?"

An uncomfortable silence passed as I tried to think of what to say. *I'm not ready.* My father deciphered what I could not bring myself to say aloud. He turned toward Yosef. "We will consider the contract, Yosef, although I cannot determine if we'll have an answer just yet."

There was a gleam in Yosef's eyes indicating he knew something we did not. It made me uncomfortable. We soon finished eating, and I tried to help my mother clean in hopes of delaying Yosef's proposal even longer, but my mother shooed me away. I hesitantly walked toward my father and Yosef.

Yosef already had the parchment in his hands. He obviously wasn't wishing to postpone any longer. My father patted the space beside him, and I slowly took a seat next to him. He rolled out the paper and began reading.

I noticed the disbelief in my father's eyes as his eyes scanned the contract. Once finished, he slid the parchment over to me, and I began reading. It read much the same as I expected until I began reading the price Yosef was willing to pay for me. It began with ten pieces of silver. My parents were poor, and I was their underprivileged daughter. In the world's eyes, I was not worth ten pieces of silver.

I read on. *A section of land on the south side.* Yosef was also offering my father a piece of his land? This happened often when the bride's father wished to increase the size of the lands he already had. But my father had never owned his own piece of land. This would greatly improve my parent's stature of living.

Continuing on, I saw that I was to receive all of the jewelry passed down from each generation. Since Yosef was the only son, it was custom that his wife would take over the family heirlooms.

I finished reading but struggled to digest the words. My marriage to Yosef would turn my parents' lives around. No longer would my father have to struggle so hard in the fields. He would be able to hire a servant to do most of the harsh labor.

My head shot up at the sound of liquid being poured into a glass. Yosef had poured wine and was now setting it in front of me. The decision now lay with me. If I drank from the cup, it would indicate my acceptance of his proposal. I would then be betrothed. After that, there was no turning back.

What was wrong with me? If he had proposed just a few weeks before, I would have drunk from the cup without hesitancy. What had changed?

I looked up at my father, who was regarding me with tenderness. I was willing to marry Yosef for my father, to give him a better life. Timidly I reached my hand toward the cup, my hand beginning to shake almost violently.

My eyes met those of Yosef's. And my hand froze midway. What was it I read in his expression? Domination? Control? Power? My father obviously saw the same thing, for he pushed the cup back toward Yosef and stood to his feet.

"We need time to discuss this, Yosef. We'll have an answer for you next week."

"What if the offer doesn't stand next week?" Yosef's words were harsh and angry.

"Is that what you are saying? She needs to decide this moment, or you withdraw your proposal?" My father was a kind man, but he was not one to be manipulated. I unconsciously moved closer to him.

Some of the anger left Yosef. I think he realized his chances were better if he waited a few more days, rather than trying to force an answer immediately. He stood up, rolled up the parchment and walked toward the door. "I'll be back next week." And then he was gone.

Three nights later, I was helping my mother clean up after supper when a knock sounded at our door. I watched as my father left his comfortable seat and hobbled toward the door. He had tripped over a rock yesterday in the fields and had twisted his right ankle. Watching him now made me question my indifference to Yosef's proposal. My father's health was failing. My marriage to Yosef would change everything for him.

"Good evening, Heli."

I recognized his baritone voice before I ever saw him. Joseph entered our home and his brown eyes met mine briefly, before he turned back toward my father. They exchanged a few pleasantries, and then my father offered for him to take a seat.

"Actually, this includes Mary as well," Joseph said. "Would you mind if she joins us?" I liked his respectful demeanor toward my father. Joseph clearly saw my father as an elder and wanted his opinion.

"Mary," my father called. "Would you please join us?" I handed the dish rag to my mother and gently dried my hands on my apron.

I entered the room and took a seat next to my father, then Joseph sat down across from us. "How can we help you, Joseph?" I watched Joseph's eyes and noticed they lacked their usual confidence. He seemed nervous. Uneasy.

"Honestly, I feel foolish for coming. And yet, I fear the consequence if I do not relay to you what is on my heart and my mind." Joseph's eyes met my father's. "From the first day I saw your daughter, I knew she was special. And not just to you as her father, but to our heavenly Father. Of course, I soon learned that she was all but pledged to Yosef. And I intended to stand back, honestly I did."

"What changed your mind?" Heli asked.

"A few things, actually." Joseph's eyes turned to me and then back to my father. "We unintentionally crossed paths, and I felt a connection with her unlike any I've experienced before. After feeling that connection, I need to admit the next few times we met may have been intentional on my part."

I looked at my father and saw that he had succeeded in hiding his smile on his mouth but not in his eyes. His eyes were smiling, much like they did when I pleased him. "Go on."

"I asked God to take away this longing. But it only continued to grow. And then…" He stopped talking as if wondering if he should continue.

"And then?" my father prompted.

"And then, I happened along Yosef a couple weeks ago…with…with someone else."

"Someone else?" Heli questioned. "As in…another woman?"

"Yes."

"Could it have been his sister?" I finally entered the conversation. "He has a sister."

"It was not his sister. You speak of Zillah, correct?" I nodded. "It was not Zillah. They bolted apart when I came upon them. It was…it was the girl from the well that day."

"Dinah?" I knew my surprise echoed in my voice. I watched as he nodded his head. *"Dinah?"* I heard myself say again. But I couldn't believe it. Yosef knew how cruel Dinah had been to me. I had confided in him on numerous occasions. "I don't believe it. I don't believe Yosef could do such a thing."

"You think I'm lying?" Joseph's eyes betrayed surprise and then hurt.

"You just admitted you have feelings for me," I heard myself say. "And Yosef offered me a contract of marriage just a few days ago."

"He did? And you accepted." Joseph stood to his feet, disappointment written in his eyes.

"Sit back down, Joseph," I heard my father say. "She has not accepted. Nor has she rejected the offer. She is to give him his answer in four days' time." My father leaned forward in his chair. "Now, are you here simply as a friend to let us know the probable character of the man who has made an offer to my daughter? Or are you here to offer your own proposal?"

"Father!" I gasped.

"The second," Joseph's soft voice answered in assurance.

"You are?" I was sure my face revealed the shock I felt inside at his admission. *He was offering for my hand as well?*

"I do not have a lot to offer as far as monetarily," he said. "But I promise to love, protect, and honor your daughter all the days of my life. And as long as I am living, you and your wife will have a roof over your heads and food in your bellies. I pledge ten percent of my profits to you as well."

Joseph reached into his cloak and withdrew the contract. "I will wait however long it takes your daughter to decide."

I watched as he rose to his feet, his eyes briefly connecting with mine before he handed the contract to my father, nodded his respect, and left the house.

I lay awake most of the night pondering Joseph's surprise proposal. I was disappointed in myself and how I had reacted to his unease of Yosef. I had seen all hope drain out of Joseph's eyes at my defense of a man I hardly knew anymore.

Yosef and Dinah? If it was Yosef's intentions to hurt me, he could not have chosen a better way to do it. If the rumor was true, that is. Yet, hadn't I noticed Yosef's lingering glances toward Dinah? My heart refused to believe such a thing could be true, but my mind…my mind knew that it was.

In the morning, I quickly delivered our daily supply of water to our doorstep before running off in search of Zillah. I found her outside her home, beating dust from a large woven rug. She dropped the wooden stick in her hands and ran toward me, her hands grasping my own. She swung me around in circles until we were dizzy, laughing with joy.

"If you are looking for Yosef, you should have come earlier," she said. "He already left for the fields."

"I came to see you, my friend." I tried to smile, but Zillah could read me like no one else could besides my father.

"You're sad. But why?" Zillah pulled me into a hug. "I thought perhaps you had come to your senses and were here to accept my brother's proposal. What's wrong, Mary?"

"I heard something…yesterday."

"What did you hear?" Zillah studied me intently.

"Zillah, you are my best friend. I trust you more than anyone. If you knew something that concerned me, you would tell me, wouldn't you?"

"Of course," Zillah voiced. But her voice lacked its usual certainty.

"Have you ever noticed Dinah and Yosef spending time together?"

Her pause made my heart ache more. "Yosef loves you, Mary."

"But that doesn't answer my question."

"All right, a few days ago Dinah stopped by our house. We were eating supper. She asked for Yosef. But Yosef didn't want her here. You could read it in his eyes. He was very angry. He asked her to leave. But she leaned near and whispered something in his ear. Then, he looked worried. He told us he was going to walk Dinah home and would return shortly. He wasn't gone long, and when he returned, he said Dinah's brother wasn't feeling well and had asked for him."

"And you believe he is telling the truth?"

"Later, outside with him alone, I told him he could say goodbye to any kind of relationship with you if he were seeing Dinah behind your back. He assured me it was nothing like that. He said he'd die inside if he didn't marry you because anyone else would be second best."

"But why didn't you tell me? We've never kept secrets from each other before."

"Yosef made me swear I wouldn't tell you. He said it would only hurt you with the growing tension between you and Dinah." Zillah grabbed my hands in her own. "I regretted not telling you since the moment I agreed to do so. I'm so relieved you know now." Zillah looked into my eyes with sorrow. "You forgive me?"

"Of course." But even as I said the words, I knew that our relationship would never be the same again. "Thank you for telling me."

As I walked home, I contemplated the last few months and began to see everything in a new light. It had started with Dinah's jealously over Yosef. At some point, her jealousy had turned into a haughty anger, as if she had prevailed over something that belonged to me. And then, the last few weeks, a spirit of resentment had taken over, as if I had in fact ruined her life.

And perhaps in her eyes, I had. She had wanted the man I planned to marry. And she had seemingly succeeded in garnering his attention—for a while. But in the end, he still wanted me. Even I could read the desire in his eyes.

Only his desire wasn't something beautiful, not like Joseph's desire for me. Yosef's desire stemmed from dominance. A need to control me. A need to know I belonged to him and only him. Joseph's desire was a deep yearning. A longing. A longing to protect me. A need to love me.

And I finally knew without a shadow of doubt which desire I was going to give in to.

The next four days were seemingly endless. I was nervous, fidgety. I couldn't think straight. Had I known how overwhelming choosing a life partner would have been, I would have had my father send me to the temple to prevent myself from ever having to make a heartrending decision such as this one. Letting go of Yosef was more difficult than I imagined.

I continually replayed memories in my head. One memory in particular was of two years ago when Yosef had given me a gold bracelet.

"This is for you, Mary, to remind us of our promise to each other." Yosef gently unwrapped the item wrapped in leather. His eyes lit with joy at my intake of breath when he held the bracelet before me.

"Yosef…it's beautiful! But it's worth too much. I couldn't possibly wear it…"

Yosef reached for my hand and tenderly clasped the gold band around my arm. "I want you to wear it, Mary. Wear it every day. It is worth a lot, but not worth nearly as much as you are to me."

I had worn it nearly every day until recently. I couldn't remember the day I had taken it off. I had probably been washing our supper utensils and had sat it on the shelf as I normally did. Why had I not put it back on afterwards?

A knock sounded at the door. I turned to my father. "May I walk with him, Father? Just down the road and back. Neither of us envisioned our lives turning out this way, and I want to give him the news in the gentlest way possible."

Father hesitated. Then he nodded his head. "Stay within sight of our window, Mary."

I nodded and hurried to the door. Yosef stood in the doorway, his eyes uncertain. "Shall we take a walk, Yosef? It is a beautiful evening." Yosef waited for me to take my outer cloak off the hook. I turned and, with one last nod toward my father, we made our way down the dusty road.

"How are you, Yosef?" The tension between us broke my heart. It never used to be this way.

"That depends, Mary, on your answer."

I had hoped to waylay my refusal a bit longer, but I should have known Yosef would want to get straight to the point. "Yosef, I love you…"

He reached for my hand and firmly grasped it in his big strong one. "I love you, too, Mary. I'll always love you. I know things have been stringent between us lately, but that will change after we are betrothed."

"Yosef, I can't marry you…"

"But you just said you love me."

"And I do. But I've noticed over the last few weeks how much we've changed. You don't look at me the same anymore."

"That's absurd, Mary. I look at you as I've always looked at you."

"No, you don't. You used to look at me with innocent eyes, with adoring eyes, but now…now your eyes have changed."

Yosef stopped walking and turned me toward him. "You're refusing my offer because my eyes have changed! Mary, you're losing all sense of reality."

I could see that he wasn't going to take my refusal without actual proof. I hadn't wanted to bring Dinah into the situation, but I could see no other way. "I know about you and Dinah."

As soon as the words left my lips, I could read the certainty in his gaze.

And then an intense guilt passed through his eyes. "What did she say?"

"Enough. Enough that I question your devotion to me."

"She promised! I told her…" Realizing he was yelling his voice left off and he turned away, desperately trying to still his emotions. "Please, Mary. I promise you it meant nothing. And nothing like that will ever happen again."

It was then that I realized how far from Nazareth we had traveled. It would be dark in the next several minutes. I turned, and we began to retrace our steps back toward town. "I'm sorry, Yosef." I realized how odd it was that I was the one apologizing for his behavior.

"Please reconsider. I'll do anything, Mary. I'll wait longer. I'll prove my devotion to you and only you." Yosef studied me in deep earnest. "Please?"

"I've had…another proposal, Yosef. And I feel certain he is the right man for me."

"Let me guess. Would this man be Joseph?" Yosef's voice suddenly changed from one of regret to one of arrogance. "You would honestly choose Joseph over me? You truly are deranged, Mary. It's your father, isn't it? Your father has always disliked me—"

"My decision has nothing to do with my father. He has left the decision entirely up to me because he loves me and wants the best for me. If I were choosing merely for my father, Yosef, I would choose you. If I were choosing merely for our comfort, I would choose you. I'm choosing a man who will respect my father and honor him with his words and his actions. I am choosing a man who will love me unconditionally. A man I never have to doubt will remain true to me. A man I can depend on…"

We had stopped walking and were now standing face to face, Yosef's hands clutching my shoulders. "You can't marry Joseph. I forbid you to do so."

"You're hurting me." I tried to step away, but I couldn't budge from his grasp. "Please, Yosef—"

"Promise me, Mary. We just need more time. Yes, I made a mistake, but it's a mistake we can move on from."

Darkness had descended, and I could just barely make out the lights of town. An eerie noise broke through the night. We both turned toward the sound. Feeling Yosef's grasp lessen, I managed to break away from his grip. I bolted, knowing he would be unable to catch me. I had always been the faster runner.

"Mary!" I heard Yosef screaming my name, but I continued on toward town. The dusty road beneath my feet was hardly visible due to the darkened sky. I passed the vineyard and the fields but didn't slow as I pushed forward toward the safety of home—toward the safety of my father's arms.

Suddenly, I stumbled on the uneven ground, my arms reaching out to break my fall. And then all went black.

I awoke to a heartbeat vibrating in my ear. I was being carried. By Yosef? I felt a chill run down my spine. I turned my head slightly, just enough to see if I could identify the man carrying me, but it was too dark to make out his features. I didn't know if we were headed toward town...or away from town.

And then his scent reached my nose, and I drank in the woodsy smell of cedar wood. The tension began to leave my body. "Joseph," I whispered.

He stopped walking and looked down at me. "Mary, you're awake? I was up in the tower tonight keeping watch over the fields, and I saw you running toward town. And then suddenly you disappeared from sight."

"It was dark, and I fell."

"But what are you doing out here in the dark...alone?"

"I wasn't alone. I was with Yosef." I felt his arms stiffen at the mention of Yosef's name. "I thought if I gave him my answer...if I refused his offer..."

"You refused his offer?" The hope in his voice bolstered my confidence.

"Yes." I waited for him to ask me my decision about his offer, but he didn't. And then I heard my father's concerned voice.

"Is she hurt?" Heli voiced, his hand brushing away my long hair so he could look into my eyes.

"I'm fine, Father. Yosef didn't take my news as well as I'd anticipated. I fell trying to outrun him in the dark."

"Did he hurt you?"

"No, Father. He just needs a few days to himself. He'll get over me and move on."

"Very unlikely," I heard Joseph whisper. We entered the house, and Joseph gently sat me in my father's favorite chair. "You're hurt…"

I looked down and saw blood seeping through my cloak. I felt the heat rising in my cheeks. Would I forever be a nuisance to this man?

Gently lifting my cloak, my father inspected the damage. "You skinned your knee. It will heal up in a few days. He quickly dropped my cloak to prevent further indecency.

I waited for Joseph to reiterate his proposal from a few days before. But he didn't. He shook my father's hand, offered me a smile, and then left.

I explained to my father what had happened and then, in exhaustion, made my way to the ladder leading up to the rooftop. Barely emerging at the top, I heard the door to our home burst open and bang against the stucco wall.

"Where is she?" Yosef's voice was calm now—eerily calm.

"She fell on her way here…"

"Is she all right?"

"Yes, Yosef. Just a few scrapes and bruises. But she will mend."

"Please, Heli, please give my proposal more time."

"I'm sorry, Yosef, but Mary has made her decision."

Something shattered. Was it my mother's clay vase? "You will regret your decision, old man. Mark my words."

I paced back and forth on the rooftop, beseeching Yahweh to protect my father. Should I go back down?

And then I saw him. Joseph. He was standing across the way and had now stepped out of shadows under the moonlight. His eyes shifted to the window below and then back up to me. *I'm here*, he was telling me. And I knew he would stay until Yosef decided to leave. He would intervene if my father needed him.

Yosef railed a few moments longer before stomping out of the house. Joseph had barely managed to step back into the shadows before Yosef's exit. As Yosef disappeared from sight, Joseph once again stepped out, offered me a smile, and followed after the man I had just refused.

The next morning as I was gathering water from the well, I noticed Dinah. She was at the back of the line waiting to fill her pitcher. I adjusted the pitcher on my shoulder and made my way toward home, pausing briefly to exchange pleasantries with the other women. After a few moments, I realized Dinah was intentionally avoiding me. This was an unusual occurrence compared to her normal behavior, in which she went out of her way to bring attention to herself.

Havilah, who was standing next to Dinah, noticed it first. "What happened, Dinah?"

Dinah turned then, and I felt my knees tremble. The right side of her face was bruised and puffy, her eye barely open. "I stumbled and fell. Are we going to stand here and chat all day, or may I take your place at the well, Jemima?" Jemima waved her forward.

As soon as Dinah had left the group, they began speaking among themselves. "It was probably her father. He doesn't control his temper very well…" I left them and continued on toward home.

Soon after, rumors began circulating that Yosef had stormed into Dinah's home the night before, calling her a liar and a manipulator. And then he had struck her twice before another man had intervened. There were discrepancies about who the man had been. Dinah's brother, Amos? Her father? There was also a third man mentioned, the man who had just recently moved here from Bethlehem—Joseph.

I knew at once who the man had been.

I waited for Joseph to come back to ask my decision. I waited an entire week, only he didn't come. Had he changed his mind? And then my menstruation came again, and I was once again homebound. By the end of the second week, my mother's patience was wearing thin.

"I think I know why he hasn't come," my mother voiced over supper one evening.

"Why?" I was desperately searching for a reason.

"What were his last words to you, Heli, after his proposal?"

I watched my father sit in silence, replaying that night in his mind. Suddenly Joseph's words came back to me. *I will wait however long it takes your daughter to decide.* He was waiting for me! I jumped up and ran toward the door.

"Daughter, you unfortunately cannot go today, perhaps not even tomorrow. You have yet to be cleansed by the mikveh." My mother's words stopped me dead in my tracks. I slowly returned to my seat on the floor. My father reached across the table and patted my hand, even though he'd have to wash that hand three times before touching anything else. His reassuring eyes brought me peace.

Three days later, I made my way up the hill toward the mikveh. Taking extra care with my cleansing, I was chilled to the bone when I began the trek back down. I passed my house and continued on toward the edge of town where Joseph lived with his father and brother. Hearing noises from the back, I walked around the house and stopped when I saw him.

He was sanding the top of a wooden fixture that looked to be a chest. I watched as his hands gently caressed the top, feeling the smoothness of the wood. As if sensing my presence, he turned, his brown eyes connecting with mine.

"I've made my decision."

"And you've been to the mikveh, I see." He walked toward me, his eyes taking in all of me, from my wet hair to my bare feet.

"Do you want to know my answer?"

"Yes, when you are certain." No pressure. No demands.

"You are invited to our house for supper this evening, along with your father and your brother. After supper, we will sign the contract."

"And you will become my betrothed?" He stepped even closer, reaching out and fingering my damp hair with his fingers.

"And I will become your betrothed." My affirmation brought a smile to his lips. A smile I knew I would never tire of looking at. His thumb traced down my soft cheek.

"Come," he voiced. "Let me walk you home."

Joseph asked for a six-month betrothal period, while my father wanted a full year. I believe Joseph would have given in to my father, but I suggested they both compromise. We all agreed on nine months.

For several days afterward, I walked around as if in my own little world. My mother jested, saying I might as well marry Joseph now for how much help I was to her. A seemingly simple task took me much longer to accomplish than normal, because my thoughts were elsewhere. In the law's eyes,

I was already a married woman. We were bound together, forever. The only demand requested of me during the next nine months was to remain faithful.

I smiled to myself. That would not be a difficult task in the least.

Joseph and I began a nightly custom of walking to the top of the hill and back, my father or mother following at a much slower pace from behind. I finally found the courage to ask him the question that had been on my mind for a long time. "What happened the night you followed Yosef?" He looked over at me, perhaps curious about my need to know.

"Yosef made his way to Dinah's, where he barged in as if he owned the place. They had all retired for the night, but he demanded that she show herself. When she finally did, he called her the most lying, conniving, manipulating woman he had ever known. And he said if this was her way of forcing him to marry her, he'd rather die than be tied to a woman of her quality."

"But how could she force him to marry her?" I felt Joseph's hand on my arm as my foot slipped momentarily on the loose dirt.

"The same thought crossed my mind as well."

"Did he hit her?" Part of me wanted to know the answer, and part of me didn't.

"Yes…twice."

"And then you stopped him?"

"Yes. I waited for her father to step in, but he did not."

"But wasn't he angry with you?"

"Who? Yosef?" We crested the top of the hill, and Joseph turned to look at me. "What reason would he have had then to be angry with me?"

I felt my face redden. "I had refused him."

"And?"

"And I may have suggested I was going to marry you instead." I looked down at the ground, embarrassed by the jovial glint in Joseph's brown eyes.

"You knew then that you were going to accept my proposal, and you still waited two more weeks before telling me?"

"I was waiting for you."

"Waiting for me? But I had told your father—"

"I know, but I had forgotten. And by the time I remembered, it was… that time…of the month."

"You could have sent a messenger. You have no idea what that delay did to my heart."

We were now standing beneath my favorite sycamore tree. "Let me guess. You couldn't eat or sleep…"

"Or think straight." His chuckle brought a smile to my own lips. "Although the day I turned around and saw you standing there beneath my canopy, your hair wet, your cloak damp, your beautiful bare feet…"

My father cleared his voice, and both Joseph and I dissolved into laughter. I looked to my father and saw the laughter in his own eyes. "That is now at the top of my most favorite memories," Joseph whispered.

"Tell me another memory." There was so much I wanted to learn about him.

"You running like the wind that day on this very hill."

"Any without me in them?"

There was a pause, and the atmosphere suddenly turned serious. "I have several memories of my mother."

"Tell me about her. What was she like?" I reached up to pick up a leaf, twirling the stem between my fingers.

"According to my father, my mother and I resemble each other quite a bit. Dark brown eyes, brownish-black hair, and the same carefree smile."

"I love that smile." The words escaped before I had time to restrain them. I felt the blood rush from my face at my admission, and I glanced downward. I sensed him waiting for me to look up. Finally, I did.

"A good thing," he said, "since it shows itself quite often."

"What happened to her?"

Joseph sighed. "She had a hard time during childbirth. After she bore me, it took her a long time to recover. And then five years later, she gave birth to Cleophas, and she never did quite regain her energy. Cleophas was three and I was eight when we learned she was expecting another child. I could see the concern in my father's eyes, but she was so excited about becoming a mother again. Seven months into the pregnancy, she went into early labor, and I woke up the next morning to my father sitting with his head in his arms and my mother lying on the table with a baby girl in her arms, both of them still and lifeless."

I reached out to him, a deep sadness penetrating my heart. "I'm sorry. Tell me a happy memory that you have of her."

"She loved to walk, much like you, and we often went on little adventures together. She knew the Judaean mountains better than my father, and we'd often pack picnics and spend the day looking for special plants to make oils out of when we'd return home."

"I think I would have enjoyed her."

"I know she would have loved you." He reached out to brush a tear from my cheek. "You remind me of her, Mary. It's what drew me to you. Your spontaneity and adventurous spirit are the two things I loved about her most. I've craved them since she left me, but now for the first time in thirteen years, I feel as if I've recovered her best traits through you."

We began our trek back down the hill, my heart full and yet free. My mother had often warned me my adventurous ways would get me into trouble. But instead, Yahweh had led me to a man who would cherish me fully, as my father always had.

A month had passed since Joseph and I had become betrothed. And I found myself wishing I had sided with Joseph when he had requested a six-month betrothal. Each moment we spent together, I found myself growing more attached to him. He was so much like my father—patient, kind and lighthearted. I saw my father's respect growing for Joseph as well. I felt at peace with my decision. Joseph reflected a calmness unlike any man I'd known.

Mother and I spent each morning working on the wedding apparel I would wear during the ceremony. The adorning of the bride was often costly and elaborate, but because my father was of little means, our neighbors and friends had each given something from their own supply. Mother sat quietly in Father's chair, diligently working on a white satin robe I would wear the night Joseph would come to collect me. I sat next to her while she sewed beads to the veil that would cover my face.

I hadn't given much thought to the preparation of the bride until now. Every evening before I retired, I washed my face with a formula that had been passed down through our generations. It was important that my complexion be shining with a luster like unto marble. This stemmed from the words of David, "that our daughters may be as corner stones, polished after the similitude of a palace." The first week of using this procedure had given me a red, chapped face. But as I continued to use the concoction, my skin began to take on a beautiful sheen as well as a smoothness I couldn't deny.

A soft knock at our door brought me from my reverie, and I rose to answer it. I was both surprised yet pleased to see Zillah standing there. So many times, I had thought about going to see her, but the possibility of seeing Yosef was too much for me to bear.

"May I come in?"

"Of course! It is so good to see you, my friend." I pulled her into the warmth of the house. I saw her eyes surveying the veil in my mother's hands. And her eyes filled with sadness. Sensing the awkwardness in the room, my mother got to her feet, tucking the robe into her outer cloak.

"I'll prepare something for us," Anna voiced before leaving us alone to visit.

We sat in silence for a few moments, each trying to decide the best words to open the conversation. This was an odd occurrence. Zillah and I had been companions since birth. She was my best friend, a sister to me growing up.

"I've had many days to ponder your decision, Mary, and I can't even begin to understand why you chose Joseph, a man we barely know, over my brother." Zillah looked down at her long, slender fingers. "I thought you loved him, Mary. We were meant to be sisters." Tears slid down her cheeks and mine as well.

I knelt on my knees before her, gathering her hands into my own. "I'm so sorry, Zillah. Three months ago, if anyone had foretold this outcome, I would have never believed them." I released one of her hands to brush away a tear from her cheek. "It was always my dream for you and me to be sisters. But as time transpired, I began to see a different plan unfold for me. And suddenly, I had two choices. One was familiar, the other strange and unknown."

I looked deeply into my friend's eyes, hoping she would understand. "Have you ever felt one choice would lead you to a place that wouldn't necessarily be wrong, but another choice would unwrap a destiny to something you couldn't even begin to comprehend?" Zillah squeezed my hand, encouraging me to continue.

"I'm not choosing Joseph over your brother because he is a better man. I'm choosing Joseph because I feel Yahweh chose him for me. I understand your pain because I feel it too. I have long dreamed of Yosef as my husband

and you as my sister, but Yahweh has chosen something different for me. And in the end, it is Yahweh who I aim to please."

"You always find the right words to say to calm my mind and heart." Zillah pulled me into a fierce hug.

"There's still the possibility you and Mary could be sisters, Zillah. Doesn't Joseph have a younger brother?" Zillah smiled as my mother laid the tray of cheese and figs on the small table beside us.

"Yes, but he's not nearly as handsome as his older brother," Zillah said with a laugh.

"But he's only sixteen, Zillah," I teased. "In two years' time, Cleo may indeed be the more handsome of the two."

"Will he indeed?" a familiar husky voice asked. I turned to find my intended standing behind me. "I knocked. But you couldn't hear me over your deep and profound conversation, I assume." Joseph's eyes baited me while Zillah dissolved into laughter.

"What are you doing here?" I tried to hide my embarrassment but knew I was failing miserably.

"I was hoping to show you something, but I see you have a guest, so I will come by later."

"What is it?" I prodded.

"A surprise."

"What kind of surprise?"

"You are aware, are you not, of the meaning of the word surprise? If I told you now, I would ruin the unexpectedness of it."

"You are aware, are you not, of my dislike of the unknown…?" I realized at that moment I had forgotten we had an audience. I could see Joseph had as well. He quickly bid us goodbye, and I watched until he was out of sight.

"I've never seen you so animated, Mary. He brings out the best in you." She reached for my hand as our eyes connected. I could tell Zillah meant the words she spoke.

A woman's cry pierced the air. It wasn't unusual to hear voices throughout the day. But this sound was different. It was a cry of panic. I stood to my feet and made my way to the window, peering outside to get a better view. There were people leaving their homes and making their way toward the center of town.

I turned toward my mother, who was now standing beside me. "Where are they going?"

"I'm not sure. Shall we find out?" Anna sat the veil on the table. I did likewise with the robe and proceeded her out the door. We followed the crowd of people until they came to a halt. I could hear a woman sobbing, but I couldn't see her over the heads of the people standing in front of us.

"My daughter is with child, and I demand the father to step forward and take responsibility." This was the voice of an older man. I stood on my tiptoes, desperately trying to make out who the voice belonged to.

"Ask your daughter, Alad. Surely she knows who the father is," a woman voiced from behind me. I cringed at the laughter that followed. Alad? Dinah's father?

"She refuses to tell me anything, this harlot daughter of mine." The noise of his hand slapping her face echoed through the crowd.

"Would she rather be stoned to death along with her unborn baby? Speak, fool child," another voice called from among the crowd.

I finally managed to squeeze through the crowd and could see Dinah crouched beside her father. Having not seen her since my betrothal to Joseph, I was startled at how much she had changed. She had lost weight, and her hair was unkempt. Her cloak was dirty and disheveled. Her eyes were clenched shut, as if she indeed was hoping for death to transport her to a better place.

I stepped forward, unable to keep what I knew to myself. Her eyes opened, as if she knew what I was about to say. I opened my mouth, but at the shake of her head, I paused. *Why?* my eyes beckoned. Again, she shook her head. I pleaded with her in silence to let me speak for her, to make things right, but she refused my offer. I didn't understand why she would do so.

Then I saw him, standing a ways off. Standing there watching. A look of contempt; a look of hatred for this woman on her knees. This woman he had placed in this predicament and yet refused to atone for. A simple word from him would change everything for Dinah. The fine was fifty shekels, which he well could afford. And then they could marry, and they could raise their child. In time, everyone would forget the circumstances surrounding her pregnancy. All in good time.

But instead Yosef turned and walked away.

I gasped as a stone flew by my head. The stone was followed by another one and then another. Rational thought eluded me, and I ran toward her until an arm wound around my waist and dragged me farther and farther away from a place I would always wish I had never been. A place that from this day forward would change me forever. I fell to my knees, a loud sob springing from deep within me.

Strong arms picked me up and held me close. "I'm here," his voice caressed.

And I knew he would be. Always. This man that Yahweh had chosen for me.

For the first time in several weeks, Joseph did not come by to see me. I had been in a daze since that morning, and the thought of going to bed frightened me. I knew what I'd see if I closed my eyes. The silence following Dinah's death was oppressive. I could not function.

"It is late," my father finally stated as he stood to his feet. "It is time for bed."

"I'm not ready." Never before had I objected to my father's direction.

He placed a hand on my shoulder. "It will get easier with time, daughter."

"I could never sleep, and if I did happen to fall asleep, I'm afraid of what I'd dream about."

"Come, daughter. You can bring your mat into our room, and we will pray until we sleep."

I followed my father to the back room and lay on my mat, my eyes taking in the stars from the open window. "I don't understand, Father. Why would Yahweh allow something so horrible?" His hand found mine in the dark, and he squeezed it tight.

"I don't have an answer for that, daughter. But I will never doubt Yahweh's love for me or your mother or for you."

A new thought appeared unexpectedly, and I sat up. "Father, what will happen to her body? Will she receive a proper burial?"

"Due to the circumstances surrounding her death, she will not receive a traditional Jewish burial."

"Dinah dishonored her family's name, and therefore to honor her would create confusion among our people." My mother's words sounded so heartless; callous even.

"But what about mercy and grace? What about forgiveness?"

"Even though the penalty of sin is death, Yahweh says He will not forsake us," my father whispered.

"Father, will you bury Dinah?"

"She is being taken care of even as we speak."

"By whom?" I felt my eyes growing heavy but refused to close them.

"I noticed her brother Amos beside her body just before dusk. I made my way toward him, intending to help, but Joseph came upon me and told me to go home to my family. And then he approached Amos. Together they carried her outside of town."

I finally lay back down on my mat. "Joseph is a good man, isn't he, Father?"

"I've prayed since your birth that Yahweh would provide a man worthy of you. I believe Joseph was sent here just for you, Mary."

I fell asleep then, my distraught mind finally at peace.

The next morning, I made my way out of town, my eyes scanning the ground for any signs of dirt that had recently been dug up. Many Jewish families buried their dead in caves. After the deceased body decomposed, the dried bones would then be collected and placed in a stone box known as an ossuary. But my father reminded me earlier that Dinah would not have been placed in her family's tomb due to the nature of her death. Usually, after a stoning, the body was left as a reminder to others that the wages of sin resulted in death, and then later their bones were scattered outside the city.

Hearing footsteps from behind, I turned to find Joseph. "Come with me." He motioned for me to follow him.

We veered off the well-traveled trail. It was then that I noticed the beautiful stone box tucked under his right arm.

"Did you make that last night?" I knew he had but couldn't help asking the question. He slowed his pace and waited for me to come up alongside him. He held the burial box out to me, and I gently took it into my hands. It had been obvious from the first moment I had seen Joseph's work that he was exceptional with his hands. I ran my fingers along the outer edges before turning the box over.

There, engraved in the middle, was the word *Dinah*, and underneath her name was the inscription, ***Blessed are those who mourn, for they shall be comforted.***

My vision clouded with tears, and I felt Joseph's hand on my arm to steady me. "It's beautiful," I whispered when my voice felt steady again.

We came upon her grave not long later. Standing there in silence, I felt a comforting warm breeze caress my skin and hair. Without words spoken, Joseph gently lay the burial box next to where Dinah had been buried. Finding some red pereg flowers nearby, I began making a bouquet to place at the gravesite.

"All flesh is grass, and all its beauty is like the flower in the field." Laying the flowers on Dinah's grave, I closed my eyes, listening to the words Joseph spoke. "The grass withers, the flower fades when the breath of the Lord blows on it; surely the people are grass. The grass withers, the flower fades, but the word of our God will stand forever."

During the next few weeks, words were spoken, some insensitive and some just plain spiteful. I suppose many assumed I approved of Dinah's sentence. In their eyes, she had taken something belonging to me.

But I no longer saw it that way. Dinah had been looking for fulfillment, for someone to love her. And in the process, she had found someone who had exploited her. I held no ill will toward Dinah, but the same could not be said for Yosef. And Joseph discerned it before I did.

We were returning from Dinah's gravesite one evening when Joseph voiced his concern. His words completely took me off guard. "Mary, I've been so wrapped up in your selfless compassion for Dinah that I couldn't see at first the contempt you've begun to harbor for Yosef."

"I don't dislike Yosef." But even as I said the words, I knew they were untrue. "I am angry with him. But I don't hate him." Joseph, sensing the opposition in my voice, remained silent, allowing the internal conflict going on within me to work itself out. "You don't believe me, do you?"

"I think you've transferred your resentful feelings over everything that has happened onto Yosef." Joseph stopped walking and turned toward me. His gentle brown eyes looked deep into my own, begging me to be truthful with myself.

"Mary, you are the kindest, most beautiful woman I've ever known. And I can't bear to let this unresolved bitterness toward Yosef fester any longer. I was hoping it would work itself out, but it has only worsened."

I felt my face flush with irritation. "He took advantage of her."

"From my viewpoint, he wasn't the only one to blame, Mary. She was offering herself as well."

"But he's a man. As a man, he is to protect and comfort and support—"

"And he fell short—"

"Fell short! He did more than fall short, Joseph. He let a woman die!"

"Which he will carry with him until the day he dies. Mary, please…"

"I hate him!" Even I was surprised by the vehemence behind my words. "I hate him," I said again as a sob tore from my body. I felt Joseph's arms come around me, and I rested my head on his chest. The wall from within began to crumble, slowly at first until it finally was forced to collapse due to the unsteady foundation it had built itself on. I cried until I was so weak, it was Joseph holding me up and no longer my own two legs.

"I'm sorry," I finally whispered, my tears finally spent.

"You're sorry? For what?"

"For not being stronger. For falling short."

"Mary, you could never fall short in my eyes. When you are weak, you can rely on my strength just as when I am weak, I know I can rely on your strength." Joseph tipped my chin up so I had no choice but to look into his eyes. "Pray for him, Mary."

"Pray for Yosef?"

"He began making unwise choices somewhere along the way, but it's not too late for him to turn back."

"How can you be so forgiving and kind?"

"It would have been more difficult had you chosen him."

"But still…still you would pray for him, even if I had chosen him over you?"

"Yes, because bitterness once yielded to changes even the best of people. So, will you? Pray for him?"

I nodded my head, knowing I was making a difficult promise but knowing it was the right one.

My heart toward Yosef didn't change overnight or even after a week of routinely offering up a prayer for him each morning and evening. But eventually I noticed the anger begin to slowly change to sorrow. A deep, grieving sorrow. I cried several more times, as if my body was being emptied of a bottomless reservoir of grief. At first I was embarrassed, but Joseph assured me it was a process of letting go. My heart was emptying itself of dreams long harbored.

Yosef's betrothal to Atarah was announced during this time. It did not go unnoticed the similarities between Atarah and myself—our dark hair, dark eyes, olive skin, slight figure. She was a year younger than me.

"She doesn't have your adventurous spirit," Joseph whispered into my ear during synagogue when he caught me staring at her. I felt my cheeks flush red. And then his hand brushed mine ever so briefly, causing my heart to beat erratically.

I passed through the doorway of the synagogue, my footsteps picking up speed until finally I was running up the pathway toward the top of the hill. Once I crested the top, I continued on until I was completely out of breath. Pulling the cover from my head, I stood there, the wind blowing my dark hair. I closed my eyes and began twirling slowly at first and then faster and faster.

All at once, I began to feel dizzy. Losing my step, I felt strong arms encircled me from behind. "Lean back," his masculine voice said softly against my hair. I leaned back against his strong chest and waited for the lightheaded feeling to subside.

"These last three months have been torturous," he said.

I couldn't see his face, but I certainly felt his discomfort. I, too, wished we had chosen a shorter betrothal. "The next six months will pass by in the blink of an eye," I teased. I turned to face him. Joseph's brown eyes gazed lovingly into my own.

"I love you, Mary." His gaze dropped to his sandals, and I knew that he hadn't meant to say the words quite yet.

"I love you, too," I whispered, tracing the outline of his jaw with my fingers. He wasn't expecting my reciprocation, but I could tell my words moved him deeply.

As I stepped out of the cold water, I braced myself for the chilly wind against my bare skin. But instead, a warmth enveloped me, and I felt a presence I had only felt one other time in my life. It was Yahweh's presence. I closed my eyes, wondering why I was feeling Him so tangibly, here, now.

"You are honored very much."

My eyes opened wide as I turned to see where the voice was coming from. Across the way, standing in front of the entrance to the mikveh, stood a man. He was tall, stout, with eyes that were bright and full of joy.

"You are a favored woman. The Lord is with you, and He has chosen you from among many women."

I took a step back, and then another, my eyes scanning the stone wall for another way of escape, yet knowing there was not another way out. I was troubled by his words. Chosen by the Lord? For what purpose? Who was this man?

"Mary, do not be afraid. The Lord has sent me. I am His angel, Gabriel. You have found favor with God. You are to become a mother and have a Son. You are to give Him the name Jesus. He will be great. He will be called the Son of the Most High."

I shook my head. "How will this happen? I have only recently become betrothed." I felt my face redden. "I have never been with a man."

Gabriel came toward me, his countenance bright, and his eyes full of light. "The Holy Spirit will come upon you. The power of the Most High will cover you. The child you give birth to will be called the Son of God." He paused to look into my eyes before continuing. "See, your cousin Elizabeth, as old as she is, is going to give birth to a child. She was not able to have children before, but now she is in her sixth month."

"How can this be?" Elizabeth was indeed my cousin and lived in Jerusalem. But she had been barren for many years. Even the physicians had concluded she would never have children.

"God can do all things, can He not?" Gabriel spoke with such authority, his confidence bolstering my own. "Are you willing, Mary? Are you willing to be used of the Lord?"

"I am willing. Let it happen to me as you have said."

A bright light flashed through the cave, temporarily blinding me, and then he was gone. I felt Yahweh's presence leave before I could see clearly enough to confirm Gabriel's absence. A smile slowly spread across my lips. *Elizabeth pregnant?* I had to go and see her, if only to confirm that it was so.

The smile quickly fled when I thought of Joseph and how I would ever explain what had just happened to me.

For three days I kept Gabriel's words to myself, hiding them in my heart. Normally, after my cleansing at the mikveh, I would immediately seek out Joseph. It was an incredibly long week during my menstruations, when we were forced to be apart from one another. But this time I stayed at the house, replaying over and over again the scene at the cave, one minute sure I had envisioned the entire thing, and then the next moment criticizing myself for doubting it.

"Are you well, daughter?" my father asked one evening over the supper table.

I looked up into his concerned eyes. "I need to go and see Elizabeth." It was true. I needed to see her belly swelling with child. In seeing her prophecy foretold, I could then believe in my own.

"We will go together, Mary, in a few months to observe the Feast of Weeks."

"No, Father. I need to go now."

"Why, Mary?" My father studied me. I rarely defied him.

I looked over to my mother, her eyes rebuking my opposition to my father. I felt within that it was not yet time to tell her. Looking back at my father, I said, "May we walk...later this evening?"

"You and Joseph? Where has he been, by the way?"

"No, you and I. I will see Joseph...later." Both my parents eyed me with perplexity. I helped my mother clear away the dishes but instead of letting me stay to dry them, she shooed my father and me out the door.

Once out of earshot of any passersby, I relayed what had happened to me in the cave. My father stopped walking and stared at me, his eyes full of disbelief and wonder. "Tell me again." I relayed the story once more, in exact detail, just as I had the first time.

"And you want to go see Elizabeth to determine the accuracy of Gabriel's prophecy?" My father reached for my hands, holding them in his large warm ones.

"I need to go."

"Mary, are you sure you didn't dream this up? Did you fall…become unconscious prior to the angel coming into the cave?"

My father didn't believe me. I looked down at my feet, doing my best to blink away the tears trying surface. "It was not a dream, Father. If you take me to see Elizabeth, you will believe as I do."

My father leaned forward and kissed my forehead. "Then we will go. Tomorrow."

I thanked Yahweh for the father He had blessed me with. Even though my father questioned my story, he didn't question my belief in the story. And he was willing to journey with me to Jerusalem, if only for me to gain answers.

"What shall I tell Joseph?" I wanted to tell him everything just like I had my father, but did not feel the same liberty to do so.

"Wait until we return from our visit, Mary." *In case the tale proves false.* He left those words unsaid.

Hearing footsteps approaching, both my father and I turned to find Joseph. "Mary!" His eyes showed how glad he was to see me. I hoped my eyes reflected the same. He then looked to my father.

"May I walk with her?" At my father's nod of approval, we began walking down the pathway, my father several feet behind us.

"You didn't come by the house. Why?"

"My mother needed help…"

"When were you at the cave?"

I should have known he'd ask that question. And he knew I would not lie. "Tuesday," I voiced with hesitation.

"Tuesday? Three days ago?" He stopped to look at me. "Is something wrong?"

I couldn't quite look him in the eyes, which only furthered his skepticism. "I'm leaving in the morning. My father and I are going to Jerusalem to visit my cousin Elizabeth."

"Mary, there is something you are not telling me. Are you having second thoughts?"

I grabbed his hand and brought it to my lips. "No," I whispered against his fingers. "I am sure of my love for you and my desire to be your wife." I saw some of the fear leave his eyes. "But there is something I need to share with you upon my return."

"When will you be back?"

"Before our ceremony," I teased, trying to lighten the tension surrounding us. His lopsided smile emerged when he saw the twinkle in my eyes. Had I known the accuracy of those words, I never would have articulated them.

It was a five day walk from Nazareth to Jerusalem. Thankfully, the roads were dry. We started down our familiar road and then began circling around the Sea of Galilee. From there, the road widened as it followed alongside the Jordan River. As the water picked up momentum, so too the road picked up more travelers, although not nearly as many as when we traveled to Jerusalem to attend the Passover. When I was a small child, I would often collect items along the way; smooth stones, colorful feathers, sometimes even things dropped by other travelers.

We followed this road nearly to the Dead Sea. And then we began an uphill ascent into the Judean hills. I replayed Joseph's stories in my head of how he and his mother would play in these very hills.

As we climbed, the air became thinner and we left behind the salt and stone. Even though our progress was slowed by the steepness of the climb, this was my favorite part of the journey. The land was productive in this area, with fields of wheat on one side and groves of palms and olives on the other side. We began seeing people regularly, whether other travelers or people working in the fields. Houses began springing up along the roadside, and instead of sleeping on the ground, we were invited instead to sleep indoors. Meeting new people was always something my father and I looked forward to.

And then the walls of Jerusalem came into view. The walls always reminded me of David and Solomon. The stories surrounding their royalty, valor, honor, and bravery both on and off the battlefield brought a certain element of excitement every time my father spoke of them.

"David was the smallest brother, but he possessed an inner strength…a courage that even his brothers couldn't measure up to. At a very young age, David talked with God, and God showed David His will. I've often thought of you like David, Mary. You are courageous, yet you have a kind and gentle spirit."

My father stopped walking and turned toward me. "The scriptures mention a Messiah who will come to save the world. And if indeed Yahweh has chosen a mother for His Son, I do not doubt it could be you."

I wrapped my arms around him. "Thank you, Father." I stepped back upon hearing the giggle of a small child observing us from the side of the road.

"We aren't far now," Father said, as we continued on our journey.

He was right. Elizabeth lived with her husband, Zechariah, in a small village on the western outskirts of Jerusalem. We would reach our destination by early evening. Not having time to notify them of our visit, I wondered several times as we drew nearer how they would react to us showing up on their doorstep.

Finally, we arrived. Both my father and I stood outside their home, perhaps prolonging an uncertain outcome. But then my father knocked and walked in. I followed behind him. Elizabeth stood in the kitchen, flour on her hands, in her hair, and all over her apron. She looked up, her eyes widening in surprise. The rolling utensil fell from her hands to the floor and she ran toward me, bypassing my father completely. She fell to her knees, her hands gently caressing my flat belly.

"You are the most blessed of all women, and blessed is the child that you will have." Tears slipping down both cheeks unchecked, Elizabeth struggled to her feet, the weight of her own child making her unsteady on her feet. My father rushed forward to help her.

Once standing again, she cupped my face in her floured hands. "I am blessed that the mother of my Lord is visiting me. As soon as I saw you, I felt my baby jump for joy! You are blessed, Mary, for believing the Lord would keep His promise to you."

I looked over Elizabeth's head into my father's loving eyes. The doubt in his eyes from before was gone. He believed. He stepped forward and pulled both Elizabeth and me into his arms.

Over supper that night, Elizabeth regaled us with story after story of Zechariah and several humorous incidences involving his lack of communication. We couldn't help but laugh at the paradox of it all.

"He was chosen by priestly custom to go into the Lord's temple to burn incense. Then, suddenly, to the right of the incense altar, an angel appeared. Zechariah trembled with fear, but the angel said to him, 'Don't be afraid.'"

Zechariah motioned with his hands, a familiar occurrence during Elizabeth's accounts. He didn't like it when she left out important elements. My father and I shared a smile. It was quite odd to experience Elizabeth as the verbal communicator, since usually it was Zechariah who did most of the talking.

"The angel said, 'Don't be afraid, *Zechariah*.' He called him by name!"

"Gabriel said my name as well," I exclaimed.

"It certainly makes the prophecy more personal, does it not?" Both Zechariah and I nodded in unison at my father's words.

"Then the angel told Zechariah that I would have a son and that we were to call him John. He will be our pride and joy, and many people will be glad that he was born, although none more than I." Elizabeth laughed with joy. Zechariah motioned for her to continue, so she did. "He will go ahead of the Lord with the spirit and power that Elijah had. Can you imagine?"

Elizabeth's right hand rested on her large pregnant belly. She was already well into her sixth month. "Where is that scroll, Zechariah? I can't remember what Gabriel said next."

Zechariah stood up and walked across the room to fetch the scroll. He had written in detail the experience he had in the temple with the angel Gabriel. Elizabeth took the scroll and then scanned the writing until she reached the place where she had left off. "John will change parents' attitudes toward their children. He will change disobedient people so they will accept the wisdom of those who have God's approval. He will prepare the people for the Lord."

Elizabeth set the scroll down, her eyes twinkling with delight. "But of course, my husband had to question the angel. 'What proof is there for this? I am an old man! My wife is beyond her childbearing years!'" We all laughed, excluding Zechariah who rolled his eyes. "I wish I had been there to see the angel's face as my dear husband questioned the Lord." Again we laughed.

Elizabeth once again looked at the scroll. "The angel said, 'I'm Gabriel! I stand in God's presence. And yet you do not believe what I have told you? You will see, Zechariah, everything will come true at the right time. But because you didn't believe, you will be unable to talk until this day happens.' As soon as the angel spoke the words, Zechariah was unable to speak. The angel vanished, and Zechariah left the temple. But he was unable to communicate, so he began motioning to the people, but they did not understand him. Sure enough, within days of the prophecy, I became pregnant. I didn't go into public for five months, not sure of how people would receive the pregnancy of an old woman!"

Tears slipped down Elizabeth's cheeks, and I reached across the table and took her weathered hand in my own. "Look, Mary, look what the Lord has done for me! He has removed my disgrace." My own tears flowed freely, as did my father's and even Zechariah's.

We stayed a week, but the morning we planned to depart, Elizabeth took my father aside. Seeing that she needed to speak with him in private, I walked outside to watch the sunrise. Jerusalem rests upon four hills— Mount Zion, Mount Moriah, Bezetha, and Akra. Between these mountains is a large valley. Mount Zion held much significance, and it was frequently mentioned during King David's reign. The Upper City, located on Mount Zion, was where many of the wealthy resided. It was also where David and his successors were buried.

I had always loved Jerusalem. It was surrounded on the west, south, and east by deep ravines, some nearly four hundred feet deep, making it impossible for an enemy to attack. Only the north side was approachable, but a wall over one hundred feet high stood tall with numerous towers. I always felt safe here, as though God Himself was protecting it.

Hearing the door open, I turned to find my father exiting. "Mary, how do you feel about staying here with Zechariah and Elizabeth for a while? I'll return for you when…when the time is right." My father rarely stuttered over his words, and I could read the concern in his eyes.

"What is it, Father? I don't like the idea of you traveling alone…"

"I used to travel alone all the time. If anything, traveling with a young beautiful woman is more dangerous."

I swatted him playfully. "Father, you're older now. What if you fall?"

"It's a road well-traveled, daughter. I would be found quickly and given aid. What other reason is there for wanting to return to Nazareth so soon? Besides your betrothed, that is." My father's eyebrows rose in humor.

"I do miss him."

"But you'll be married soon, and time like this to bond with your cousin will most likely not present itself again."

"How long?" It wasn't that I didn't want to stay. I did. If Joseph wasn't waiting for me in Nazareth, I would have been thrilled. How many times had I begged to stay longer after the Passover and had never been able to.

Again, my father hesitated. There was something he wasn't telling me. "Three months," he finally stated.

"Three months? What will Joseph think? I cannot possibly keep this from him that long. By then, my pregnancy could be evident to all. What would he think?"

"Elizabeth had a dream last night."

"A dream?"

"Your pregnancy was found out and…and…the outcome was the same as Dinah's."

I felt my knees go weak. "I was stoned to death?"

"Elizabeth feels there is danger if you return now. After three months, the danger will lift and you can return home."

"But what if it is still there when I return?"

"I will be praying for wisdom, as will you. Yahweh will give us peace when the time is right." My father drew me into his arms and held me tight. "I'm sorry, daughter, for doubting you."

I laid my head against his chest, memorizing the smell of him. "So many times, I doubted myself. How can I blame you for doing the same?"

"So, you forgive your miserable father?"

"I forgive you." I stood up on my tiptoes and kissed first one cheek and then the other. "Be safe, Father. I love you."

As he began to walk away, I remembered Joseph. "Father, what about Joseph? What will you tell him?"

"I'll tell him your cousin is pregnant and needs a companion during this last trimester. And if the Lord prompts me to tell him more, I will. But telling him more without the guidance of our Lord could bring about adverse consequences." I nodded and waved, watching until he faded into the horizon.

Two weeks after my father's departure, I began to feel nauseous. It had been relatively easy to disregard the idea of being pregnant. Until now. At first I thought I was sick, but after three days of being unable to keep anything down, Elizabeth expressed she thought I was experiencing morning sickness, a common symptom of pregnancy. My sense of smell seemed to have heightened, and I had a strong aversion to meat of any kind. And I was so tired. I went to bed early and woke up late, still feeling as if I hadn't gotten a full night's rest. So much for helping Elizabeth during her pregnancy.

I awoke one morning to the smell of broth simmering. Vegetable broth. I was relieved to finally feel tempted to eat something. It sat well and was the only thing I ate, several times a day I might add. Elizabeth made a fresh pot every few days. Fresh air also helped, and I often sat out on the rooftop, especially during the evenings.

I began to distract myself by keeping a journal. Zechariah's detailed description of the angelic visitation made me want to record my own. I also recorded my fear of losing Joseph. Would he understand? How would he feel about me carrying a child that was not his own?

One evening while writing, I saw a group of Roman soldiers climbing the hill toward Jerusalem. I was surprised when one of the men veered away from the other men and made his way toward me. At first I thought he was looking at me, but soon realized he was studying the house. He then moved toward the door and was no longer in my view. I heard him talking to Elizabeth but could not make out what they were saying to each other. Several minutes later, the man came back into view. His back now to me, he continued on into Jerusalem with his fellow soldiers.

Hearing laborious breathing, I turned to find Elizabeth. I was amazed at how much her belly had expanded in just the short time I had been here. She still had two months left, and I couldn't help but wonder how the baby could stay put much longer. It was then that I noticed the item she held in her hands. My veil—the one I had been working on at home. And some folded parchment. Elizabeth handed me the items before taking a seat beside me.

"Who was that?" I asked.

"His name is Julius. He is a Roman soldier stationed outside of Nazareth, and when your family learned he was traveling this way, they asked him to deliver these items."

Unfolding the parchment, I saw there were three letters. One from my mother, one from my father, and one from Joseph. Just the sight of his name brought tears to my eyes. A part of me wanted to read the letter right away, but another part of me wanted to wait and savor it just a little bit longer. The latter desire won out, and I read my father's missive first.

I made it back to Nazareth. Your mother was not happy to find I had traveled so far alone. Like mother, like daughter! I did miss your company.

And it is too quiet in our little hut without you, which makes me dread the day you marry and leave us for good. My only consolation is knowing the man you are betrothed to loves you and will take care of you better, I think, than I have.

I met a Roman soldier on my journey home. His name is Julius. He is stationed just outside of Nazareth and travels between Nazareth and Jerusalem on a regular basis. When it is time for you to return, I believe I will have him escort you. I think you would be safer traveling with a group of armed soldiers than with an old man such as myself. I will write again when it is safe for you to return.

Much love, Father.

Next, I turned to my mother's letter.

Mary,

First you startle me with a sudden trip to go see Elizabeth with little notice. And then, your father returns home without you. I sense there is more going on than you or your father are willing to tell me. But having kept things to yourselves for years, I know better than to complain now.

I'm sending your veil for you to finish. Without knowing how long you plan to stay, you may not have time to finish it when you arrive home.

Joseph stops by often. He is such a good man, and you are blessed to have found a man such as him. Come home soon. He seems lost without you.

Love, Mother.

I tenderly traced the name *Mary* written on the last folded letter. I desperately wanted to bring the letter to my nose to see if it smelled of cedar, but sensing Elizabeth's gaze, I managed to resist. Finally, I unfolded the parchment and began to read.

Mary, the woman I've prayed for, the woman who fills my heart with every good thing, the woman who makes me feel whole, the woman I wish to lie next to until my dying breath…

"He obviously writes a good letter," Elizabeth whispered in response to my flushed cheeks.

Once again, I had almost forgotten her presence. "Yes, he most definitely does."

…the woman I dream of every night, the woman who fills my thoughts each day, Mary, Mary, where are you, Mary? I may one day in the distant future forgive you for staying in Jerusalem with your cousin. How disheartened I was when your father returned without you. And then to find you plan to stay another three months… I'm not sure my heart can survive that long without you near, but perhaps if I daily remind myself that upon your return we will only have two months to wait until our wedding day, it may relieve some of this agony.

Your parents are doing well. Although your father also feels somewhat misplaced without your presence. Do you realize the void you fill in each one of us? Do you understand your value? You are more precious than rubies. All things desired cannot be compared to you…

Is this how he felt about me? I had always sensed his desire, his longing, but never could I have guessed what lay in his heart…for me.

"Tell me about him," Elizabeth asked.

"Joseph?" At her nod, I continued. "He is a carpenter. He is from this area. He and his mother used to play in these Judean hills, but sadly she died when he was a young boy. And he has a brother five years younger."

"What drew you to him?" Elizabeth was asking for details I had never shared with anyone, details I kept hidden in my heart. But I found myself willing to share them with her.

"From the moment I first laid eyes on him, I knew he was different. He's kind, compassionate, and hard working. He's dependable, and I know he'll remain faithful. And just now, I found another quality I didn't realize he had. Romantic letter writing!" I waved the piece of parchment in my hand. "What I love most about him is how he treats my father with such honor and respect. And he smells of cedar and makes beautiful things with his bare hands."

"And how does he feel about you carrying God's son?"

I looked down at my hands. "I haven't told him yet."

"If you wait too long, he'll find out on his own." Elizabeth spread her hands over her large belly. "Pregnancy is rather hard to hide, wouldn't you say?"

"I'm scared, or rather terrified, he won't believe me. Who has this ever happened to? I hardly believe it myself. Which brings me to a question of my own, Elizabeth. Why was Zechariah made mute for questioning Gabriel? I also questioned him but I still have my voice…for now, that is!"

We both laughed.

"I've wondered the same thing," she answered. "And I've come to this conclusion. Though you both questioned the angel, there is a subtle difference in the way you questioned him. Zechariah was questioning in doubt, perhaps asking the angel for proof. The only basis for his doubt was my old age! Hadn't Yahweh already proved that old women could have children when he answered Abraham and Sarah's prayer?

"You, on the other hand, were not questioning whether you could trust God at His word. You were asking in amazement and wonder, *How can this be?*—a justified question since no woman has ever before conceived without being with a man. And once the angel explained how it could be, you did believe. Were not your words, *'Let it be as you say'*?"

At my affirmation, she continued. "Perhaps even greater is how often Zechariah and I prayed for a child. And then when the angel announced that Zechariah's prayer was going to be answered, Zechariah essentially was doubting the answer to his prayer. But have you, Mary, ever prayed to have a miraculous child out of wedlock?"

I shook my head.

"I didn't think so," she said with a laugh. "So, your questioning of the angel was perhaps more understandable than that of my unbelieving husband."

Seeing a shadow behind me, I turned to see Zechariah standing there, shaking his head at his wife's clever comparison of our faith. He had his writing tablet and he made his way over, taking a seat beside his wife. We waited while he wrote out his response. Finally finished, Zechariah turned the tablet toward us so we could read his words.

I was challenging God, almost defying that even He could accomplish such a thing. I had become prideful in my old age. But God has certainly dealt with that, wouldn't you say?

"You did have a certain self-assuredness," Elizabeth teased her husband. "But not now. Now you're nearly like the man I married all those years ago."

It's a good thing, too, since we are facing the largest responsibility of our lives.

"Raising your son?" I asked.

Raising a son who will be a forerunner to your son. John will be born into a priestly family, but God has already enlightened me that he will not follow in my footsteps. Instead, he will preach and prophesy in an effort to prepare a way for Jesus.

It felt surreal when we would talk about our sons' futures and what God would do in each of their lives. I often found myself wondering if they would be friends. How often would they see each other? Would they know one another well? I watched as Zechariah wrote in fervor, trying to relay what was on his heart.

This is a two-thousand-year-old prophecy, Mary! A child of God will be born. *Who would have thought it would be in my day or even in this family? We are blessed indeed.*

I was sitting inside, working on my veil. I spent most early mornings and evenings on the roof when it was cool outside. But the middle of the day proved to be warmer than I could handle. Heat never used to bother me, but my tolerances of many things had changed since I had become pregnant.

Elizabeth and Zechariah had gone to the market to purchase some produce. I had gone before, but the outing proved to be too taxing. I was looking forward to the next part of the pregnancy when this sickness eased and my fatigue lessened. The door was open to let in the gentle breeze. I closed my eyes, enjoying the wind as it lifted my long hair.

I'm not sure how long I sat with my eyes closed. But when I reopened them, I flinched to find a man standing in the doorway.

I recognized him as the Roman soldier who had delivered the letters just a few days before. Standing to my feet, I walked toward him, slightly embarrassed he had caught me daydreaming in the middle of the day.

"I apologize for interrupting," he said. "My name is Julius." He had kind eyes. "I'm on my way back to Nazareth and was wondering if you have any letters you would like me to deliver before I depart."

Julius stood over six feet tall and was solid in build. I could see why he made a good soldier. "I do have some letters," I confirmed. "Thank you for stopping. If you could wait just a moment…"

"Take your time."

I hurried to the back room to retrieve the letters I had written. The two to my father and mother had been relatively easy to write. But Joseph's…

I fingered the letters of his name, wishing he were not so far away… Joseph's letter had been much more difficult. Perhaps if he were aware of the situation I was in, it would have been easier. But I wasn't sure how much to share with him. If I told him I was not feeling well, he would wonder why my ailment was lasting so long. Instead, I stuck with simple, mundane things that were sure to bore him. And I emphasized my love for him. But to me it was lacking, especially after receiving his letter so full of emotion.

I returned to the front room, handing the letters over to Julius. "You met my father on his journey home?" I asked.

"I did. He's a very kind man, and we had many good conversations. Did he mention I would escort you on your return home?"

"Yes, he did. Was the journey so hard on him that he will not be returning to retrieve me?" There was a long delay in his answer, and I could tell he was preparing an answer to best suit me.

"It may have been too taxing, yes. But no worries, I will get you home safely when the time comes." After a brief pause, he continued. "Do you need me to relay anything that you didn't put in the letters?"

"I believe I covered everything. Thank you for taking the time to deliver them."

Julius nodded and turned to leave. Hesitating, he turned back around. "Are you well? The day I delivered the letters, you were on the roof, your eyes closed. And today, your eyes were closed again." He studied me as if trying to diagnose me himself.

So, he had seen me on the roof. "I am well," I answered. I barely knew the man, and was not about to divulge my most private thoughts. My father was usually a good judge of character, and seeing how he trusted Julius even to the point of allowing him to bring me home should have brought me peace. But the soldier would need to earn my trust before I'd tell him any secrets from my heart.

Hearing voices, we both turned as Elizabeth and Zechariah came upon us. Introductions were made. I watched Julius closely, wondering how he would react to Zechariah and his lack of speech. But he seemed to take it all in stride, as if he had been aware before he'd ever arrived. My father must have told him.

"Your son, he is due soon?"

"Yes, only a few more weeks. I look forward to not having this extra weight to carry around. I am an old woman, and this child has certainly slowed me down!"

Elizabeth hadn't noticed Julius had said *son* instead of child. But I had. Just how much had my father shared with him?

We all turned to look at Zechariah's tablet. *You will still have the extra weight to carry around, my wife, as he will grow heavier by the day!*

"Yes, well, at least when my arms grow weak, I can simply hand him over to you, my husband!"

I should not have married such a feisty woman!

Julius stayed for the midday meal before departing. We learned he had lost both his parents at a young age, and his grandparents had raised him here outside of Jerusalem. His grandmother was now gone as well, although his grandfather was alive and well and now resided in Nazareth. His grandfather's name was Gavriel. And while I didn't know him well, I knew of him.

I felt Julius's eyes on me during the meal, aware that I ate only vegetable broth and none of the other items on the table. Had my father told him?

Herod the First, better known as Herod the Great, ruled over Judea long before I was even born. I had heard many stories, some perhaps exaggerated, but each one alarming. He was known as a ruthless man who did not hesitate to kill anyone who stood as a threat to his throne. Banishing his first wife, Doris, along with their three-year-old son, he replaced her with Mariamne, the granddaughter of Hyrcanus II in hopes of increasing his credentials as a Jewish ruler.

But after seven years and five children, Herod accused Doris of attempting to dethrone him and had her executed. He married several more times, and he later had two sons executed in the belief that they had become a threat to his own life and reign.

Herod's most fatal flaw was his obsession of being dethroned. It was often said in secrecy, "It is better to be Herod's dog than one of his children."

Aside from his family, Herod did have many positive accomplishments as a builder. His most famous project was the massive expansion of the Temple of Jerusalem. This building project began many years before my birth. But I vaguely remember coming for the Passover as a little girl and being part of the dedication ceremony. It was a magnificent building. The Holy of Holies was covered in gold. Walls and columns were constructed of white marble. And the floors were hewn from Carrara marble, giving it a tinge of blue which gave the impression of walking on water.

Herod had placed at the main entrance a large Roman eagle, which many of the Jews saw as sacrilegious. When a group of Torah students saw fit to destroy the emblem, Herod had them hunted down, dragged in chains, and burned alive. Herod's persecutions were notorious, and he was both hated and feared alike.

Previous to Herod, Rome had dominion over Israel. In order to keep control over the Judean people, Julius Caesar had installed Herod as king. We had long been a people under foreign rule. There were often mandates and decrees issued by Caesar Augustus, so the latest one was not a surprise. Zechariah brought it home that evening. He laid it out for us to read.

A census shall be taken and every individual counted. Every person must return to the city of his ancestors to be registered and taxed. Failure to comply will result in land being forfeited.

I looked up at Zechariah for answers. He took out his tablet and began writing.

The emperor wishes to be able to tax the people with greater accuracy. How else will he fund his military or build his projects?

Elizabeth's hand rubbed her belly. "How long do we have?"

"Here, at the bottom, it says six months from the date the decree is issued." I pointed to the words on the parchment holding the seal of Caesar.

Plenty of time. Zechariah pulled his wife near and kissed her cheek before sitting down at the table.

It had been three weeks since Julius had left for Nazareth, and I had expected him to return by now. I didn't want to admit how much I was yearning for another letter from Joseph. After nine weeks apart, I was afraid he would forget me or at the very least grow accustomed to life without me. I sat down at the table next to Zechariah, hoping he would elaborate on the meaning of the census, but he did not. I felt a warm hand cover my own and looked up into Elizabeth's kind eyes.

"Where is Joseph from?" she asked.

"I believe his ancestors are from Bethlehem. He is from the line of David."

Zechariah's hand scribbled quickly over his tablet. *No wonder he is such a good man.*

I smiled at his words. Joseph was a good man. A very good man. I watched Zechariah lunge from his chair and stride across the room, pulling something from the mantle on the wall. Sheepishly, he walked toward me. He sat the pile of parchments on the table and pushed them toward me. I cautiously picked up each one. A letter from my father, another from my mother, and *one, two, three, four...*four letters from Joseph.

"When did these come?"

Yesterday, when you and Elizabeth went to market.

"Julius was here?"

Zechariah nodded.

"Go ahead." Elizabeth excused me from the table with a smile.

I quickly climbed up to the rooftop, eager to find out news from home. Once again, I started with my father's letter. He spoke of the well running out of water for three days and Joseph bringing them their supply from an abandoned well a mile from town. He also spoke of Gavriel, Julius's grandfather, and how he was joining them for supper almost every evening now. I found it odd that my father hadn't mentioned how work in the fields was going, since most of his days were spent there.

My mother's letter also mentioned the concern with our town's well and the lack of water. She asked that I pray for rain. She also revealed that my dress was finished, and she couldn't wait for me to try it on. I felt the color drain from my face. The beautiful dress my mother had spent so many hours creating would not be worn for my ceremony. How had I overlooked that detail? By the time Joseph and I married, I would be five months along.

The first four weeks I had lost weight, as I was unable to keep any food down. But lately, the nausea had been lessening week by week. I was beginning to make up for my lack of eating from before. My waist was expanding, only noticeable by me, but just looking at Elizabeth's figure day in and day out assured me that it would only be a matter of time before the entire world knew that Mary of Nazareth was pregnant.

All of a sudden I felt faint, as if I were going to pass out. I leaned back against the mortared wall.

Had I made a mistake not telling Joseph before I left Nazareth? His letters were clenched in my fist, but I couldn't bring myself to read them. His letters were speaking to another woman. A woman I had left behind. A woman he didn't know.

I came to think of my time with Elizabeth as a time of preparation. It was a great relief to be able to express my doubts without any fear of reproach or ridicule. Whether I had questions about pregnancy or uncertainties about my future, Elizabeth seemed to have an answer for everything. It had been over a week since I had received Joseph's letters, and I still had not read them. Finally, I brought up my struggle.

"You haven't read his letters?" Elizabeth asked in surprise. "Well, hand them over. Lord knows I need something stimulating right about now."

I couldn't help but smile at her words. "He is writing to a woman who is not expecting a child. I feel like I am deceiving him."

"Perhaps if he were here and this much time had passed, it would be considered deception, Mary, but this isn't something you can put in a letter."

Of course, she was right. But I was also questioning why I was still here in Jerusalem. Was I hiding?

"And you're not hiding!" I looked at her in surprise, and then we shared a smile. Elizabeth and I had spent so much time together we now knew what the other was thinking.

"If you remember, I had a dream—and it was so real, I knew if you were to return with your father, it would not go well for you." Elizabeth drew near and took both my hands in her own. "Ask God for wisdom. He will lead and guide you, Mary, in your words and your deeds."

"Are you afraid, Elizabeth, of childbirth?"

"I thought about it often during the beginning of my pregnancy. But I think I've entered the stage where I am so uncomfortable, I'm willing to endure some unpleasantness in order to have my body back again." Elizabeth laid a hand on my cheek. "Read your letters, Mary. They may contain news you'll regret not hearing now."

I nodded and went to the back room to retrieve them. Sitting down on the mat where I slept each night, I unfolded the first letter, forcing my eyes to read the print on the page.

As I lay here on my mat each evening, I find myself trying to bring up the image of your beautiful face, and it becomes more and more difficult the longer you are away. And it frightens me. I find myself fighting off a foreboding feeling so intense at times, it feels as if I have already lost you. To what? To whom? That has not been answered. In three weeks, you will have been gone three months. Come home to me, Mary.

I felt the trepidation in his words. Was God preparing him for what he would find when I returned? I opened the next letter, no longer reluctant but desperate to feel his words, his heart.

I put flowers on Dinah's grave today. Nazareth has returned to its original way of life, oblivious to the fact that she is missing from our community. Oblivious to most, that is. I see signs that Amos visits her gravesite regularly. Yosef and Atarah married yesterday. They were betrothed for only two months, Mary. I think we made a mistake in waiting for so long. Six months would have been plenty long. Has Elizabeth had her baby yet?

Yosef, married? For so long I had thought he would be my husband, but I found that the realization that he had moved on didn't hurt anymore. In fact, I felt relieved that he had let me go. It made it easier for me to move on, without wondering if he'd be all right. The third letter was longer than the first two. Joseph spoke of the extra room he had built on to their dwelling. Our room.

…where we'll truly become husband and wife, where we'll make all those babies we plan to have, where we'll share our dreams and fears…

Where he'd become aware of every curve of my body. If he couldn't see I was carrying a child upon my arrival back to Nazareth, he certainly would be able to see it that night, our wedding night. Of course, I would tell him before he committed himself to me, although at times the thought of waiting until it was too late for him to back out of our betrothal did appeal to me. Until I realized how selfish it was. How heartless.

The final letter was about his father, Jacob. He had fallen and broken his hip. And now he was bedridden for at least six weeks. It was concerning to Joseph because his father was already weak, and he wasn't sure how his already weakened body would recuperate after being bedridden for so long. How I wished I were there to help Joseph. Trying to handle the carpentry orders and take care of his father was taking its toll it seemed. Cleophas provided help in the evenings, after he was done working in the fields.

And then he wrote something strange.

Your father has only been back on his feet for a mere two weeks, only to have my father take his place, it seems.

The words were so out of place, so unexpected, that at first I read over them with barely a thought. But it didn't take long to comprehend that something had been amiss in my family, something they had hidden from me. And I began to question other things—things said by Julius and how he had met my father on his journey home. Hadn't I sensed he was hiding something from me? It was why I did not trust him.

He was hiding something. As was Joseph, it seemed. And my parents. I left the room in search of Zechariah, and found him sitting with Elizabeth in the front room.

"Do you know where Julius is staying?"

There is a Roman fort just outside the city. He stays in one of the barracks. Why do you ask?

"Because I need to see him. There is something I need to ask him." I made my way toward the door.

"Mary," Elizabeth called as she struggled to get up out of her chair. "You can't just go out to the Roman barracks. It is unseemly."

I stopped and turned. "I won't be able to sleep unless I talk with him about something."

"Are you wanting to return home?" Elizabeth studied me, concern in her eyes. She was hoping I would stay through the childbirth.

"Eventually, but not quite yet. It is something else I wish to enquire him about." I looked over at the tablet Zechariah had raised.

If it cannot wait, I will go out and find him myself. It is not safe for you to venture out there alone. He rose from his chair slowly before kissing his wife's cheek, and then mine. He then made his way outside and down the dirt-covered path.

I helped Elizabeth with some mending, and then we began preparing supper. Finally, Zechariah returned with news that he had been unable to locate Julius but had left a message with one of the men in his barrack to have Julius come by when it was convenient for him. He didn't come by that night, nor the evening after. I guess our definitions of *convenient* were completely different. The third day, Elizabeth's contractions began.

The two greatest imperatives in life were to get married and to have children. People depended on their adult children to look after them later in old age. Without a son to assist them, the aged were in serious trouble. Another reason was that the more children one had, the more workers. More workers meant greater wealth. Children brought a sense of security offered by no other means. Elizabeth and Zechariah had been childless up until now. But today that would change.

I did my best to keep Elizabeth comfortable, while Zechariah went to fetch Adina, the midwife. I heated water and set out clean linen beside the bed so it was readily available. While Elizabeth lay on her side, I massaged her lower back with oil. It was said to quicken the labor process as well as increase the flow of breastmilk, something she would require much of in the months to come.

"Sing to me," Elizabeth's wearied voice requested.

"Sing?" I did love to sing but never sang in front of anyone, not even my parents. It was something exclusive between myself and God. I at first began to hum an unfamiliar tune. After a few minutes, I brought forth words with the music.

> *My soul praises the greatness of the Lord.*
>
> *My spirit exults in God, my Savior, because He has looked favorably on His humble servant.*
>
> *All generations will call me blessed because the Almighty has done great things for me.*
>
> *His name is holy.*
>
> *His mercy lasts from generation to generation for those who fear Him.*
>
> *He displayed His mighty power with His arm.*
>
> *He scattered people who were proud in mind and heart.*
>
> *He pulled powerful rulers from their thrones and lifted up humble people.*
>
> *He filled hungry people with good things and sent rich people away with nothing.*
>
> *He helped His servant Israel, remembering to be merciful, according to the promise He made to our ancestors, to Abraham and His descendants forever.*

I turned to find Elizabeth staring at me, her eyes full of joy. "Again," she whispered. I obliged her, singing the same words over and over again until Zechariah and Adina entered the room.

I was happy to let Adina take over. I would simply observe so when my time came, I would be prepared. I watched as Adina placed a small stool in the center of the room. She then moved to the mat where Elizabeth was lying and began a thorough examination.

"You are close, yakira. An hour or two at most. We will move you to the birthing stool when the time is right. For now, you rest. You will need your strength."

I smiled at Adina's term *yakira—dear.* She treated Elizabeth with such tenderness and respect. "Is there anything I can do to help?"

"Take the water off the fire, please. We don't want it too hot when the time comes."

I nodded and hurried from the room. I found Zechariah sitting at the table writing with more fervency than I had ever seen before. Glancing at the words, I realized he was writing out the Psalms. Many men would chant the words outside the doorway to their wives' birthing chamber. But since he was unable to speak, he was offering up the words in his own way.

I returned to the room to find Adina laying out her supplies. There were sponges, pieces of wool bandages, a pillow of some sort, and strong-smelling herbs. I wrinkled my nose, which brought a slight smile to the serious woman's face.

"We can't have Elizabeth fainting, now can we?"

"I don't think any of us are in jeopardy of that." My comment earned a chuckle from Elizabeth and a wider smile from Adina.

"This needs to be heated." Adina handed me a glass jar of olive oil, and I took it to the kitchen to put it near the fire.

"How far along are you?" Adina asked when I returned. Her question caught me off guard. I glanced down at my belly, wondering how she could tell.

"I've been delivering babies for over twenty years. It is in the way you walk."

"Three months," I whispered. She could see my fear, my hesitation.

"You're not married?"

"Betrothed. He doesn't know yet." The words slipped out before I could stop them.

"You are not the first woman to be carrying a child before the actual ceremony. Marry soon, and no one will know the difference…no one perhaps but the midwife, that is."

The child is not his, my conscience admonished. But I ignored it and did my best to aid Adina. Mostly I observed and ran back and forth from the kitchen, delivering one item and taking another. I watched as Adina massaged Elizabeth's stomach with the warm olive oil, reducing the pain of each contraction.

Finally, Adina decided it was time for the baby to come. Together, we moved Elizabeth to the birthing stool, placing her feet on the warm stones that had been heating by the stove earlier. Adina wrapped her hands with the thin papyrus she had already laid out and then knelt before the stool. I stood behind Elizabeth and steadied her body the best I could. The rest was a blur, but the loud wail of a newborn baby filled the air, bringing me back to my senses.

"It's a boy! A strong, healthy son." Adina gently handed the baby to Elizabeth, and I watched as their eyes connected for the very first time. Tears slipped down my cheeks.

Noticing Zechariah's head peeping into the room, I waved him forward. He gently lifted his wife and child and lay them back in the bed, now lined with clean linen. He then took his son into his arms and blessed him. Several minutes passed before Zechariah turned toward me, his eyes wide. He pointed to the doorway, adamant that I must leave at once.

At first I was surprised, and then hurt. My time here was done, it seemed. I left and walked into the front room to find Julius standing there. He stood staring at me, as if he wanted to point out some peculiar detail but couldn't bring himself to do so.

I looked down at my hands and cloak, and gasped. They were stained with various red colorings, and no one need guess what had happened in the room next door. I felt my face blush several shades the same color.

"You chose a rather *convenient* time to come, did you not?" My voice was laced with irritation, and I instantly regretted my words. When my eyes finally found the courage to meet his, I was surprised by the gaiety I found in them.

"I came an hour ago. Zechariah seemed like he needed the company, so I remained. But when he heard his baby's cry, he forgot I existed." Julius took a seat, intending to stay, it seemed. "You wanted to see me?"

"Has my father been ill?"

"Ill?"

"You always answer my question with one of your own, I've noticed. Especially when you need more time to answer. Why is that?"

"Why?" He smiled at me, trying to bait me, it seemed.

"Has my father been ill or not?"

"Joseph talks about you in the most endearing words possible, and I have yet to see any of the qualities he has described. Are you by chance deceiving him?"

Deceiving him? His words caught me off guard. I turned and walked out the door and into the dark night, my feet taking me on a journey my mind was uninformed of. I clenched my fists in effort to keep my emotions from unraveling.

"Where are you going?"

I hadn't realized Julius had followed me until his words pushed through my reverie.

"Where am I going?"

Julius chuckled. "Playing my game, are you?" We walked a little farther. "Your father is doing well, by the way."

"But he wasn't, was he?"

Julius cleared his throat before continuing. "He was attacked by thieves on his journey home. I came upon him, scaring the robbers away in the process, although your father said they hadn't taken anything of value, only his dignity. They had beaten him severely enough that another soldier and I had to carry him on one of our injured soldier cots. Several ribs were cracked and his right leg broken, which prevented him from working in the fields. He didn't want you to know until your return to Nazareth. He didn't want you to blame yourself."

"Who has cared for him?"

"Your mother and Joseph. Joseph came by often, making sure your dad was moved about daily to prevent bed sores. He also made sure they had food and water for the duration of your father's healing. He is back in the fields again, with a slight limp but working hard as usual."

Somewhere along the way, Julius had turned our feet back toward the house. "Thank you for coming to his aid."

"If it makes you feel any better, Joseph wanted to tell you. He didn't like keeping anything from you. He begged your father to reconsider. But your father was very obstinate in his decision, almost as if he thought you'd come home if you knew."

I looked up into Julius's eyes. He knew. He had to know. "What did my father tell you?"

"The first night was uncertain for your father. I think he had some internal bleeding and quite honestly, I thought he was going to die. He studied me for a long time, as if trying to decipher my character. And then I told him of my grandfather, Gavriel, who lives in Nazareth. You see, my father, a Roman centurion, fell in love with Gavriel's daughter, a Jewish girl."

"You are a Jew?" I stopped walking and stared up at him in surprise.

"Partly, although it isn't something I share with just anyone." Julius winked, his lopsided smile growing on me. "Your father then enlightened me with this absurd story that he had a daughter who was impregnated by the Holy Spirit and would soon deliver a child, the Messiah. He wanted to make sure you were taken care of if anything should happen to him. He told me of your betrothal to Joseph, but he was not sure how Joseph would react when he found out. And in case Joseph disowned you, he wanted my oath that I would protect you if need be."

"And did you believe this strange story?"

"Of course not. I thought perhaps he was hallucinating. But I promised to watch out for you. It was his dying wish, and I didn't think it would be too hard to look in on a young girl every once in a while. But then I met Joseph. You have nothing to worry about. He will stay by your side."

"Even when he finds out I carry a child that is not his?"

"One can never tell for sure, but the way he loves you, I can't imagine him letting you go."

We were standing now in front of the house. I looked down at my soiled hands and clothing. "I better clean up," I finally voiced.

"I leave for Nazareth in three days. Your father seemed to think it was safe for you to return. Are you ready to go home, Mary?"

I nodded. "He mentioned in his letter that I could return if I felt…felt inclined to." I looked away from Julius's piercing stare.

"What are you hiding from in Nazareth?"

"I'm not sure. But I am ready to return." I turned and made my way toward the entrance of Zechariah's home. "Have you…have you mentioned my situation to anyone else?" My eyes were closed, my back toward him, as I waited for his response.

"While the story does seem farfetched, I like your family, Mary, and I will keep my word to your father. Besides, if you do carry the *Messiah*, perhaps I will be rewarded with my own place in heaven one day. I'm not holding my breath, though."

I heard his footsteps fade away, and it was several minutes before I entered the house. Adina was still there, attempting to aid Elizabeth in the ways of nursing. I listened intently, knowing one day soon I would have a son of my own.

I left Jerusalem, both thankful for the time Elizabeth and I had been blessed with, and distraught over how much distance lay between us. Kissing both her cheeks, I then placed a gentle kiss on John's soft forehead.

John. An unusual name since it was customary to name a son after his father. But Zechariah was determined his son's name was to be John. There was a reason John was born before my son. I had a feeling one day I might fully understand. All I knew now was that John and Jesus would be close companions.

Julius had made arrangements for another family to travel with his *contubunium.* The family consisted of a man and wife and their two daughters. I was relieved I was not the only female among the group of eight soldiers. The family was quiet, and they mostly kept to themselves, although I slept in their tent each evening when the sun went down. Vida, the mother, and her two daughters, Alizah and Maya, helped with supper preparations each evening, as did I.

One evening, after supper, we all sat around the fire. I asked Julius what the qualifications were for becoming a soldier.

"Well, first off, you must be a Roman citizen."

"And you must be recommended by someone already in the army," another soldier, Johan, added.

"And don't forget the most important aspect, which is to be physically fit," Leander, another soldier, announced with a smile. "Are you aware of the meaning of my name, Leander?"

I tried to hide my smile, especially when Julius raised his eyebrows in sarcasm. Alizah, who was near the same age as myself, studied Leander with admiring eyes.

"Leander means lion-man."

"And you never let us forget, do you?" Johan voiced with irony. "The most important aspect is actually to be of good character, which is as it should be, as we can't control how tall or stout we will be, but we can control our character."

"Very true, Johan," Julius stated with a smile.

Each of the eight soldiers ranged in age from eighteen to twenty-two. They were all fairly new recruits. I found it fascinating that each army had twenty-eight legions. And each legion had between five thousand to six thousand men. These men were then divided into ten cohorts, and each cohort had six centuries of about eighty men, led by centurions. Each century was split into groups of eight men who shared a tent, also known as a barrack. These eight men made one group and were led by a Roman centurion, Ludovic.

"So, is that every soldier's goal? To become a centurion?" Alizah asked.

"It is what we strive for," Julius answered.

All the soldiers were up at sunrise, so we made good time as we traveled. As we drew nearer to Nazareth, I felt myself begin to draw away from the group, not just physically but emotionally as well. As much as I wanted to see Joseph, the fear of telling him was almost too much to bear.

Over supper the last evening, I picked at my food, pretending to be interested but not able to take one bite. Finally, I sat the dish aside. Looking across the fire, I noticed Julius's eyes studying me with concern. When I stood up to leave, he stood as well and followed me away from the group.

"Are you well?" he whispered from behind so the others were sure not to hear him.

"I'm fine."

"You're not fine. I've watched you all day. You're restless, anxious even. Are you sick?"

"Look at me," I cried in frustration. "This is not going away." I pressed the cloak against my growing belly.

Julius quickly stepped in front of me, hiding my figure from the on-lookers sitting near the fire. "No one has noticed as of yet. Marry Joseph as soon as you return to Nazareth, and no one will be the wiser."

"And what if he won't marry me once I tell him?" I looked up into Julius's eyes, hoping to find strength…courage…something.

"Do you have to tell him? Couldn't you wait until after…after the ceremony?"

"And if you were my betrothed, how would you feel about that? Would you not hate me for the rest of your life if I first hid my pregnancy and then trapped you into a lifetime commitment? Would you not have even more reason to mistrust my story? Would you…"

Julius grabbed my hand and led me farther away from the small group of people. "Shhh, Mary, you need to let God take care of this situation. Is He not the one who gave you this child? Is He not the one who can work out all the details?"

I fell against him, sobbing. I sensed his hesitation before he finally enfolded me into his arms, allowing me to release all the tension I had been carrying for the last three months. Once my tears were spent, I stepped away.

"You are right." I forced myself to look up into his eyes. "God must have a plan. I must only let it unfold." I walked away, knowing Julius followed behind at a leisurely pace. He had made my father a promise. And until I was legally Joseph's, I knew he would honor it.

As we neared Nazareth the next day, I found myself scanning the faces of the people we crossed paths with. It was only a matter of time before my family and Joseph heard of my return. I found myself wishing for more time to prepare, even though I had already had over three months of time. I realized I would never be ready for this day, no matter when it came.

I saw my father's face first. He hobbled toward me as fast as his awkward gait would allow him to. And then I was in his arms as he kissed both my cheeks, whispering, "*Mo-tek, mo-tek,*" over and over again. *Sweetness.* I was his sweetness, no matter what circumstances might befall me, of God's doing or my own.

"Mary."

I heard his voice and knew he was standing behind me. Joseph. The man I knew I was destined to share my life with. The man who held my rapidly beating heart. I released my father and turned to face him, drinking in the sight of him, his beautifully chiseled face and tender brown eyes.

"*Ya-fa-shel-li,*" he said as he drew me into his arms. *My beauty.* He cupped my face in his hands. "I've missed you," he whispered. Then he kissed my forehead, lingering just long enough for me to drink in the smell of him. Finally, we turned toward my traveling companions. My father and Julius were talking, and we waited politely for them to finish. Once done, Joseph stepped forward to shake Julius's hand.

"Thank you for bringing her home safely."

"Of course. I am only glad she is in your hands now. You didn't warn me of her adventurous spirit, nor the temptation she has to roam." Julius and Joseph both laughed.

Finally, we turned toward home, my father informing me my mother was busy at home making all my favorite foods in preparation for my arrival. I felt Joseph's hand capture my own, his fingers gently intertwining with mine. I looked up, and we shared a smile.

"I have not forgotten you have something you wish to tell me now that you have returned. You've made me wait a very long time, Mary. Had I known you'd be gone so long, I would have made you tell me before you left for Jerusalem."

"And just how exactly could you have forced me to tell you?" I couldn't keep the banter from my lips.

"I would have thought of something, like holding you down and kissing you until you were breathless." He leaned near when my eyes shifted to the dirt below. "Have I embarrassed you?"

"You've always had a talent for that."

He squeezed my hand. "So, the news?"

"After supper, I promise."

"After supper," he agreed, having no idea his world was about to be upended.

I studied him freely over supper that evening, secretly trying to commit to memory every angle of his face—his strong cheekbones, his kind eyes, the dimple in his left cheek that only showed when he gave his full-fledged smile. He caught me staring a few times, and his eyes mirrored my own.

Yearning. A deep yearning. Three months apart had only deepened our love for one another.

"You've gained weight, I see," my mother announced.

Had Father not told her? I looked up at my father. He quickly looked away. "She needed to gain a few pounds," my father said. "She looks healthier than I've ever seen her before."

"Yes, she looks perfect," Joseph agreed, his hand brushing mine as we both reached for a piece of bread.

"As long as you fit in that dress I've spent countless hours making," my mother acknowledged.

I couldn't look her in the eyes, not when I knew I wouldn't be wearing that dress, not anytime soon anyway.

"I'll help clear away supper this evening," my father offered, waving Joseph and me away. We made our way into the front room. I waited for Joseph to take a seat before I sat down across from him. I felt sweat trickle down the back of my neck and into my cloak.

Joseph looked at me expectantly, and I prayed within that my news would be accepted without question. If any man was to believe me, it would be him, I tried assuring myself. I had rehearsed so many times the words I might say, but they never seemed to come out quite right.

"You're starting to frighten me," Joseph voiced with a half-smile. I realized he was staring at my hands clenched in my lap.

"I'm with child." Never, in all my rehearsed words, had I started with those three words. And as soon as they escaped my lips, I wished I had chosen another path. I watched as confusion clouded his beautiful eyes. Then denial.

"You've known this since…since that day you asked me to wait until you returned from your cousin's?" His voice held disbelief, as if he couldn't believe I could hide something of such importance from him. "Why? Why would you let me believe you intend to marry me?"

"My love for you has not changed. I still want to marry you."

"Yet you gave yourself to someone else…"

"No, I didn't…"

Joseph stood to his feet and walked to the window. I could no longer see his face, judge his emotion. "Who is the father?"

God. "An angel appeared to me."

He quickly turned from the window, his eyes questioning me. "An angel?" The suspicion behind his words was disheartening.

"Yes, an angel. His name is Gabriel…"

"Gabriel?" Joseph once more interrupted. "The same Gabriel who appeared to Daniel?"

Hope seeped from my body. The condescension in his tone worried me. Never before had he ever treated me as less than him. I questioned whether I should tell him more.

"And what did Gabriel say to you?"

I felt a hand on my shoulder and looked up into my father's loving eyes.

The warm squeeze of his fingers assured me he would tell the rest. "Joseph, if you love my daughter, I ask that you sit back down and listen to what I have to say."

Joseph hesitated briefly before finally returning to the seat he had recently vacated. My father took a seat next to me, continuing to hold one of my hands.

"This story you are about to hear will sound completely fabricated. Unbelievable. In fact, when Mary told me, I questioned her reliability, even her sanity. But please, please listen to what I have to say in its entirety. And then, if you have any questions, we'll do our best to answer them."

Joseph reluctantly nodded his head, his eyes mistrustful. But at least he hadn't left yet. I listened as my father told him of my experience in the cave four months prior. He then described our journey to Jerusalem to see Elizabeth and how everything matched up with complete accuracy. I watched Joseph's eyes as he took in the words my father spoke. He wanted to believe, I could tell he did, but without being there, how could he?

I watched as he fought between skepticism and longing. When my father finally finished speaking, there was a long, awkward silence. Finally, Joseph's eyes collided with mine. And the grief in them brought tears to my eyes. He stood to his feet.

"I'm sorry," was all he could utter before he turned and walked out the door.

I fell to my knees beside my father's chair, placing my head in his lap, deep sobs wracking my body. "Don't worry, Mary," my father consoled, caressing my hair. "He'll come around. It's a lot to take in. But he knows your character. And the story, while profound, is too miraculous to be imagined."

"You're with child?" I turned to find my mother staring at me from across the room. "And you expect all to believe you carry the Messiah?"

"Not all," I whispered before turning toward the ladder and climbing to the top.

Later, as I lay on the roof, I tried to reassure myself. But deep down, I knew how our minds questioned the miraculous. Even I, who had seen the angel, had traveled all the way to Jerusalem just to determine if the angel's words were indeed accurate.

An entire week passed by. Then another. And still, Joseph did not stop by.

I felt eyes lingering on me as I made my way into the synagogue. Was it my expanding figure? My slight figure did little to hide the pregnancy, yet I had hoped my cloak would hide it for a few more weeks. I looked up to find Joseph staring.

Believe me, my eyes begged. But he slowly turned away, and I felt the ache within intensify. Joseph, his brother, and his father took their customary seats beside us, but the chasm between us was so profound, we might as well have been sitting on opposite sides of the room.

After worship, I climbed the hillside to my favorite tree. Finding a piece of loose bark, I peeled a piece from the tree, and then another, and another. Was not my life being peeled back in similar fashion, layer after layer? Would I be required to give up everything I held dear?

"Why, Father? Why do You ask so much of me?" My tears fell to the dry dirt below. Finally, I knelt to my knees in exhaustion, my tears spent. The warm sun lulled me into a deep sleep. I awoke some time later to a shadow standing over me. My eyes, now open, turned upward in hopes to find Joseph, but I was disappointed. It was Julius.

"My grandfather says you've been by to see him several times. Thank you for taking the time to visit a lonely man." Julius sat down beside me, his back leaning against my big, strong tree.

Gavriel was the sweetest old man I had ever met, and I enjoyed our talks. "He's a kind man, so much different than his grandson. I can hardly believe they are related."

Julius grasped his heart as if he had been wounded. His antics made me smile. Reaching into his cloak, he pulled out a piece of parchment. "From Elizabeth," he voiced as he handed it to me.

So desperately in need of something encouraging, I opened it right away. Elizabeth had the most exquisite handwriting. I traced a word with my finger. How I missed her.

Dear Mary,

How blessed I was to have you here with me. I miss you something fierce. John is doing well, still healthy with the same loud wail you witnessed upon his birth! Takes after his father, I'll have you know. All of the neighbors have been so very kind, bringing meals and gifts daily.

*When we went to the temple to circumcise John on the eighth day, the priest intended to name our son Zechariah, but I spoke up and said, 'His name is to be John!' The priest then went to Zechariah for approval, and Zechariah took his tablet and wrote in large letters, **His name is John**. And as soon as the priest read the letters Zechariah was able to speak! And he hasn't stopped since.*

What does the future hold for this child? For it is clear that the Lord is with him. I think of you often, Mary. And I pray for you daily. You've been chosen for something extraordinary. It won't be easy. But it will be worth it…

Would it? Would it be worth it? The man I loved could no longer look me in the eyes. My own mother was embarrassed by my predicament. I could read it in her eyes, feel it in the way she spoke to me. She blamed me for Joseph's aloofness. Would it be worth it?

Julius, having sensed my need for deep thought, continued to lean against the tree, his eyes now closed. And then suddenly, a quickening in my belly left me breathless, not from the movement but from the realization that there was life inside of me. And not just any life. I had been chosen to be the mother to God's only Son.

"*I'm sorry,*" I whispered, a tear escaping my eye and running down my red, windblown cheek.

"Mary?" Julius was now looking at me, concern in his eyes. "Are you all right?"

"I will be," I answered. I stood to my feet, suddenly realizing I was weak with hunger. "Supper should be ready by now. Shall we return?"

We returned to my parents' house, where I found Gavriel waiting with my parents. He and Julius stayed for the meal. It was nice having them with us. Their conversation mingled with smiles, even some laughter, and served as a respite from the gloomy meals as of late.

I hastily finished off my bowl of lentil stew and reached for a second helping, but paused when I noticed my mother's disapproving gaze. My father took the ladle from my hand and poured another generous serving into my wooden vessel. Julius broke off a piece of barley bread and held it out. I hesitantly took it from his offered hand. For so long, I had felt nauseous. The very thought of food had made me ill. But that sensation had lessened considerably over the last few days.

I must be entering the next phase of pregnancy.

Elizabeth had reminded me often to enjoy this season, as it was only a few weeks of reprieve when my body would feel somewhat normal before it would then become uncomfortable as the baby grew within.

When the meal was finished, I stood to help my mother gather the dirty dishes, but she dismissed me with a wave of her hand. She was angry with me. And I didn't blame her. I was their only child and a girl at that. And now I was pregnant out of wedlock, and the father was not Joseph. She believed I had ruined my life and perhaps theirs as well. For who would ever want to marry me now? And who would take care of them later in life when they could no longer work and provide for themselves?

My mother was busy in the kitchen. And my father and Gavriel had ventured up to the rooftop to admire the grain in the fields. Julius and I remained in the courtyard, an awkward silence building between us.

"Your mother doesn't believe." It was not a question. Julius spoke the words with certainty. "How can that be? Is she not aware of the prophecy?"

"She does believe the Messiah will come," I quickly defended her. "But Micah foretells the Messiah being born in Bethlehem." Mary looked down at her hands. "And I am from Nazareth."

"Isaiah also foretold that the Lord Himself will give us a sign—for a virgin will be with child and will give birth to a son, and He will be called Immanuel." Julius stood to his feet and walked over to the rock-hewn cistern. With so little rainfall as of late, there was barely any water in it.

Immanuel. *God with us.* The Messiah was referred to by many names. *Wonderful, Counselor, The Mighty God, The Everlasting Father, The Prince of Peace.* Such beautiful descriptions of who He was and would be. My hand rested on my belly. "His name is Jesus."

"Jesus?" Julius turned to stare at me.

I nodded. "The angel, Gabriel, was very clear when he appeared to me."

"Where is Joseph?" Julius finally asked the question I knew had been plaguing him since his arrival.

I felt tears rise to the surface. Would it ever stop hurting? "I haven't seen him…not since I told him the news."

"I expected better of him…"

"You expected better of me?" Joseph's voice brought me to my feet. He stood at the entrance to the courtyard, his eyes angry and his voice bitter. The dark circles under his eyes and his unusually pale skin were evidence he had slept very little during the time of our separation. Joseph strode across the courtyard, and I watched as Julius took a step back, his back nearly pressed against the wall. "Tell me. If your betrothed came to you expecting a child that was not your own, how would you react?"

"This is different." Julius stood to his full height, the soldier in him beginning to emerge. "Mary isn't expecting just any child."

"You believe her then." Joseph stepped back, his eyes briefly appearing hopeful. But a cloud of mistrust fell over him again. "You want me to believe her story. Why is that?" And then another form of doubt crossed his features. "Are you the father?"

Julius shoved Joseph backwards. "You need to leave…"

"Stop," I screamed. "Please…please stop." They both turned toward me, their anger momentarily forgotten as I fell to my knees in despair.

Seconds later, I felt two strong arms gather me close. Thinking it was Julius, I began to push away until the scent of cedar reached my nose. I pulled him closer, my hand clutching his tunic, fearful he'd put me down and walk away. Instead, he backed against the stone wall and slid down until he was sitting on the ground. He sat holding me for quite some time, his chin resting on my head. I knew without looking that Julius had left.

"Mary." His forlorn voice crushed my heart. "I can't marry you."

I pulled my head off his chest and looked up into his betrayed eyes. "I need you," I whispered. *I need you.*

"I've tried, Mary. I've tried to come to terms with it. Perhaps I'm weak. But the hurt would fester. And there's one thing worse than not having you, and that is lying next to you with a great divide between us."

I knew within there was nothing I could say; nothing I could do that would change his mind. I felt him slipping from my grasp. *It will be worth it.* Elizabeth's words came back to me. I repeated them over and over again in my head.

"I will not expose your…predicament. I harbor no hate or disregard and vow not to publicly shame you. My plan is to quietly dismiss the contract so as not to alert the elders of the synagogue."

I nodded my head in acceptance only because I knew I could form no words. I brought his strong, rough hand to my lips. And then with a sob, I stood to my feet and ran into the house.

I loved Yahweh and desired to serve Him with all of my heart. I was a poor girl from an insignificant town in the hills of Galilee. Unknown by most, God had taken note of me. For as long as I could remember, I knew of God's promise to send the Messiah. A Messiah who would rescue my people and become our King. For four hundred years, God had been silent. No prophets had spoken. No new Scripture had been written.

I had no great expectations that my life would be any different than my mother's or than Zillah's. My mother had trained me to be a good Jewish wife and mother. And there was nothing that I wanted more than to be Joseph's wife—to be the mother of his children.

But God had a different plan for me. I didn't pretend to understand, but I accepted that He knew best.

I left the house early one morning, the water pitcher resting on my hip. The sun had barely risen in the sky, but I wanted to be the first to the well. I could no longer hide my protruding belly, and the whispers were difficult to ignore. I saw Lillian's face staring out the window of her home. I waved. She smiled and raised her hand to wave back, but her mother caught her lifted hand in her own and pulled her away from the opening, disapproval evident in her eyes.

Ironic. I had been chosen as the mother to the long-awaited Messiah, yet I had never felt more like an outcast. I breathed a sigh of relief as I approached the well. There was no one else around. I pulled the rope until the leather bucket came into view and then filled my pitcher nearly to the top.

"Mary?"

I turned to find Zillah, surprise written on her face. "Hello, Zillah."

"Jemima said…you were with child…but I didn't believe her." She stared at my protruding stomach in shock. "I still can hardly believe it. Why haven't you married?"

"Joseph has dismissed our contract." I wondered if the humiliation showed on my face.

"Whatever for…?" I saw the light register in her eyes. "The child is not his?" It was part question, part statement.

"The child is not." I stepped away from the well, situating the pitcher on my shoulder for the walk home. "It's good to see you, Zillah." I moved to walk away.

"I'm betrothed." Zillah's voice stopped me in my tracks. She stepped toward me instead of the well. "Calev offered a contract yesterday evening."

I reached out and touched her shoulder. "Oh, Zillah!" I felt tears rising to the surface and was thankful they were happy tears for once. "I'm so happy for you."

"Thank you. I wanted you to be the first to know. It was all we talked about at one time."

I remembered. But gone were the days of running across the hillside, carefree and unrestrained, dreaming about the men we would one day marry and the children we would have.

Zillah grasped my free hand in her own. "What happened, Mary?" She stepped closer, her eyes intently searching my own. "You love Joseph, do you not? Why would you give yourself to another?"

Zillah had been my closest friend for as long as I could remember. Would she believe me if I told her the truth? I felt my hope begin to fade when I reminded myself my own mother didn't believe me.

My friend must have sensed the battle within me. "Mary, you are my closest friend and confidant. You can tell me anything."

"I was at the mikveh one morning…when an angel appeared to me."

"An angel?" Was that awe and wonder I heard in her voice? *Please let it be.*

"It was the same angel that appeared to Daniel. Gabriel." The pitcher of water was growing heavy. I slowly bent to sit it on the ground. "He had a message for me."

"What was the message?"

"He said I would conceive and bear a son."

"A son. And the father?" Zillah's eyes were full of curiosity.

"The Holy Spirit." I said the words so quietly, I wondered if she even heard them.

"The Holy Spirit?" Zillah whispered. She stepped closer. "Are you saying you are carrying God's Son?"

"You shouldn't be speaking to *her,* Zillah." Havilah was standing near the well, her eyes observing me with contempt. "She is a fallen woman. Disgraced. You taint yourself just by association."

"Havilah…" Zillah began, but she quieted when I shook my head. I didn't want Zillah to tarnish her own reputation simply by being near me. I bent to pick up the pitcher, my eyes briefly connecting with Zillah's. *Thank you for listening.* I then turned down the dusty path toward home.

Hours turned into days and days into weeks. I must admit, at first I struggled with despondency. The only time I felt it lift was when I trekked to the top of the hill just before dark. Standing on the hill next to my sycamore tree, I felt alive and free. But the closer I came to Nazareth, as I trudged back home each evening, the heavier my steps became.

"Will I ever be happy again, Father?" I led the way, as darkness was descending quickly and my father's leg still gave him trouble.

"You do realize, daughter, that happiness is determined by our circumstances. Perhaps you should ask Yahweh for joy instead."

I looked over my shoulder into my father's compassionate eyes. "To be happy or joyful, are they not the same?"

"Many may think so, but they most certainly are not." He paused to catch his breath. "Happiness is temporal. It comes and goes, depending on how well our situation in life may be. But not joy. Joy is constant because God is constant. Joy is dependent upon God and His faithfulness. As our awareness of our Father increases, our joy increases."

"And as our awareness of our circumstances increases, our joy decreases," I finished for him. *The joy of the Lord is my strength.* Even the prophet Nehemiah had known the value of a joyful heart.

"Your problem is not rooted in your circumstances, Mary. Your problem is in the way you think about your circumstances. You can focus on what you've lost. Or you can focus on what you've gained."

The baby leaped inside of me, and tears of joy flooded my cheeks. We had reached the bottom of the hill, and my father came up alongside me, his large weathered hand enveloping my small one.

"Would you like to know one of the reasons God chose you?" He stopped walking and turned me to face him. "He chose you because of the strength that resides within you. You will endure trials, Mary. But you will triumph in the end."

My father gathered me close as I cried on his shoulder. Finally, my tears spent, I reached up and kissed his worn cheek. "I love you, Father."

"Oh, I almost forgot." He reached into his cloak and pulled out a piece of parchment. "Zillah pressed this into my hands as I passed by her house today.

I took the paper and unfolded it.

I believe you.

Three words. Three words that spoke volumes to my battered heart. My father pulled me back against him as tears flooded my cheeks once more. I cried even harder when a chuckle rumbled across his chest.

Barley bread was a feature of every meal. And I gladly took over the preparation. The process reminded me of my life. I was beginning to realize the importance of not overlooking the journey to the amazing destination God had planned for me.

The art of making bread was a long, drawn out, time-consuming process. I'd begin by using two grinding stones to crush the barley into a fine grain. The grain was then mixed with water. Some fermented dough that had been set aside from a previous batch would be added to the new batch. And finally, I would knead the dough before leaving it to rise.

By the time the dough was left to rise, my hands were weary, but I felt triumphant that I had completed the task. I thought about how trials of life scrape away the rough edges. And then came the water to cleanse and purify. Lingering in God's presence intensified my yearning for Him above all other things. And then finally, He'd begin molding me into something he could use.

Ultimately, He expected me to take all that I had learned and use it to minister to those who were struggling. And the process would happen over and over again, just as in the process of making bread.

At first, the task was helpful in lessening the tumult of emotions residing within me. I would knead the dough with such fervency, desperately trying to keep my emotions in check, the deep reservoir of tears at bay. But during the last week, I began to feel a shift take place. The words of Isaiah came to me daily in the form of a song. I knew much of the writings by heart, as I had memorized them as a child.

For as the rain comes down,
And the snow from heaven,
And do not return there,
But water the earth,
And make it bring forth and bud,
That it may give seed to the sower,
And bread to the eater,
So shall My word be that goes forth from My mouth;
It shall not return to Me void,
But it shall accomplish what I please,
And it shall prosper in the thing for which I sent it.

I stopped kneading the dough, the words I had just spoken enlighten-ing me, building my confidence in Yahweh. I took my floured hands and placed them on my rounded belly. "You shall prosper, matok. *Sweet one.* God will accomplish what He has set out to do."

Resuming the kneading, I glanced across the room at my mother. She was sitting on the raised platform at the far end of the room watching me, tears coursing down both her cheeks. Her eyes held wonder. Admiration even. I then noticed the item she held in her hands. My wedding veil?

"What are you doing, mother?"

She swiped away her tears, only to have them replaced by more. "I'm finishing your veil," she finally managed to utter.

My mother was one of the most practical women I knew. She was sen-sible… levelheaded. And never once in all my life had she gone about a task without reason behind it. I knew I had been a frustration to her with all my lighthearted ways. Our personalities were as different as night and day.

"Why?" I asked in confusion.

"Well, the gown is a lost cause." She was evading my question—also very unlike her.

"Mother, I am not in need of the veil either." I punched down the dough one last time and placed it near the warm fire to rise. I tried to hide the grief from my eyes upon seeing the veil in her hands. It had been packed away since my return from Elizabeth's. My mother continued to sew another bead upon the beautiful lace.

"Why?" I voiced again, tears pooling in my eyes.

"I've set about to complete several tasks this morning, but I find I am unable to do them. When, finally, I asked Yahweh what He wanted from me, He insisted I finish the veil. I know not why, daughter. But I do know until this veil is completed, I will be unable to accomplish anything else, it seems."

Hearing a flock of noisy boys outside on the streets, likely on their way to the synagogue for their lessons in the Torah, reminded me I had yet to get our daily supply of water. I had used the last of the water this morning while mixing the dough. With one last confused glance at my mother so engrossed in her task, I reached for the pitcher and then opened the door.

"Your father believes it is time for me to begin collecting the water." My mother began to rise from the cushion.

"One last time, mother. You can collect the water this evening." I hurried out the door lest she try to stop me. I didn't want to be a burden to my parents, but it seemed that was unavoidable. As a pregnant woman with no husband, I had become an enormous burden. Their lives would only become more difficult with each passing day.

It will be worth it. I continued to repeat the words in my heart.

I smiled when I noticed his small shadow. "Following me again, Matteus?" He had been trailing me for weeks now. I knew my father must have been paying him to watch over me. Although he couldn't be paying him much, not with our minute savings. But it seemed Matteus took his job seriously.

"Off to get water again, Mary?" the young boy asked. "I find that I am thirsty as well." He stepped out of the shadows of the house and waited until I was a few steps ahead before he set the same pace as me. When I had brought up my handsome follower to my father over supper one evening, he had only smiled, a gleam in his eyes. Oh, how I loved him!

We passed house after house and finally the synagogue. There were several women already waiting in line at the well. I should have come to get water before the preparation of the bread. Matteus saw my hesitation. He stepped forward.

"Step into the shadows, Mary. I will fill the pitcher this time." His smile reached his eyes. I handed him the pitcher and watched as he got in line.

A deep, unfulfilled longing resonated within as I watched the women visit and laugh with one another, waiting to draw water. This was the time of day to discuss life. It seemed forever since I had enjoyed conversation with anyone other than my parents.

It was now Atarah's turn. I studied her as she went through the motions of pulling the bucket of water up out of the well. I couldn't help but wonder if she was happy in her marriage to Yosef. Did he treat her well?

Finally, Matteus stepped forward to take his turn. The women were so engrossed in conversation, they hardly noticed him. I watched as he poured the bucket of water into the pitcher at his feet. As he bent to lift the pitcher, I could see his arms strain beneath the weight. When it began to slip from his shoulder, I stepped out from beneath the shadows, and all eyes turned toward me. Matteus righted the pitcher, his bright eyes suddenly cautious and alert. He slowly walked toward me.

"Harlot," a voice cried in anger.

As soon as Matteus was within reach, I took the pitcher from him and slid it onto my own shoulder. We turned and hastily moved down the dirt path away from the well.

"Always so high and mighty. Look at you now!" The words of my accusers were not fading away but were, in fact, drawing nearer.

"Go, Matteus. Go home," I pleaded. He was such a beautiful little boy. I didn't want him involved. I gently pushed him away from me. "Go!"

Matteus looked up into my face. "I promised…"

A stone hit me from behind, and I fell to my knees, the pitcher shattering into pieces on the ground beside me, water seeping into the dirt. I was roughly hauled to my feet and forced to walk down the street toward the synagogue. Their pace too fast for me, I tripped several times, the firm grasps of those beside me keeping me from falling.

We entered the outer stone walls of the synagogue, and I found myself surrounded by women on all sides. And not just any women, but women I had known all my life. Had I known that God's plan would cause such turmoil and pain? Was I aware when I submitted to the angel's request that all my dreams for the future would be shattered?

No, I hadn't known the cost. But I would gladly accept God's plan for my life again and again, no matter the outcome.

A heavenly peace flooded me. I could see everyone's mouths flinging insult after insult, but I couldn't hear the spoken words. And then a white-robed rabbi stepped into the crowd and made his way toward me. Immediately, I could hear again.

"Mary?" he questioned. "You have no husband?"

"I do not." I looked into his troubled eyes.

"Let us bring her to the entrance of her father's house and stone her to death." The voice belonged to a man. More and more people were flooding through the outside entrance of the synagogue.

"Hush," the rabbi demanded. "Where is the man who had relations with this girl? Pay her father fifty silver shekels, and take her as your wife." A brief silence fell over the place as people looked for someone to step forward.

"Mary," the rabbi whispered for my ears alone. "Who is the father of your child?"

"Please, let her go." My father fell to his knees before the rabbi. "She has done nothing wrong."

"Her belly suggests otherwise," another man screamed from the crowd. He bent to retrieve a stone from the ground. Others around him did likewise.

"I am the father."

I heard his voice before I actually saw him. Firm. Decisive. He stepped into the circle, his eyes quickly finding mine. His gaze didn't waver as he made his way toward me. He reached out and dropped fifty silver shekels into my father's hands.

Joseph picked me up and carried me away from the crowd. Suddenly he stopped. Turning, he said, "Rabbi, there's to be a wedding celebration this evening at the home of Heli." He then turned toward the crowd. "Any friends of my betrothed are welcome as well." He left the synagogue and continued down the path toward my home.

When his eyes had connected with mine back at the synagogue, there was a clarity within them. "Joseph," I whispered against his chest.

"Later," he replied. He sat me down on the stoop in front of my door. "I will tell you everything later." He tenderly kissed my forehead. "*Ya-fa-shel-li*," he whispered against my skin. And then he was gone.

A Jewish wedding was one of the cornerstones of the Jewish life and a great cause for celebration. Its tapestry was woven from many threads: biblical, historical, cultural and legal. The marriage ceremony was a reenactment of the marriage between God and the Jewish people that took place at Mount Sinai. It was also very personal and perhaps one of the holiest day of one's life.

Under normal circumstances, the bride and groom were to refrain from seeing each other for a full week prior to the wedding, so as to increase their love and yearning for one another. Although I had briefly seen Joseph just that morning, I felt that our recent month-long separation since he had learned of my pregnancy certainly qualified. I had never ached for his nearness more than I did in this moment.

It was customary for the bride and groom to reside in adjacent rooms at the beginning of the ceremony. An ornate, throne-like chair was brought in, and I was instructed to sit in it. Friends and family began to arrive. First to appear were Zillah and her betrothed, Calev. She bent and tenderly kissed my left cheek and then my right.

"I wish you beauty for ashes, the oil of joy for mourning, and the garment of praise for the spirit of heaviness." She moved on to the other room to exchange words with Joseph. More and more people came through the door offering their heartfelt wishes and words of encouragement. From across the way, I could hear songs being sung. The loud, boisterous voice of Joseph's brother, Cleophas, brought a smile to my lips.

Then came the signing of the wedding documents. There were two— the *tenai'm* and the *ketubah*. The *tenai'm* was the contract Joseph had offered to my father several months ago. His hand brushed mine as he reached for the quill pen. The lift of one side of his mouth suggested he noticed the enjoyment it caused.

After the signing of the *tenai'm,* it was custom for the mothers of the bride and groom to break a plate. My mother broke two, one for herself and one in memory of Joseph's mother, Aliza. The meaning of her name, *filled with joy,* did not escape my notice during this moment. Joyous shouts of *Mazal Tov* echoed throughout the house and down the street. In this way, they congratulated us and wished us good fortune.

After the signing of the contracts came the veiling ceremony. Joseph took the beautiful veil from my mother's outstretched hands—the veil she had finished just hours before. I looked into her eyes, hoping that she could read my appreciation, my love. Her eyes filled with tears as she placed her hand on her heart.

Joseph stepped forward and gently covered my face with the veil. The covering of the bride's face originated with our matriarch Rebecca, who covered her face when meeting her groom, Isaac. It emphasized that the groom was not solely interested in the bride's external beauty, which would fade in time, but rather in her inner beauty which would never fade. My face would remain veiled for the duration of the ceremony, affording me privacy during this holy time.

Now, the blessing. My parents approached me with reverence. Never had I seen such devotion in my father's eyes. "May God be with you always, daughter." He placed my hand in Joseph's as a symbol of relinquishing me into Joseph's care. His sorrow was evident. I was his little girl, and it was hard for him to give me up.

The ceremony moved outdoors to the courtyard where a *chupah* now stood. The canopy sat atop four poles and was ornately decorated. I began to wonder how all of this had been orchestrated in so little time. Neither my parents nor I had been aware there was going to be a wedding today. I looked across the way to where Joseph stood with his entourage of well-wishers. The wooden chair…the canopy…where had it all come from? Joseph? And if Joseph had constructed it, he hadn't done it today. These items had taken days to create.

I looked up into the open night sky, recalling God's blessing to Abraham that his descendants would be as numerous as the stars. Tears filled my eyes as I became aware of the awe and magnitude of this moment. Just this morning, I had been called shameful, disgraceful. The accusations hurled at me were intended to make me feel worthless and undeserving. And now, this evening, I felt like a queen worthy of her King.

I heard a whistle and felt my face flush red as I realized Joseph was already standing under the canopy awaiting the arrival of his bride. I moved toward him slowly, my eyes never leaving his. I circled him seven times, each time around creating an invisible wall into which I then stepped into, excluding all others. *I honor you now and forever with all that I am.* He smiled and took my hands in his.

Marriage was a two-step process. The first step was called *kiddushin,* known as sanctification. It was effected when the groom gave the bride the wedding band. Joseph took my left hand, gently kissed my palm, and waited for the rabbi to proceed.

The next step was called *nisu'in,* where we sipped wine from a cup held by the rabbi while he recited blessings over us. Joseph then placed the ring on my finger. Hesitating briefly, he looked into my eyes and proclaimed, "With this ring, you are consecrated to me according to the law of Moses and Israel." He slipped the gold ring in place.

After Joseph placed the ring on my finger, the *ketubah* marriage contract was read aloud. Marriage was more than a physical and spiritual union. It was also a legal and moral commitment as well. Joseph was now obligated to provide me with food, clothing, and affection. The passion I read in his eyes made me realize he'd struggle little with his promise of affection.

My mother had tried to prepare me for the consummation that would come later tonight when we would unite as one. My face must have given away my thoughts, for when I looked up into Joseph's face, his smile and lifted brows gave evidence that he was also thinking the same thought. As the rabbi finished reading the *ketubah,* he then handed it to Joseph. Joseph then handed it to me. It signified his promise to faithfully love and provide for me as long as we both were alive.

Friends and family approached the canopy where they passed around a cup of wine, each reciting a blessing while they held it. Once the cup had made it around the circle, both Joseph and I took a sip from the cup, symbolizing that we were now one soul and would forever delight in one another. The cup was then wrapped in cloth and set beneath Joseph's foot. He brought his foot down, shattering the cup. This symbolized Jerusalem, and even amidst our personal joy was a yearning to return there. Shouts of *Mazal Tov* echoed throughout once again.

A line formed as a procession of people escorted us out of the court-yard and into the street. We made our way toward Joseph's house. Finally, we stopped in front of his door, where we turned to face our well-wishers. With a loud, triumphant shout, Joseph swung me up into his arms and carried me across the threshold. With a swift backwards kick, he shut the door, the chants and blessings still loudly heard outside.

Joseph leaned back against the door, a deep sigh resonating from his chest. *"Ish'to"*, he whispered before he lifted my veil, his mouth finding mine. *Ish'to*. His wife.

I knew I would never tire of the word. Becoming his wife was all I had ever dreamed of. From the time I was a little girl, I had envisioned marry-ing a man who would love and adore me. This man who now held me in his arms was even more than I had imagined. *Thank you, Yahweh.*

Also more than I imagined was his kiss. His lips caressed mine with such tenderness. My fingers crept up into the back of his hair as I pulled his head closer, deepening the kiss and allowing him to feel my desire for him.

Suddenly he stopped. Setting me on my feet, he strode across the room, his hands now in his hair. Disappointment now replaced desire. Unease crept up my spine. Was he having second thoughts? I took a step back. And then another.

"Wait…" he hoarsely whispered. "It's not you."

"You're still angry?" I questioned, tears rising to the surface.

"No, I'm not angry. Come." He motioned for me to join him. "I'll show you our separate quarters. And I'll explain."

I timidly crossed the room and took his outstretched hand. We crossed the main room and walked into a separate room. "You built this recently?" I asked. The stone was new as was the mud-bricks. There was little wood used, as wood was expensive. The room was cool, comfortable and pleasant.

"I added it after you accepted my betrothal." He pulled me toward the raised platform at one end, where he sat down and patted the cushion next to him. I started to sit and lost my balance. The increasing weight of the baby was proving to be awkward. Was that why he was pushing me away? Did my changing figure repulse him?

"An angel appeared to me last night." Joseph drew me close.

"Did he…say anything?" I questioned with surprise.

"He said quite a lot, actually."

"Tell me," I requested, as I leaned against him, enjoying the sound of his calm, baritone voice.

"He said I was a senseless man…"

"I don't believe you," I giggled against his chest. "What did he really say?"

"He said, *'Joseph, son of David, do not be afraid to take Mary as your wife, for that which has been conceived in her is of the Holy Spirit. And she will bear a Son; and you shall call His name Jesus, for it is He who will save His people from their sins.'* " Joseph reached out and wiped a tear from my cheek.

"Could you ever forgive such a fool?" he whispered. Bringing my hand to his lips, he kissed my wrist and waited for my reply.

"Of course." I leaned forward and kissed him on the mouth. He closed his eyes and pulled back.

"There's more." I could see this was a struggle for him, so I patiently waited for him to continue. "I woke up from the dream with a growing assurance that you did indeed see an angel that day so long ago. I wanted to believe your words when you confided in me the day of your return, but there was a conflict raging within my soul. Knowing you as I do, a part of me believed you told the truth. But the rational side of me was determined you were too good to be true; that I had made you into something you were not. The thought of living with an unfaithful wife for the rest of my life was too much to bear."

"And now?" I questioned.

"And now I could care less what any wagging tongue might suggest. I'm honored to be your husband. I'm honored God would grant me the privilege of being the father to His Son."

"But you are not attracted…"

He laid a finger on my lips. "You have no idea how you tempt me without even meaning to." Joseph pushed a hand through his already disheveled hair. "The angel requested that I…that you…that you remain a virgin until after you give birth to His Son."

I stared at him, surprise written on my face. Was he serious? Five more months? The look on his face proved that he was indeed serious. "Perhaps we should have waited?" My face reddened at the words I had just said aloud. He was now aware of my attraction to him as well.

"The thought also crossed my mind. And then Matteus showed up at my door, screaming that you were being taken to the synagogue." Joseph shrugged his shoulders. "Stoning or marriage? I don't know. Marriage seemed like the better alternative at the time."

I laughed. A laugh so freeing, I felt tears roll down both cheeks. As I thought of all that I had gained in this one day, my emotions began to get the best of me. Joseph pulled me near.

I awoke sometime in the night, his arms around me, a hand lying gently on my belly, his deep breathing indicating he was sound asleep. I closed my eyes in gratitude, once again thanking Yahweh for his goodness before falling back into a deep, restful sleep.

I awoke to the sound of hushed voices speaking from the other room. Sunlight was streaming through the two small windows in the room. I pushed myself up off the cushion, suddenly conscious of how late in the morning it was. Why hadn't my mother woken me?

I paused, taking in the unfamiliar room. Realizing the voices I was hearing were masculine, I rose to my feet. It was rare to hear so many different manly tones. I smiled when I recognized Joseph's.

My husband! The events of the past evening came back in a rush. I brought a finger to my mouth, tracing where his lips had touched mine just hours before.

"*Isha.*" Wife.

Joseph stood just inside the doorway. How long had he been watching me? Long enough, it seemed, for his lopsided smile suggested he knew exactly what I had been pondering just moments before. I felt my face flush red.

"Are you hungry?" He still wore that irresistible grin. I looked down at my feet.

"Yes. Shall I make us something?" I moved toward him.

"My father already prepared something. He usually does. We haven't had the privilege of having a woman cook for us in some time."

I followed him into the other room. It had been dark when I had arrived the night before, and I hadn't been able to survey the area. Joseph's father, Jacob, stood across the room near the cooking area, where there was a circle of stones with a fire burning in the center. This was the main room of the house, holding both an eating area and a sleeping area. A raised area across the room indicated Jacob and Cleophas both slept there. There were small niches cut into the wall, used for storage items like bed rolls and clothes. A niche near the kitchen area held food and utensils for cooking.

"Shall I go get water?" I asked hesitantly, trying to find my place among them.

"I did that already." Cleophas stepped into the room from another entryway. I assumed it led to the courtyard. "Never have I seen so many beautiful women in all my life. I see now why Joseph insisted he retrieve the water each morning."

Joseph playfully nudged his brother as he passed him. "I had eyes for only one woman."

"Ah, but has she only had eyes for you?" Cleophas said with ire. I felt my face redden as his eyes assessed my pregnant stomach.

"Cleo," Joseph warned. "I don't expect you to believe anything I say, but you will not disrespect my wife again. Understood?"

The tension between them was nearly tangible. Cleo stoically stood, staring at his brother, perhaps debating whether he would give in or not. Finally he nodded before stalking across the room back out into the court-yard.

I'm sorry, Joseph's eyes apologized.

I expected skepticism. Had, in fact, grown used to it. I could read doubt in Jacob's eyes as well, although he was too polite to acknowledge it. My heart went out to Joseph. Did they think him a fool? I realized in that moment that he would live with the gossip of an unfaithful wife for the rest of his life. By marrying me, he had turned the scrutinizing eyes of the people toward him. *What had he gained in marriage to me?*

My Son. Peace that surpassed my finite understanding instantly calmed my spirit. When I looked up at Joseph, I could see he felt His presence too.

I followed Joseph and Jacob into the courtyard where we ate a light meal consisting of grapes, melon, nuts and raisins. Joseph held a platter toward me, containing oven-baked bread with honey drizzled over the top. I took a piece, and when the plate lingered in front of me, I shyly took another.

"Thank you, Jacob, for preparing this meal for us." Jacob nodded his head in acknowledgement. I then looked at my husband. "And thank you for allowing me to sleep so late. It won't become habit, I hope." Joseph winked at me, the corner of his mouth suppressing his smile.

"Wish he'd let me sleep late once in a while," Cleophas muttered before tossing a grape in his mouth.

"Don't want you becoming soft," Joseph said with a playful grin.

We then ate in silence. I felt Joseph's eyes on me several times. With his brother and father there, I refused to look up, embarrassed to display such feeling in their midst. As the meal came to an end, Joseph turned toward me.

"There's a rather nice sycamore tree on top of that hill, there." He pointed in the direction of my favorite tree. "Would you like to join me on a walk?"

A feeling of freedom overcame me. After trying so hard to conceal my pregnancy in the previous weeks, I now realized I didn't need to hide anymore. I was now a married woman. And even though the circumstances surrounding my condition were precarious to say the least, I was free to roam once again under the protection of my husband. Tears rose to the surface. He had to know how hard my confinement had been, could read it in my eyes.

I stood to my feet and turned away, lest they all see the tears that had now fallen down my cheeks. Immediately, I felt his presence behind me. He put his hands on my shoulders, gently kneading away weeks of distress. "Come," he whispered over my shoulder. I put my hand in his offered one and allowed him to lead me from the courtyard and out into the street.

As we came to the trail leading up the hill, Joseph stopped and motioned for me to walk ahead of him. I felt my breath quicken when I saw the lovely flowers that had recently sprung up over the hillside. White Sacred Lilies, purple Rosemary and red Pereg Poppies. I stooped to pick some, their scent reminding me of the words of Isaiah.

All flesh is grass, and all its loveliness is like the flower of the field. The grass withers, the flower fades, because the breath of the Lord blows upon it; surely the people are grass. The grass withers, the flower fades, but the word of our God stands forever.

Remembering Joseph, I turned toward him, embarrassment surely evident on my face. So caught up in the moment, I had forgotten he was there. He stood watching me, amusement twinkling in his eyes.

"Are you laughing at me?" I quipped with humor, hoping to lessen my awkwardness.

"No. I'm simply enjoying your enthusiasm for life." He came up beside me, placing in my hand a fistful of blue Lupines. His eyes stared into mine. "You surprise me."

"How so?"

"Your rare strength. Your unfathomable trust."

My gaze dropped to the bouquet of flowers I held in my hand. "I'm not without flaws."

"I don't expect you to be. And neither does He." He tipped my chin up. "You carry something priceless within you—a deep love for God and an obedient spirit." Joseph smiled. "Who else would God choose to be the mother of His Son? Who else would love and nurture His Son more sincerely than you?"

"And yet I often wonder why Yahweh has given me this incredible gift." My free hand caressed my stomach. "I possess no wealth or family inheritance to pass on to Him. I can boast of no fame or social status to help Him make His way in the world."

"And yet I believe you'll give Him gifts of more infinite value than material advantages."

"Like what?" I whispered in uncertainty.

"Like purity of heart. Obedience. And love."

We turned and resumed our trek up the hillside, my mind pondering Joseph's words. I felt invigorated as I hadn't felt in days. "Would you like to know why you were chosen to be His father?"

Joseph laughed. "Why yes, I would."

"You're an extremely skilled carpenter…" I began giggling and couldn't stop.

"Are you laughing at me?" Joseph asked from behind as I stopped to catch my breath. My laughter ceased as his lips gently touched the back of my neck. He then turned me around to face him. "I'm one of the best carpenters in these parts," he whispered, his eyebrows lifted in humor.

"You're also one of the most honorable and faithful men I know," I whispered back before my lips found his. He deepened the kiss, and when he finally stepped back, my body trembled.

"One hundred twenty-five."

"One hundred twenty-five?"

"The days left until our Son is born." One hundred twenty-five days until we could fully become husband and wife.

"You forget the time of purification," I corrected, a blush creeping up my neck and face.

Joseph moaned. "How long?"

"Forty days."

He looked up into the sky. "You obviously believe I'm stronger than I think I am."

For seven consecutive evenings following the wedding celebration, it was customary for friends and relatives to host festive meals in honor of the married couple. The first night we accepted an invitation to join my parents in their home. How odd it felt returning home as a guest instead of a member of the household. My mother had prepared my favorite meal—baked salmon and warm bread dipped in olive oil. As we entered the courtyard, I realized my father was not alone. Seated with him were Gavriel and Julius.

Julius stood to his feet as soon as he saw me. His eyes were filled with pleasure at the turn of events in my life. He took my hands in his and briefly kissed one cheek and then the other.

"Congratulations," he whispered. He then turned to Joseph. There was an awkward hesitation between them. Finally, Julius extended his hand, and Joseph reached out and shook it firmly.

"Came to your senses, I see," Julius jested.

Joseph glanced over at me, humor evident in his eyes. "Yes, it seems I have."

Our conversation was light and enjoyable as we shared supper together. Julius brought us up to date on the places he had been the last few weeks since I had seen him last. He spoke of Sepphoris where he was stationed, just a mere three miles away.

Sepphoris was the center of trade for the area. It was also beautiful and wealthy. Herod the Great had conquered the city and made it his Galilean capital. I had never been there. My people despised the Romans and had extreme distrust for the soldiers. Julius was the only Roman soldier I had ever been around to any extent. But I knew enough stories to know he was one of the more respectable ones.

"I may have some work there in the near future," Joseph said. "I was supposed to meet the man today, but something unexpected came up." He turned toward me, amusement dancing in his eyes.

"I know most everyone there. Is it carpentry work you plan to do?" Julius asked between bites of fish.

Yes, carpentry. A man by the name of Ludovic. Do you know him?"

Julius paused. "I do know him. Actually, I know him quite well. He's the Roman Centurion over all the soldiers, including myself."

"Is he honest? Fair?"

"Yes. You shouldn't have any issues with him, although he's quite demanding and expects nothing less than perfection."

I looked over at Julius. "Then he should be quite pleased with Joseph because his work is impeccable."

After supper, I helped my mother gather the dirty dishes and clean them in the basin inside the house. Once they were dry and put away, we returned to the courtyard with the men. I sat down next to my husband and did my best to remain attentive, but the late hours of the night before had taxed me beyond what I could usually handle. I stifled a yawn. Joseph stood to his feet and gently took my hand, pulling me up to stand beside him.

"My wife is tired, it seems. I believe I should get her home so she can regain her strength for tomorrow."

I hugged my parents and thanked them for the meal. After goodbyes were said to Gavriel and Julius, we made our way out of the courtyard and down the street, much like the evening before but this time with no procession to guide us.

"A beautiful evening, is it not?" Joseph whispered beside me.

I looked up into the sky where the moon and stars shone brightly. With no breeze, the air was calm. It was a beautiful evening. "Yes, it is."

We arrived at the house and Joseph led me inside, through the first room and into the second. He guided me to sit and gently removed my sandals before easing me onto the cushion. He then removed his own sandals and joined me on the cushion, cradling me as he had the night before, one hand gently resting on my belly. This time I fell asleep first as I listened to the prayers he offered up for our Son.

And so began the process of covering my hair while in public. It was Jewish law for married women to do so—a safeguard served to protect my privacy, creating a personal, sensual space reserved only for my husband.

I awakened early and, the pitcher firmly placed on my hip, I made my way toward the watering well. I was relieved to be the first in line. "Mary?" a voice questioned from behind me. I turned to find Zillah.

"How are you?" she asked.

"I'm well. How are you?" I pulled the water up over the edge and now began pouring it into my pitcher.

"I'm fine. If I were married already with a home of my own, I would invite you to share a meal with us this evening. But…but unfortunately since I'm living at home…still…"

"I understand," I voiced. Her parents had not attended my wedding celebration. They had been almost like second parents to me growing up, but they believed I was defiled now. And in an effort to keep their home clean, they would not associate with me any longer.

"I don't feel the same way they do. You believe me, don't you?" Zillah said, worry lining her eyes.

I reached out and squeezed her hand. "I believe you." The same words she had written to me just days before. Her eyes filled with tears. She nodded and moved to fill up her own pitcher.

I walked toward home, the snide remarks from the other women not as loud as usual but still being whispered among them. Marriage had saved me from being stoned to death but obviously hadn't changed their hearts toward me. I realized then that there would be no more invitations to dine with anyone the rest of the week. I felt my eyes fill with tears.

Standing now in front of the house, I quietly waited outside, trying to still my emotions. Several seconds passed as I took a few deep breaths. Finally, I turned the handle and walked inside.

"Mary? Are you all right?" Joseph said from across the room.

I squared my shoulders, desperately trying to be strong. I swallowed and turned to face him. "I'm fine," I responded with a wobbly smile.

"You are not."

"Yes, I am." I sat the pitcher on the stone countertop. Seeing the compassion in his eyes undid my composure. I looked down at my feet and when that wasn't enough, I moved toward our room hoping he wouldn't follow, but he did.

"Did someone do something…"

"No."

"Say something?"

"No."

"You are wishing you hadn't rushed into a marriage with a feeble-minded carpenter?"

I smiled. "No."

He took my hands in his and brought them to his lips. "What's wrong?" he beseeched me. "I'd like to share your burden…your pain."

"It's silly actually. I realized we won't be receiving any other invitations for supper. And I guess I'm feeling sorry for myself."

Joseph tipped my chin up. "And yet you've received the most important invitation of all mankind." He kissed my nose. "Mary, mother of Jesus."

Mary, mother of Jesus.

Joseph's words ignited something within me. My concern for what the rest of the world thought of me began to be replaced with a deeper concern for the magnificent life I now carried inside of me. God had chosen me to love and nurture His Son. It was my responsibility to raise him in the knowledge of God. And although I felt inadequate in myself and what I could offer, I knew that God had selected me for a reason. Perhaps that reason was my awareness of my utmost need of Him.

I was ordinary, but God saw me as extraordinary. I was poor, but God saw me as prosperous. I was young, but in God's eyes I was established. People saw me as defiled, but God saw me as pure. For some reason beyond my limited understanding, He had chosen me to be a part of His plan of redemption for mankind. And I was determined to live up to what He saw in me, even if at times I doubted myself.

And I wasn't alone. Against all odds, God had blessed me with Joseph. And the better I came to know him, the more I realized what an exceptional man he was. He was perhaps one of the most gracious men I knew. Although of meager means, he seemingly managed to provide for our needs.

He usually worked in his carpentry shop just beside the house. But over the last month, he had been remodeling a home for Ludovic in Sepphoris, which required him to be gone away from home during the day. He awoke each morning much earlier than I and insisted I stay abed. And each morning when I'd awaken as the sun came up, I'd find a note tucked within the covers with me.

Ich hob deer leib. These were the words he had written this morning. *I love you.* Each and every day he reminded me of my worth. I had been accused of the worst thing a virtuous woman could be accused of. It was a shadow I knew I would live under for the rest of my life. But Joseph knew the truth. And he made it his mission in life to make sure I remembered it too.

One month passed by and then two. My body began changing in appearance, my belly taking on a much rounder, fuller shape. I also began to notice swelling in my ankles and feet when I stood for prolonged periods of time. There were a few extra aches and pains but nothing to complain about. Remembering Elizabeth's exhaustion during her last phase of pregnancy, I tried to enjoy the remaining few weeks of respite I had. I felt the telltale signs of awkwardness beginning but did my best to ignore them.

As a newlywed, I feared the culmination of the fascination Joseph and I held for one another. I couldn't help but wonder if Joseph's attraction for me would wane the more my body underwent the changes of pregnancy.

I was standing at the well, waiting for my turn. Havilah stood in front of me, her body beginning to show signs of being with child. Having married before Joseph and me, she could only be a few weeks along. She was unusually quiet, which was unlike her. Normally she took great pleasure in reminding me and anyone else within hearing of my defilement. The day before yesterday, she had been whispering to Jemima about Joseph.

"*Yold*," I had heard her say. *Easily duped.* I had managed to keep quiet, but it was difficult. It hurt when I heard people insulting his character, especially when he had endured so much in an effort to protect me.

When Havilah turned toward me, I could see she was not well. Her face was pale. Morning sickness? She spilled more water onto the ground than she managed to pour into her pitcher.

"Let me help," I said softly as I approached her. Setting my own pitcher aside, I lowered the bucket back into the well and brought it up, pouring the contents into her pitcher. She reached for the pitcher but was unable to heft it onto her shoulder. I gently pried the pitcher from her hands and hefted it onto my own shoulder.

"Come," I said.

"I don't need your help," she managed to rasp.

"I realize you don't want my help, but you do need it." I took a step forward and then two. She unsteadily began to follow me. Thankfully, she lived only a few houses away from the well and wouldn't have far to tread each day to retrieve their supply of water.

Havilah's mother had passed away six years ago during childbirth. I still remembered the midwife's tale the morning after and how the baby had been too large to pass through the mother's birth canal. Havilah, like me, had no other siblings. Her father had been devastated by the news of his wife's passing and the loss of a son. Mentally, he had been unstable ever since.

And Havilah's husband was older than she by forty years. He was set in his ways. I couldn't imagine him offering to retrieve their daily supply of water. Many men refused to do so. It was demeaning to their manhood. They'd pay to have someone else retrieve it rather than do it themselves.

"Eat," I admonished. "And then rest." I sat her pitcher on the floor inside the house and made my way to the door. "Leave your pitcher just outside the door each morning, and I'll fill it for you." I left her house and returned to the well to retrieve my own water. I was surprised to find my pitcher already full. Hearing a giggle, I turned to find Matteus in the shadows.

"Are you still following me?" I hadn't noticed him since my marriage to Joseph and had assumed my father had relieved the boy of his obligation toward me.

"Occasionally," Matteus said with a wide smile. "You have Joseph now and are no longer in need of my protection each and every day."

Not wanting him to feel unappreciated, I tried to hide my smile. "I thought perhaps my father would no longer need you to watch over me, since I am now married and out of harm's way."

"Your father?" Matteus questioned. "I do not work for your father." He smiled again. "I work for Joseph."

"Joseph?" I tried to reason in my mind why that would be. Joseph had intended to break our betrothal. He had been angry with me. Why would he hire a young boy to watch over me?

I returned home and sat the water indoors before making my way around the side of the house and into the carpentry shop where Joseph worked today. He had finished his work in Sepphoris last week. I stood in the open doorway watching as he sanded the plank of cedar. "You hired Matteus?"

Joseph's hand paused in motion as he turned toward me. "He was looking for work. His father died last year. And his mother has another little one younger than him. They've returned to live with the mother's family, but Matteus wanted to contribute in some way."

"Wouldn't he be better help here…in the shop?"

"No."

"No?" I stepped inside the shop. "Why did you hire him?"

"To keep you safe."

"But why? Why would you hire a boy to watch over a woman you didn't intend to marry?"

Joseph began sanding again, and after a long pause, I began to wonder if he planned to answer me or not. "I still loved you. I still cared about your well-being." He turned toward me. "I had this foreboding sense that something horrible was about to happen. I prayed night and day for your protection. And had Matteus not been with you that day…" He swallowed, unable to finish the sentence.

He set the piece of rough paper on the board and walked toward me. "I was wrestling with what to do. When I'd make plans to go to the synagogue to quietly end our contract, I couldn't do it. I suppose deep down I knew I was wrong and just didn't want to admit it."

Joseph cupped my face in his hands, his fervent eyes searching my own. "Letting you go seemed an impossible venture." He kissed my nose. "From the moment I first saw you, I knew you were meant to be my wife." He kissed one cheek and then the other. "And now I finally have you as my wife but am restricted in another area." He smiled and then kissed me softly on the lips. And then with more urgency. My back against the wall, I drew him closer still.

Suddenly he released me, gently pushing me toward the door. "You need to go," he quipped, "before I end up breaking my promise."

I backed out the door, my eyes never leaving his, a smile on my lips. His love for me was profound. I felt it to the tips of my toes. "Ich hob deer leib," I whispered before turning and hurrying toward the house. *I love you.*

As I passed by Havilah's home the next morning, I was surprised to find the water pitcher sitting outside her door just as I had instructed. I honestly thought she'd either force herself to gather the water or ask someone else. I grabbed it with my free hand and made my way to the well. Matteus escaped the shadows of the wall and made his way toward me.

"Why do you help her?" he asked as I drew water from the well and began filling her pitcher.

"She's too weak to gather her own water."

"But why do you help her?" He looked up at me, confusion in his eyes. "She's the one who led the group of women that day."

The day I was nearly stoned to death. It was a day I was unlikely to ever forget. "We can't control the way people treat us, but we can control how we treat them." I situated the pitcher on my hip and delivered it to Havilah's door.

I turned to find Matteus making his way toward me, his tiny arms wrapped around my pitcher, water sloshing out one side and then the other with each step he took. At this rate, I'd be returning to fetch water at lunch time. I offered him a smile of encouragement and gently took the pitcher from him.

"Thank you," I voiced, noticing his eyes were staring at the pitcher of water sitting in front of Havilah's door.

"She doesn't deserve that water," Matteus whispered in frustration.

"We are all undeserving, Matteus." I reached down and tenderly took his small hand into my free hand. "And yet God delights in me. He rejoices over you with singing. Mere words cannot accurately express the thoughts and feelings He has for me and for you. And even for Havilah." I gently squeezed his fingers. "Whenever I struggle with forgiving someone, I remind myself of how God feels about them. He doesn't love Havilah any less than He loves me…"

Matteus stopped in the middle of the road. He looked up into my eyes. "He does love you more. He chose you to be His Son's mother," he whispered, his eyes sparkling with admiration.

Surprise surely showed on my face. "Who told you that?"

"I overheard the women at the well arguing about it one morning."

"And you believe the story?" I studied his charming face, in awe of his certainty.

"Of course. Don't you?"

I laughed. "Yes. I believe it also!"

"Tell me," he asked. "How did it happen?"

We had reached my home, and I sat the pitcher down by the side of the door. I leaned my aching back against the wall and closed my eyes. "An angel appeared to me."

"A real live angel?"

I smiled. "Yes, a real live angel. At first, I was afraid. It was the first time

I had ever seen an angel."

"I wish an angel would appear to me," Matteus said with enthusiasm.

"Perhaps one day you will see one." I shifted my weight to my other foot. "The angel said I'd have a baby boy."

"How?"

"He said the Holy Spirit would perform a miracle, and my baby would be called the Son of God."

"But Joseph didn't believe you at first, did he?"

"Not at first…" I began but was interrupted by a masculine voice standing nearby.

"I was confused and upset by the news. But not anymore." Joseph took my hand in his and pulled it close to his lips.

"Did the angel appear to you too?" Matteus asked in wonder.

"No. I had a dream. And when I awoke, I knew I was to take Mary as my wife."

"It's a good thing I saved her life, isn't it?"

Joseph laughed and reached out to ruffle the boy's dark hair. "Yes, it's a very good thing." His eyes never left mine, a lopsided smile upon his handsome face.

And so began my last trimester. With it came the exhaustion Elizabeth had warned me about. Sleep became more and more difficult. There were a few reasons for this. I began awaking periodically during the night, cramps radiating down the back of one leg or the other. The first time it happened, I sat up frantically, forgetting about the man lying beside me. Since then, I tried to keep calm so as not to awaken him. But it was hard to remain silent when it felt as if my calf was being torn from my skin. Just the change in my breathing was usually enough to alert Joseph that something was wrong.

If I managed to endure the night without leg cramps disturbing my sleep, then it was interrupted instead by the need to empty my bladder. The baby was so large and I so small that I had to relieve myself several times a day. I tried to drink less water during the evening in an attempt to limit the number of times I'd have to crawl over Joseph.

"Perhaps I should sleep on the outside," I suggested one night when I had returned from the urinal.

"I'm fine, *Akila*," he whispered. *Most beautiful.* I was beginning to doubt his words. My body had changed so significantly, I couldn't help but wonder how he could say such things.

A dark line had begun to run from my belly button downward. And perhaps even worse were the reddish-brown streaks that showed up on my thighs and stomach. I stood there one morning examining my body, recognizing that becoming a mother required sacrifice. I realized in that moment my body would never be the same again. My skin would be permanently marked forever.

Lost deep in thought, I turned to find Joseph standing just within the doorway to our private room. How long had he been watching me? I quickly snatched my robe off the bed in an attempt to cover my body. I turned from him, afraid of what I'd see in his eyes.

"What is it, *Akila*?" He was now standing so close, I could feel his breath on the back of my neck. And then I felt his lips. I swallowed past the tears. *Do not cry,* I told myself. Joseph turned me around and tipped my chin up so he could look into my eyes. "What are you hiding?"

The humor in his eyes proved he was speaking both literally as well as figuratively. "My body... I find myself wondering how you see me."

"I shall share those details with you soon. But not today."

Not today? Because he thought after I had the baby, my body would go back to the way it had once been? I bit my lip to keep it from wobbling. "I asked my mother. These unsightly marks should lessen with time, but they will never leave completely."

"Is that what you're asking me?" Joseph hesitantly questioned. "You're wondering if you need to hide from me the marks left by this pregnancy?" Joseph reached out, his fingers gently touching my long hair. "They are nothing to be ashamed of, *Akila*. Think of them as symbols of your sacrifice. Let them be a reminder of your strength. They are not scars…or flaws…but beautiful features of who you have become."

He bent and kissed me on the mouth. "If I refrain from touching you, it is only because I am well aware of my limits. And I refuse to jeopardize you or His Son."

I leaned against him, breathing in his scent of cedar, allowing his words to soothe my questioning heart. *Symbols of sacrifice.* My body was a vessel used to nurture and bring forth the Son of God. *I must not lose sight of that.*

For six weeks, I delivered water to Havilah's door. During that time, I hadn't seen her one time. From the whispers among the women at the well, I learned that she rarely left her bed, and she barely ate. Of course, I had learned a long time ago that the conversations that circulated around the well could be exaggerated.

And then one morning as I approached her house, I was startled to find the pitcher was not sitting out front as usual. At first I was alarmed. My first thought was that she had passed away during the night. And then I saw her at the well drawing her own water.

I was astonished by the amount of weight she had lost. She hadn't been considered thin before. But now—now she looked severely malnourished. I found myself wondering how she would carry her child to term, struggling as she was with eating enough to sustain the life inside of her.

Hearing my footsteps, she turned. She hesitantly studied me before timidly stepping toward me. "Thank you. For the water."

I nodded. "Are you feeling better?"

"I do feel much better."

I could see her struggle with holding the full pitcher of water, so I stepped aside to let her continue on. "It's good to see you."

"And you." Havilah stepped past me.

I watched her until she was safely within the confines of her home. My own mother had dealt with severe nausea during her pregnancies. I was the only child she had carried to term. I prayed for Havilah while I drew my own water, that God would give her strength and sustain her weary body.

I returned home to find Joseph with a letter clenched in his right hand, his eyes void of their usual humor. "What's wrong?" I asked as I sat the pitcher down.

Joseph held up the piece of parchment. "Caesar Augustus has issued a decree for every person to travel to their town of birth to register."

"And you're from Bethlehem?" I knew he had been born there. He had told me so several weeks back.

Joseph nodded. "There is a penalty for not doing so by the end of the year."

"This year?" He only had a small window of time. "Then of course you must go." Was he afraid to leave me? "My time won't come for three more weeks. There is plenty of time for you to go and come back before the baby arrives."

"I hate to leave you, especially as you are so close to having the baby. But I do not think it is wise to disobey the census. We have enough negative attention as it is." I could read the frustration in his eyes.

Joseph returned to the carpentry shop, and I began preparing our daily ration of bread. Trepidation began building within me. *Why the apprehension?* I wondered. Was Joseph in danger if he left? Was I supposed to join him? I looked down at my enormous belly. I could no longer see my toes. We would have to cover some eighty hilly miles to reach Bethlehem—a trip of several days. And I could barely walk to the water well and back each morning.

I felt tears begin to rise to the surface. Now, of all times, I yearned to stay close to home. My mother was to aid in my childbirth, along with Nala, the midwife who had delivered me. If I went with Joseph, where would I be when my pangs began? Who would deliver my child?

I lifted my chin in defiance against my own weakness. *Give me courage, Yahweh.* I felt my adventurous spirit rise up within. The last several months had been difficult. When had I become so timid? I laid the mound of dough on the counter and left the house. Standing in the doorway of Joseph's shop, I watched him work, his strong hands moving back and forth over the wood, forming it into something beautiful.

"When do we leave?" I asked.

Joseph turned, surprise evident in his eyes. Reading the determination in my expression, he strode toward me, gathering me into his arms. "This is certainly not how I envisioned the end of your pregnancy." He tipped my chin up, looking deeply into my eyes. "I'll trade something for a donkey. You'll need something to carry you when you tire of walking."

I realized he had known all along I was supposed to accompany him to Bethlehem. But being the patient man he was, he had wanted me to realize and accept it for myself.

"Likely before we get beyond Nazareth," I said with humor.

"Likely." He leaned down to kiss me, but I stepped out of reach.

"You're not supposed to agree with an enormous pregnant woman who's about to give birth."

Before I could escape, he grabbed my hand and pulled me close. "*At kol kakh yafa,*" he whispered in my ear. *You are so beautiful.* This time, I didn't step away when his lips found mine.

I suppose I was in shock when I was first visited by the angel Gabriel. The events that had unfolded since then had only proven God's infinite knowledge. For years it had been foretold that a virgin would conceive and bear a Son. Only God had the power to bring His prophecies to pass. And with each event that unfolded, I began to understand just how incredible He truly was.

Saying goodbye to my parents was not easy. Oddly enough, it was my father who questioned Joseph's judgement in traveling such a distance when I was so far along in my pregnancy. As Joseph searched for the words to reassure him, my mother stepped forward and took my hands in hers. She quoted the words of Micah, a seven-hundred-year-old prophecy which foretold the birthplace of the Messiah.

"*But you, Bethlehem Ephrathah, though you are little among the thousands of Judah, yet out of you shall come forth to Me the One to be Ruler in Israel, whose goings forth are from of old, from everlasting.*"

I watched as the tension eased in my father's eyes. My mother stepped aside as my father took her place. He bent and kissed one cheek and then the other.

"Who am I to stand in the way of Yahweh?" he whispered. "Ani ohev otach." *I love you.*

I gently wiped a tear from his weathered cheek. "Ani ohevet otcha, aba," I whispered back as I kissed both of his cheeks. *I love you, Father.* I found myself wondering when I would see him again. And then I chastised my own anxiety. We would likely only be separated a mere few weeks. I hugged him one last time before returning home with Joseph to pack.

I prepared enough food to feed us for three or four days. Finally, the day of our departure arrived. We left Nazareth at the break of day.

"We'll be so close to Judah," I said. "Do you think we'll have opportunity to see Elizabeth and Zechariah on our journey?" I rode on the donkey with our provisions while Joseph walked ahead, leading the animal.

"Yes, I think it's possible."

Our first day of travel brought us to the foothills of Mount Gilboa, where we camped for the night by the Jordan River. My father had long ago told me the meaning of Gilboa was boiling springs. It was a fitting name because bursting from the rocks was warm water, which then formed a pool of hot water for bathing.

Later that night, after we had eaten, I walked to a secluded pool nearby. I closed my eyes as I immersed my body into the water, allowing it to soothe my sore muscles. Riding on the donkey was perhaps not the easiest way to travel. How I wished I could walk beside Joseph, but the baby inside prevented me from doing so. It would be too strenuous, and I didn't want to jeopardize the baby.

Darkness was quickly falling, but I savored the moment a bit longer, hating to leave this warm haven—especially since the air had cooled considerably since the sun had gone down.

"Mary?"

I opened my eyes to find Joseph standing at the edge of the pool, a blanket in his arms. "You should come in," I invited. "It's wonderful!"

I saw the laughter in his eyes. "Thank you, but I believe I'll take my turn when you are safely settled by the fire."

I blushed, instantly understanding his reason for not joining me. I stepped from the water, careful where I placed my feet so as not to stumble under the weight of the baby. Joseph wrapped the blanket around me and drew me into his arms, the heat from his body quickly warming me.

Several seconds passed before he stepped away. He led me around the large overhanging rock and back to our campsite.

Once I was settled, Joseph left to enjoy the pool. I quickly dressed and sat by the fire, waiting for Joseph to return. The sounds of the night were both terrifying and yet soothing at the same time. Some time passed before I heard Joseph's sandals on the rocky path. Finally, I could see his form as he drew near to the fire. How handsome he looked, his hair wet and disheveled from his time in the water.

"Israel's first king, King Saul, led an army against the Philistines here… possibly in this very spot."

"Three of his sons were killed in battle," I said, my hand resting on my belly. *Could there be anything more devastating in life than losing a child?*

"The battle ended with King Saul falling on his own sword."

"And you're reminding me of this story right before bedtime because…?"

Joseph laughed. He came to stand beside me, taking my hand in his warm one. "I was remembering the words of Samuel. '*O mountains of Gilboa, let there be no dew nor rain upon you, neither fields of offerings. For the shield of the mighty is cast away there! The shield of Saul, not anointed with oil.*'"

He brought his free hand out from behind his back and handed me a beautiful purple Gilboa Iris. "The moon was shining so brightly on this lovely flower, I couldn't resist picking it for one just as beautiful and lovely."

I gently took the flower from his fingers. Bringing it to my nose, I breathed in its pleasant fragrance. "Thank you," I whispered.

Bright and early the next morning, we partook of bread and fruit before continuing on our way. Midday, we stopped to rest and nourish our bodies once again at the foot of Mount Sartaba, overlooking the Jordan Valley. The valley was long and narrow. The lower course of the Jordan River lay here; on the north end it exited into the Sea of Galilee, but on the south end it flowed into the Dead Sea. South of the valley resided the town of Jericho, which we hoped to reach by nightfall.

"My father told me Jericho was once surrounded by a great earthen embankment with a stone retaining wall at its base." I never tired of hearing of the walls falling down when I was a child.

Joseph nodded. "The walls were at least fifteen feet high. And on top of that was mud-brick, making it six feet thick and another twenty-five feet high."

"So, it may have been over forty feet tall?" I couldn't help but be astonished at Joseph's words. How the wall must have loomed high above the Israelites as they had marched around the city each day for seven days.

"Humanly speaking, it would have been impossible for the Israelites to penetrate the walls of Jericho," Joseph voiced.

"But Yahweh makes the impossible possible." My hand rested on my belly, and I smiled when a small foot kicked my palm.

Joseph had turned his head to look at me, and the sparkle I had grown so fond of over the last few months was present in his eyes. "The people of Jericho were well prepared for a siege. A spring lay within the walls, providing them with water. And they had an abundant supply of food as the harvest had just been taken in."

"And yet after the seventh trip around the city on the seventh day, the wall fell down."

"It serves as a lesson for us all," Joseph said as he sidestepped a boulder in our path. Stopping, he pushed the boulder out of the way. "We often find ourselves facing enormous walls that seem impossible to break down by our own human strength. But if we put our trust in God and follow His commandments, He is able to perform great and mighty things."

We stopped at an inn situated on the outskirts of the city, where we shared an evening meal and listened to the discussion going on around us concerning the oppressiveness of Roman rule. My thoughts turned to Julius. I hadn't seen him since my wedding day. I had visited with his grandfather several times since then, and he had relayed that Julius was permanently stationed near Jerusalem for the time being.

We listened as the group of men's discussion then turned to Herod. Herod was known to be a cruel, power-hungry ruler who destroyed anyone he feared was trying to topple him from his throne. It was said he had even killed members of his own family because he thought they were plotting against him.

Once my belly was full, I felt the exhaustion of travel begin to take over. Joseph held out his hand and helped me to my feet. I grimaced as pain radiated down my abdomen and around to my lower back. Joseph paused, his eyes examining me with concern.

"Where are you from?" a man across the way asked.

"Nazareth," Joseph replied.

"She shouldn't be traveling so far from home in her condition." The man's eyes questioned Joseph, and then he turned back around to join in on the topic of Herod once again.

I sensed Joseph's concern heighten as he walked me to our room. "Are you unwell?" he asked.

"Just tired," I answered. I didn't even remove my outer garments. Crawling onto the mat I closed my eyes, falling asleep before Joseph had time to cover me with the blanket.

I awoke to find Joseph absent. I could see from the window that the sun was already high in the sky. It was late in the morning. I smiled contentedly, knowing Joseph had purposefully allowed me to sleep longer in order for me to regain my strength.

I sat up as he walked into the room holding a tray of food. Kneeling down beside me, he gently lay the tray within reach. He pressed his lips to my forehead before standing to his feet. "I'll prepare the donkey for travel while you eat," he said as he once again vacated the room.

Famished, I ate every morsel of food, saving the grapes for last. I had craved them more than any other food during these last few weeks. Finally, I knew I could delay no longer. I made my way down the rickety staircase and found Joseph waiting for me just outside the inn.

"You look well this morning," he voiced with a smile.

"I feel well. Thank you for the extra hours of sleep!"

"I felt it necessary to increase the odds of you keeping that baby inside until we reach Bethlehem."

We resumed our journey, reaching Jerusalem well after the noon hour. We stopped there briefly to visit the temple before continuing on to our destination. I breathed a sigh of relief when I first caught sight of Bethlehem in the distance. As we mounted the hillsides, passing by olive groves which were among the last of the crops to be harvested, I found myself wondering about the history of this little village. It was too insignificant to be numbered among Judah's cities; yet it was the birthplace of Boaz, Naomi, and David, all more than a thousand years earlier.

There was a noticeable change in Joseph's demeanor the closer we came to the city. When he glanced back at me, I could see the strain of the last few days gradually beginning to decline.

We found the village to be crowded. "Is there usually this many people?" I questioned.

Joseph shook his head. "It must be the census bringing in so many people at once."

We stopped at the first inn we came to. It was already overcrowded, and we were quickly turned away. There was simply no room. Many people were already sharing rooms. We found the same results at each and every place we stopped. It seemed every room in Bethlehem was filled to overflowing.

I walked beside Joseph, doing my best to hide my disappointment. I was drained from our long days of travel. My back hurt beyond anything I had ever experienced before. And ever since our stop in Jerusalem, I had begun feeling intermittent spasms in my abdomen. All I wanted at the moment was to lie down.

We stopped at yet another inn, only to be turned away by an aggravated man trying to keep his customers satisfied. A losing battle, it seemed—for everyone around us seemed irritated about something.

A pain suddenly tore through my belly, and I nearly fell to my knees. Joseph rushed to my side, his strong arms coming around me. "You need to rest," he voiced with despair. "And I have no idea where we'll find a place for you to do so."

I leaned against him until the pain passed. A woman was talking to the man we had just spoken to. The innkeeper's wife, perhaps? The man shrugged his shoulders before finally ambling toward us. "Listen, we have a stable below the inn. It's not much, but you'll at least have a roof over your head."

"We are in your debt. Thank you." Joseph reached for my hand, helping me to my feet.

"You both look to be in for a very long night." The man turned toward a young girl serving drinks across the way. "Ada, fetch some clean linens and show these two to the stables."

When Ada returned, we followed her outside and into the courtyard where we had left the donkey earlier. We stopped for a moment so Joseph could retrieve our items of clothing and provisions. Finally, we followed her down some stone steps and into a rock hewn stable. It was surprisingly well kept.

"I wish you well," Ada said with kindness as she deposited the fresh linens into my arms. "Can I get you anything else?"

"Do you know of a midwife?" Joseph asked from behind me.

"I do. Would you like me to fetch her?"

"Would you?" Joseph sighed with relief. "Tell her my wife is in the beginning stages of labor."

Ada hurried from the stable, and I watched as Joseph climbed the ladder to the loft. Disappearing from sight, he then hollered down. "Stand back." Clean hay began falling from above. Satisfied that he had thrown down enough, he once again joined me below.

"How long have you known?" I asked.

"Since Jerusalem. You think you can hide your pain from me? I am here to share it." Joseph cupped my chin in his hands and gently kissed me. "Now, stand back while I make you a comfortable place to lie down."

While Joseph prepared a place for me, I surveyed the stone walls surrounding us. Across the way stood three goats and four sheep. Their eyes occasionally glanced at me in curiosity before they then returned to the hay they were eating.

I felt Joseph's presence beside me and turned to face him. "Would you like to lie down?" he asked.

"I believe I'll stand for as long as I am able. Riding on that donkey is not for the faint of heart."

"Try walking eighty miles," Joseph said with a smile.

"I plan to on the return trip." I nudged his shoulder playfully. He swept me up into his arms, his face nuzzling my neck. He laughed when my stomach growled very noisily. "I am hungry," I said with a smile. "And that mutton stew smelled heavenly."

Joseph gently placed me back on my feet. "Mutton stew coming up," he saluted before he left the cave.

It was then that I noticed the manger—a beautifully carved manger that would serve quite well as a crib. I walked over to admire it more closely. And that was how Joseph found me a short time later—the stone manger dragged halfway across the stable, and me panting heavily, both from exertion and contractions.

Joseph quickly set the tray of food down. "I can't leave you alone for a moment, can I?" He pulled the manger the remainder of the way, situating it next to our bed of hay while I chided myself for not waiting for him. I watched Joseph spread a blanket over the hay he had gathered earlier. He patted a spot beside him as I made my way to join him.

We ate our mutton stew and fresh bread and spoke of Nazareth and of what our families were doing at this very moment. "You should lie down, just for a while," Joseph finally said. "You need to gather your strength for what lies ahead."

I nodded. I lay there, Joseph holding my hand as a contraction passed. I closed my eyes, thanking God for the adequate shelter He had provided.

I knew what was in store for me. Women everywhere could empathize with me. Some four thousand years earlier, Jehovah had foretold that it would be the common lot of women to suffer pain during childbirth. There was no evidence to suggest that I was any exception.

I awoke sometime later when I heard voices speaking across the way. I sat up, feeling groggy and even more exhausted than when I had lain down.

"She didn't say when she'd be free to come?" Joseph's concerned voice troubled me.

"She was gone delivering another baby, but her son said he'd send her to the inn as soon as she returned. And when she comes, I will bring her to you." My eyes followed Ada as she left the cave.

Joseph's back was to me. He was hunched over as if carrying the weight of the world on his shoulders. I pushed myself to my feet and wobbled toward him. Hearing the sound of my footsteps, he turned to face me.

"The midwife is not at home," he said. "But she will come as soon as she is able."

"I was there with Elizabeth when John was born. I was observant and took mental notes of everything. Perhaps Yahweh was preparing me for the arrival of His Son even then." I took Joseph's hands in my own and squeezed them. "Would you gather some items for me?"

"Of course, anything you ask."

"You'll first need to build a fire. Then bring a kettle of water and a stool."

"A stool?"

"We can discuss that later," I said with embarrassment. I paced the stable-room floor while Joseph did as I instructed. My contractions were growing closer and closer together. I knew I'd be ready to deliver within the hour. The kettle of water had already boiled and was keeping warm near the fire. And Ada had brought a stool from the inn and sat it near our bed of hay.

"It's time for you to leave," I said to Joseph.

He shook his head. "I won't leave until the midwife is here to take my place."

I felt tears rise to the surface. I had tried all night to keep them at bay, knowing if Joseph saw my weakness, I'd never get him to leave the cave. It was customary for the men to be absent during the delivery. Blood was impure, and it would contaminate him. If he touched me or anything I touched, he would be considered unclean and would need to wash his clothes and bathe with water.

"Perhaps you could ask above if there is a woman who could aid me in delivering this child."

Joseph left to do my bidding. I turned my eyes toward heaven. *I know You are here with me. With Your Son. Please give me courage and strength.*

Soon, Joseph returned with Ada and an older woman. The woman rushed toward me. "Your time is near. Very near." She then turned toward Joseph. "You go. Go to the inn, and Ada will find you when the baby has arrived."

Joseph stood, his hands clenched at his sides. His eyes focused on me and only me. I knew in that instant if I asked him to stay, he would break custom and stay. I swallowed past my deep need for him. I nodded.

"Go," I whispered. The next time I glanced toward the entrance, he was gone.

A woman in childbirth is on the threshold of life and death. Both the pain and exhaustion consuming me brought me to a point of a dying and a birthing. I began to feel a loss of self, a loss of identity, a loss of control and dignity, a loss of all the protective layers with which I had surrounded myself.

I felt the rejection I had endured from those I loved and trusted begin to surface. The tears that had fallen silently soon turned into deep sobs of emotional cleansing.

"Are you in pain?" the older woman asked her eyes wide with concern.

I first nodded and then shook my head. I didn't know how to answer. Of course I was in pain. My body was preparing to birth a baby. But it wasn't the physical pain generating my tears, but rather the emotional trauma of the last few months. In an instant, I was brought back to the day in the synagogue when I had stood in the middle of the circle with eyes of condemnation staring me down. I frantically searched for Joseph in the midst of all the contempt, but he was nowhere to be found.

I'm not sure how much time passed. I was in a fog, as if I was suspended in time. I could hear all that was said around me but could not respond. Fear began to take root. Was this what it felt like to die?

"There's too much blood." The older woman looked into my face, worry evident in her gaze. "She's not responding. It was time to push an hour ago, and she just lies here." The woman turned toward Ada.

"Is she dying, Martha?" Ada asked, tears on her cheeks. "Let me get her husband. He may be able to reach her." She ran from the stable.

I tried to reach out to Martha to let her know I was still here, but my hand would not move. I was paralyzed. Paralyzed with what? Fear?

Soon Joseph was standing over me, my limp hand clutched between his two massive ones. "Mary?" he said, his brown eyes searching mine for life. "Mary?" he said again, this time panic evident in his voice.

He pulled me up against him, his hand now on the back of my head, his warm cheek pressed against mine. "Mary, this is not your time. You're still needed." His voice broke. He swallowed. Cleared his throat. "I need you. Jesus needs you." My cheek felt damp from the tears sliding down his own.

"Jesus," he whispered. "Jesus needs you."

My previously paralyzed hand gripped his tunic. He leaned back, his eyes staring into mine. "I'm ready," I rasped. My tongue slid across my dry, parched lips.

"She needs water," Joseph said to Ada, his eyes never leaving mine. He took the cup from Ada's hand and gently held it to my lips. I swallowed some; the rest slid down my chin and onto my bare chest.

"How can I help?" Joseph asked of the two women standing near. I knew by the sound of his voice he would not be leaving my side again. They seemed to know it too.

"If you could carry her to the birthing stool. And then support her from behind."

Joseph gently cradled my weak body in his arms. Once I was situated on the stool, he wrapped his arms around me, my back resting against his chest, the base of my head resting against his shoulder. His whispered prayers brought peace to my heart.

"*Those who sow in tears shall reap in joy. Bless and heal Mary. Give her strength and vigor, O Source of life. You have guided and sustained Mary through her time of pregnancy. Guide and sustain her through Your child's birth. Bring forth Your Son and safely entrust Him to our care.*"

I heard the lusty cry of a newborn pierce the night. "He's here, Mary." Joseph turned his head so he could kiss my perspiration-wettened cheek. "He's beautiful."

Martha held him up for me to see. A cry of relief escaped me as I reached my hands out for my son. She gently laid him on my chest. He was perfect. Absolutely perfect in every way. Joseph carried us to the bed of hay, where he gently covered us with clean linen and cradled us near, his whispered prayers still ministering to my weary soul.

"*Heal her body. May it renew its cycles of growth and life once more. Grant Mary strength of body and spirit as she begins to nurture her son. May we always cherish this precious gift from You. May we be privileged to teach him Your ways and laws, so that he will serve You all his days.*"

I felt my strength returning as I nursed my precious son. Once finished, I cuddled him close, staring into his beautiful brown eyes. Eventually, his eyes closed in contentment. Gently I kissed his smooth forehead, and then wrapping him snugly with bands of cloth, I carefully laid him in the manger to sleep, ensuring that he would be warm and safe.

The whisper of angels came with the shepherds as they arrived praising God. "The heavens rejoiced at the birth of this child." I treasured their words and pondered them in my heart. My heart had never felt fuller as I watched these rugged men crowding around the manger in delight. Their expressions of joy, reverence and even awe brought tears to my eyes. I felt Joseph's fingers intertwine with my own.

This journey had begun with the angel Gabriel coming to me so many months ago and now had transpired to bring me these strange visitors, reassuring me that my child would bring peace on earth.

"We incorrectly assume that God's favor rests on the rich and powerful. See here, see this woman and her child. This is where His favor lies," they said.

These shepherds had been tending their flocks in the middle of the night when suddenly an angel had appeared to them. "Jehovah's glory gleamed all around," one man said, his arms spread wide.

"We were terrified at first. Were we not, Manni?"

"None as much as you, Lael," Manni replied with a chuckle. He then turned toward me, his eyes full of excitement. "The angel told us not to be afraid. He said he brought us good news of great joy. The Savior, the Messiah, had just been born in Bethlehem. He said we would find the child wrapped in cloths and lying in a manger."

"And then something even more spectacular happened. The entire sky filled with light and sound as a whole host of angels appeared, praising God!" Lael clapped his hands together. "Never have I heard such a beautiful sound. Never in my entire life." A tear fell onto his weathered cheek. He roughly brushed it away. "And then the night sky faded back to its normal appearance, and all was quiet again. So Eben suggested we come into Bethlehem to see if we could find the infant."

"Well, he had to be something special," Eben said, standing over the manger, unable to take his eyes off of the infant. "Angels don't just appear for no reason."

"And to think the angels appeared to us! Wouldn't the religious leaders make a mockery of that?" The shepherds chuckled amongst themselves.

"Did it take you long to travel here?" Joseph asked.

"No, not long. We were only a couple of miles outside of Bethlehem. There's a tower. You may have passed it on your journey here. It's called the Migdal Eder, meaning tower of the flock. The sheep born there are used as sacrificial animals in the Jewish Temple during the Passover."

For so long, it had seemed as if only Joseph and I realized the significance of this child. No one else knew or believed. But in a moment, this had changed. The shepherds knew and believed. It was obvious they were changed men. I watched as they unashamedly praised and glorified God.

Naturally they told everyone who would listen about their experience. Some believed. Some did not. But everyone who heard about it was curious. I couldn't help but treasure these things and ponder them. I stored away each and every word in my heart, knowing that I would need to ponder them over and over again in the months and years to come.

A baby's cry roused me from a deep sleep. Still not fully awake, I struggled to push myself up. A large hand settled on my back. "I'll get him, Mary. You stay put."

I watched as Joseph rose from the bed of hay and moved toward where Jesus lay. He lifted the baby from the manger, gently cradling him in his arms. My love for Joseph had deepened since the birth of Jesus. Watching him father our son brought me immeasurable joy.

Unable to walk the baby back to sleep, Joseph knelt and gently relinquished Jesus into my outstretched arms. "I believe he may need something from you I unfortunately am unable to give." I drew Jesus close, smiling when I realized he was sucking on his tiny fist.

Once the baby was nursing comfortably, I leaned back against Joseph, my eyes heavy with exhaustion. "I don't believe I've ever been so tired," I whispered. "Even when I was pregnant and couldn't see my feet and would carry that heavy pitcher of water home from the well each and every day. Even then."

Joseph nuzzled my right ear lobe between his lips. "You once told me riding that donkey all the way here was not for the faint of heart."

"Yes, well, even then I wasn't as tired as I am now."

"I have to admit watching you bring this child into the world made me glad I am a man." Joseph took a tendril of my hair and curled it around his finger.

"And yet if you could have endured the pain for me, I believe you would have," I whispered, turning my head until our noses were touching.

"You are beginning to read me very well, wife." His lips touched mine in a gentle caress. He drew back. It was too dark to read what his eyes were saying. "I'll totally understand if you don't…"

"Don't?"

"If you wish to not have any more children."

"I want your children." This time I kissed his lips. "Not today, or tomorrow," I said with a laugh. "But someday I want another son or a daughter. Or perhaps two or three of each."

"You are so much stronger than I. Jesus is barely five days old, and already you speak of having more children."

"Are not children our legacy?"

"And our security," Joseph said. "Although I suppose none will offer more security than this child lying in your arms.

I looked down at my son. He had fallen back to sleep, contentment displayed on his features now that his belly was full. I fell asleep with Jesus snuggled close to my heart.

The next morning, I awoke to voices speaking quietly just outside the cave. My arms were empty. I quickly made myself presentable. Glancing in the cradle as I passed by proved it was also uninhabited. I peeked around the entrance of the cave, my heart rhythm softening when I found Jesus lying in Joseph's arms. My eyes then took in the unfamiliar man standing next to him.

"Mary," Joseph said, noticing me. He beckoned me over. "This is my uncle Remiel. Remiel, this is my wife, Mary."

I studied the robust man standing in front of me. He had strong brown hands callused from hard work, one of which he reached out to shake my own. His hair had silver in it, although I could tell at one time it had been glossy black.

"Remiel has invited us to stay in his home." My eyes met Joseph's. "I told him you were quite partial to chilly caves with noisy farm animals."

Remiel chuckled, a deep resonating laugh that startled Jesus awake. "Our last child of five children married last month, so we have plenty of room for you both. And the babe, of course."

"How did you find us?" I couldn't keep from asking. From the look he and Joseph shared, I knew Joseph had already asked him the question before I had joined them.

"In the market, just yesterday, I overheard a shepherd speaking of a child having been born. The Messiah! You can imagine my surprise. Some ignored him. Others paused to listen to the man's story. When the crowd moved on, I stayed to inquire more details from him. He said a young man and a young woman had traveled all the way from Nazareth, arriving just in time for the infant to be born. When I inquired of the man's name, he said Joseph…Joseph of the tribe of Judah and a descendant of David."

Remiel paused to take a breath. "And so I asked him where this Joseph was staying, and he sent me here."

"Do you remember the shepherd's name?" I asked curiously.

"Eben. His name was Eben."

I smiled. Even still, these shepherds were in awe of the birth of Jesus. "While I am thankful for this roof over our heads, I gladly accept your invitation, Remiel, if my husband is in agreement."

"Then it is settled," Remiel said with a pleased smile. "As soon as I saw your husband, Mary, I knew he was the son of my sister. We share the same irresistible eyes, do we not?"

I turned toward Joseph and felt heat spreading up my neck and into my cheeks. Joseph's eyes were one of the first physical traits that had drawn me to him. He had such eloquent eyes, encompassing warmth and kindness. I often felt as if he saw deeper beneath the surface, almost as if he could see into my soul. His eyes betrayed blessing and grace and had captivated me from the very beginning.

"Yes, I believe you do," I whispered.

God specifically directed Abraham to circumcise all newborn males on the eighth day. Why the eighth day? The topic had been discussed in detail on numerous occasions, and there were many possible explanations. Some said just as the blood of the offering brought atonement, so too did circumcision. Any offerings brought into the Temple needed to be at least eight days old, so of course a newborn should be at least eight days old as well.

Also of concern was the health of the baby. Waiting eight days would ensure the child would be strong enough for the circumcision. Then still, there was the mother to think about. A woman was considered ritually impure for at least seven days after giving birth to a boy, so it was only right to wait until both parents could share in the joyous occasion.

Whatever the reason, in the end we knew that the words of Abraham were inspired of God. There was a reason beyond what we understood. Circumcision signified the eternal covenant and bond between our people and our Creator. It was a matter of faith, signifying a bond that was so much higher than intellect.

And so on the eighth day Jesus was circumcised. The priest paused at the mention of his name, for it was common practice to name the first son after his father. But Joseph quickly nodded his consent. The name Jesus had been given by the angel Gabriel long before he had been conceived in my womb.

"Jesus," I repeated after the priest, tears coursing down both my cheeks. *Jesus. Yeshua. Jehovah Saves.* My son would one day grow into a man. He would seek and save the lost. This child I had delivered would one day deliver me. It was not lost on me that every time I kissed my little baby, I kissed the face of God.

I felt Joseph's warm hand envelop my own. He squeezed it, a gentle reminder that he understood my impassioned emotions. He was probably feeling them too.

"We offer this little child to you, Father. You've entrusted him to his parent's care. May he never stray from your law." The priest turned toward Joseph and me. "Please respond to the following questions. Do you promise to guide this child in the Torah?"

We nodded in affirmation.

"Do you commit to nurturing him in the admonition of our Father?"

Again, we nodded.

"Let all men know that on this day, Jesus has been dedicated to God." The priest lifted Jesus high and prayed a blessing over him. Finally, he relinquished my child back into my arms.

Later that evening, I glanced across the room, my eyes connecting briefly with Joseph's. I looked forward to retiring for the night. The entire day, Joseph and I had barely said a handful of words to each other. After the circumcision, a small group of people had gathered to help celebrate the dedication of our son. Jewish celebrations were never short. And this one was no exception.

Remiel handed me a plate of food. "You didn't eat much earlier. You need to keep your strength up."

"Thank you," I said with gratitude. "I feel as if I may fall asleep standing up! Entertain me with an interesting fact of your city."

"The Messiah was born just a few days ago in a stable filled with farm animals not too far away from here. It just may be the most magnificent fact Bethlehem has to offer."

"Yes, I met a group of shepherds who said the very thing. This Messiah, do you believe He has come to save the world?"

"Yes, I believe it. Don't you?" The merriment in Remiel's eyes reminded me so much of my father.

My eyes searched the room for Joseph once again. He was standing against the wall, Jesus nestled safely in his strong arms. "Yes, I believe it as well."

"Our little town has a scriptural heritage reflecting both great sorrow and great joy. Jacob lost his beloved Rachael here. She died giving birth to their son Benjamin. Her tomb stands just on the outskirts of Bethlehem and is a favorite place of prayer for many women. And of course, you're aware of the story of Ruth and Boaz. They fell in love in the fields just outside of Bethlehem. They were the great-grandparents of King David. And it was in Bethlehem that Samuel first anointed David as the future king of Israel, which of course is why Bethlehem is often referred to as the City of David."

"My father often told me the story of Ruth and Boaz." Oh, how I missed my father. He should be here celebrating the birth of my son. "As a young girl, I often romanticized about Ruth's situation and how Boaz saved her from what seemed inevitable starvation."

My thoughts turned to Joseph and how he had saved me from death by stoning only months before. I felt his hand on my back and turned to acknowledge him. The genuineness displayed in his eyes demonstrated he was thinking of that frightening day as well.

"I've deterred him long enough, I believe," Joseph whispered. "Our son is in need of your services."

I took Jesus from his arms and sought out the solitude of our private room. Placing the partially eaten plate of food within reach, I situated Jesus against me, sighing with relief when he began nursing with ease. The first few days, I had been apprehensive. I hadn't known much about the aspect of nursing a child. Thankfully, Remiel's wife had been able to advise me in the art of breastfeeding. Having nursed five of her own children, she was well versed in the art.

My heart was beholden for all God had brought me through. Why did I continue to doubt His provision when He so perfectly orchestrated my steps and knew at every moment what I was in need of? Closing my eyes in heartfelt appreciation, I thanked Him for taking such good care of me.

I opened my eyes, briefly confused and wondering where I was. I felt eyes on me and glanced toward the doorway. Joseph stood leaning against the wall, watching me. "I must have fallen asleep," I said, my cheeks flushing red with embarrassment.

"You've never looked more beautiful." He continued to watch me from across the room, in no hurry to return to the guests outside our door, it seemed. "I loved you before. I did. But watching you nurture our son has deepened that love into something even more profound."

I understood what he was saying because I felt the same way. Even though Jesus wasn't of his blood, still he had taken on the role of his father so effortlessly. So beautifully.

"I find myself thinking back to when we first met. How innocent I was then. How innocent and uncomplicated my life was. Had you married me then, would our life have been less troubled? Less overwhelmed? I wonder at times what I have to offer you…"

"All I desire is you, Mary. Whoever God has made you to be. I realize we are both different than we were a year ago. We've both matured. I've watched you blossom into an unwavering and secure woman of God. I feel blessed to call you my wife. And I pray daily that God will mold me into the husband you need so you can become everything He meant for you to be." Joseph crossed the room and knelt down in front of me.

"I saw how moved you were during the ceremony. I felt His presence too." Joseph took my hand, his eyes searching mine in earnest. "I saw something…a vision perhaps. When the priest lifted Jesus high, I saw people coming to him, people with all kinds of ailments."

A tear fell onto Joseph's cheek. Never had I seen him so moved. "Mary, the blind will see. The deaf will hear. The dead will live again. The lame will leap. The mute will speak. One day, He'll bring healing to this land." Joseph looked down at Jesus lying peacefully in my arms.

"This sleeping child you're holding is the great I Am."

One evening shortly after the evening meal, as we all relaxed within the courtyard, Remiel began sharing stories of Aliza, Joseph's mother.

"So full of joy she was. It spilled from her eyes." Remiel took a sip of water. "Our father loved her so very much. I wish… I wish things had turned out differently."

"I never had the pleasure of meeting him. He disowned my mother, didn't he? After she married my father?" Joseph leaned back in his seat, ready after all these years to hear the entire story.

"Aliza had Father wrapped around her finger. She got her way in most matters." Remiel looked away. "I'm not sure how much to disclose…"

"All of it," Joseph said. "My mother is gone, and so is your father. I would like to know what divided them."

A smile crossed Remiel's lips. "I'll begin with my favorite memory of her then. Aliza's internal beauty was profound. She cared deeply. And I always sensed Father admired her in this, for she often brought home the wounded and hungry and he'd help her doctor them. It began with animals—a bird with a damaged wing or a lame rabbit. My father often teased her. 'You can't save them all,' he'd say each time she'd bounce through our door with yet another stray in need of healing.

"A few, they were able to save. And he received more joy by observing her delight when she'd release them back into the wild. And then there were those who were too maimed, too broken to recover. When they'd take a turn for the worse, our father would dispose of them before she'd awake in the morning, pretending that the *faith healer* had come by in the night and taken them to a better place.

"Eventually, Aliza began bringing home people—a starving boy outside the temple of Jerusalem or a woman beaten and left for dead out in the fields. They'd stay for a few days and then move on."

"She would have made a good doctor's wife," Vada said as she gathered some of the dishes into her arms. She waved me aside when I attempted to help her. "You finish feeding your child."

"Our father made preparations for her to marry, but she begged for him to delay the ceremony just one more year. 'I'm not ready,' she'd say. He gave in as was his practice and said she could wait one more year but 'no more,' he'd then say adamantly. It was obvious she didn't care for the man my father had chosen. But he was well off, and as was custom, Father wanted her to be taken care of. He wanted us all to be taken care of.

"One day she brought home your father…Jacob. His carpentry shop had been broken into, all of his creations destroyed or taken. He had been beaten severely and left to die. None of us thought he'd live through the night, but one day turned into two and two into three. After three weeks, he forced himself to stand and limped right out the door while we were at the synagogue one Sunday morning. We thought that was the end of it. Unbeknownst to our father, she continued to check on him throughout the weeks. And then Father heard from a friend that she was seen leaving Jacob's shop. He was furious.

"'I have spoiled you too much, daughter, but no more,' he said. 'The bans will be read announcing your marriage to Rava this Sunday.'

"She begged and cried and persisted, but Father could not be moved. 'He has nothing to offer you, daughter. Nothing.' When she realized Father could not be persuaded, she snuck out in the night and married Jacob anyway."

"Without your father's consent?" I couldn't help asking.

"Without his consent. Without his knowledge. One day she was here, the next she was gone. Rumors spread throughout town. 'She was with child,' some said. She returned a week later to relay her good news, but our father wouldn't even look at her. He wouldn't talk to her. He wouldn't acknowledge her. With one final act, she broke his heart. He never spoke to her again."

"Did he read her letters?" Joseph asked. Seeing that I was finished nursing, he reached over and took Jesus from my arms, settling him gently into his own.

"Not for years. When the letters came, Mother would set them in a basket next to their bed. There eventually came to be quite a pile of them. And then one day after Mother's death, I noticed him reading one, tears streaming down his face. The letters are still here, stored in the same basket."

"I remember the day she received your letter, Remiel. When she knew that her letters were finally being read, it changed her whole world."

"I had to let her know that Father lived for her letters. If she stopped, I didn't know what would become of him. For years this continued, and then we received your letter," Remiel said to Joseph. "Father declined quickly after learning of her death. He was gone within a year."

Later, in bed, I asked Joseph a question that had been on my mind since that evening. "Did your mother ever regret marrying Jacob?"

"I suppose she did at times. I know she wished her father would have consented to their marriage. It broke her heart to have to choose one over the other."

I turned onto my side so I could see his face. Reaching up, I traced my finger down Joseph's cheek. "Is it from your mother that you learned the art of letter writing?"

"Ah, so you did like my letters?"

"They made me blush in front of Elizabeth," I giggled.

"I meant every word," Joseph whispered before his lips found mine.

The time came for us to take Jesus to the temple in Jerusalem to present him to the Lord. The Law of the Lord said each firstborn baby boy belonged to the Lord. We were also required to offer a purification sacrifice.

We awoke much earlier than normal, and after we shared the morning meal with Remiel and his wife Vada, we prepared ourselves for travel. Jerusalem was just over an hour by foot. I enjoyed the scenery as we walked.

"Does it ever frighten you?" I asked. "The task of raising Jesus?"

"I won't pretend that raising God's son isn't at times daunting, but I aim to make every effort to do it right."

I felt my heart lighten. Joseph always seemed to have an answer to calm my questioning heart.

We hadn't been in the temple long when an elderly man hobbled toward us. "Is this the one?" There were tears streaming down the man's weathered cheeks. I could see he needed no answer from us, for he was asking of one much higher than us. "This is the one!" The man fell onto his knees, deep sobs wracking his feeble body.

The man's head was bowed in reverence, his hands lifted in complete surrender. Never had I seen such adoration. Suddenly, the man rose to his feet, his eyes meeting mine for the first time. "He told me I would not die until I had seen Christ the Lord."

"He?" I asked.

"God, of course." The man reached out his hand. "I'm Simeon. I live here in Jerusalem, and I've been waiting years for God to save the people of Israel." Simeon held out his arms. "May I?"

I hesitated briefly. Was the man able to hold my son? His arms were shaking. Should I ask him to sit down first? Joseph nodded, indicating for me to release our son into Simeon's outstretched hands. I quickly relinquished my son.

Simeon closed his eyes, tears once again streaming down his face. And then he began praising God.

> *"Lord, I am Your servant,*
> *and now I can die in peace*
> *because You have kept*
> *Your promise to me.*
> *With my own eyes I have seen*
> *what You have done*
> *to save Your people,*
> *and foreign nations*
> *will also see this.*
> *Your mighty power is a light*

for all nations,
and it will bring honor
to Your people Israel."

Joseph was as surprised as I at Simeon's words. We shared a look of wonder at everything Simeon had spoken. He placed Jesus back into my arms. Reaching out, he touched my shoulder.

"Mary, this child of yours will cause many people in Israel to fall and others to stand. This child will be a warning sign. Many…many will reject him, and you, Mary, you will suffer as though…as though you had been stabbed by a dagger."

Tears of sorrow dropped onto the stone floor below. I realized this time the tears were mine.

"But all of this will show what people are really thinking," he said.

Not long after Simeon had left the temple, I noticed a very old woman standing across the way. "That woman is watching us," I said to Joseph.

"She's been studying us since we arrived." Joseph took Jesus from me. "Perhaps she has some words of wisdom for us as well." The humor in Joseph's eyes brought a smile to my lips. "She's not quite as brave as Simeon, perhaps. Should we approach her?"

A young woman who was holding a baby of her own looked up. "I apologize. I'm not in the habit of listening in on people's conversations, but I believe you are talking of Anna…across the way."

"Anna?" I repeated. "She lives here in Jerusalem?" I asked.

"She's a prophet," the woman said. "She was the daughter of Phanuel. Are you from around here?"

"We're from Nazareth," Jesus answered.

"Anna was a very beautiful woman in her day, or so my grandmother always said. She married in her youth, but her husband died after seven years. There were no children." The woman looked at her own child.

"I also was barren…for eleven years. I had nearly given up hope of having a child when Anna approached me one day here at the temple. 'A year hence you will hold a son in your arms in this very spot,' she said." The woman ceased talking as she tried to contain her tears. She swallowed. "Today marks one year. This is my son, Ezra."

I reached out and took her hand in mine. "God has blessed you."

"And you, it seems," the woman said as she gazed at Jesus lying in Joseph's arms. "Anna is 105 years old. For 84 years, night and day, she has served God in this temple, praying and often going without eating. Come," she invited. "She obviously wants to meet you and your child."

We followed the woman over to Anna. As I looked into the elderly woman's eyes, I felt a rush of His spirit. "Is this the child who will set Jerusalem free?" she asked in a raspy voice. Anna leaned over the bundle wrapped in Joseph's arms and gently kissed Jesus' forehead. "The Messiah has come," she cried. "He has come to save that which is lost."

I was the first to have the good news of a Savior proclaimed to me, but Anna…Anna perhaps was the first woman to understand fully what it all meant. Her insight into the spiritual world was inspiring. Her life evidently invigorated her, for never had I seen another her age as mobile, articulate and alert. Kissing Jesus' forehead a second time, she then began moving about the temple telling all who would listen that the Savior was born and would one day save Jerusalem.

"The Son of Man has come to seek and save those who are lost!" Her gentle voice resonated throughout the temple.

I turned to the woman once again. "She is amazing. And to have lived so long!"

"Anna is from the tribe of Asher. Do you remember the words of Moses concerning them?" The woman shifted her son and continued. "Moses said of the Asher tribe, 'Your strength will equal your days.' Anna's life surely is evidence of that!"

Joseph also was watching Anna, admiration showing on his own face. "It is rare to see one of her age without any hint of bitterness or animosity. Never have I seen such hope displayed in one's eyes."

Our hearts full and our minds pondering all that had just taken place, we slowly made our way across the temple toward the gate used for women. Joseph handed me the two turtledoves he had purchased. I look up into his eyes. These last months, I had seen his patience firsthand. His endurance. His self-control. His willingness to see to the needs and wants of others above the needs and wants of his own. I sensed his longing.

Smiling, I took the basket containing the two turtledoves from his outstretched hand and walked into a separate part of the temple, the Court of Women. I handed the turtledoves to the priest, who offered them as incense before the Lord. An organ sounded, indicating the incense had been offered on the Golden Altar.

I closed my eyes in relief. I was purified.

I felt Joseph's eyes on me when I emerged from the Court of Women and found myself blushing under his gaze. I realized in this moment how much he had suppressed his desire for me. His aspiration to obey God was so much more than his want for me, and I felt my trust in him deepen. But now, now that the limitation on our intimacy had lifted, I felt his want, his need in ways I never had before.

We left the temple uninhibited, freedom in our steps. It took a few minutes before I realized we were walking in the wrong direction. "Unless I'm mistaken, I believe Bethlehem is that way," I said, stopping in my tracks.

"You are not mistaken," Joseph said a hint of a smile. "I have another destination in mind."

"But we decided…"

"It's not Nazareth." He chuckled and began walking once again. "It's a surprise, Mary. Don't ruin it."

I continued after him, hurrying my pace in order to keep up with his lanky steps. Where was he headed? Perhaps an inn? That made sense. This was our first *night* together. Of course he'd want to make it special. Memorable. We passed one inn and then another. And then we were headed out of Jerusalem. I looked over at Joseph in confusion.

And then I noticed a familiar stone home. A lady stood just outside the home beating the dust from her woven rug. It was Adina, Elizabeth's midwife. Suddenly I knew where we were headed. Just around the corner, four homes down lay Zechariah and Elizabeth's home. Tears rose to the surface, and I realized I had stopped dead in my tracks.

Joseph turned and stared back at me. Slowly, he retraced his steps back to me.

"And here I thought this would be a happy surprise," he whispered, his thumb gently brushing away the tear on my cheek.

"It is!" I cried, my tears coming even harder. "I've never been happier."

Joseph took my hand, and we rounded the corner. And then we were standing in front of their home. It almost seemed a lifetime ago when I had stayed here, and yet really it had only been six months. So much had happened since then. I looked up, my eyes taking in the rooftop above. How often had I sat up there thinking of the man now standing beside me? Hoping…pleading…praying that he'd still want me when I returned home.

The door flung open, and Elizabeth screamed with delight. "Zechariah, they've come. They've come at last." My eyes took in the bright-eyed baby boy on her hip. John began bouncing in his mother's arms.

I stepped forward and kissed each of Elizabeth's cheeks. "Khavera sheli," I whispered. *My friend.* "How I've missed you!"

"And I, you." Elizabeth turned to Joseph, her eyes gauging the man now standing in front of her. "You're right, Mary. He does have very fetching eyes."

I felt the heat rush up the back of my neck. "Elizabeth!"

Elizabeth's joyful laugh echoed throughout the house. I had forgotten how much I missed the sound. I glanced at Joseph and found him smiling at me. *I'm going to like her,* he mouthed.

"Now, show me this baby," Elizabeth said with delight. She handed John off to me, and I marveled at his weight. He turned to look at me before reaching up with his chubby little hand and touching my cheek.

I smiled when I turned to find Elizabeth had already unbundled Jesus and was counting each and every finger and toe. "Just what sort of mischief will you and my son get into?" Elizabeth said with emotion. She gently held him up for John to see. John giggled and reached out to touch my son. Elizabeth stepped just out of reach. "Not yet, John. You'll have plenty of opportunities to manhandle him in a few years."

"Zechariah must not have heard me," Elizabeth said. "Come, he's in the courtyard. Lunch is ready. I assumed you'd be here some time ago." Elizabeth turned my way, a smile on her face. "You obviously had much to be cleansed of, Mary."

Joseph and I followed Elizabeth through the house and out into the courtyard. Zechariah jumped to his feet when he saw us. "Elizabeth, I told you to holler when they arrived." He rushed forward and hugged me, his son John reaching out for his father as soon as Zechariah stepped back from embracing me.

Taking his son, Zechariah turned to Joseph. I introduced them to each other and smiled as they quickly began talking as if they had been acquainted their entire lives instead of just barely introduced.

Elizabeth handed Jesus back to Joseph and nodded for me to follow her back into the kitchen. "I forgot the olive oil," she said. Once out of earshot of the men, she asked, "Is married life all you thought it would be?"

"It's wonderful," I said. I looked down at my hands, knowing she would be able to read in my eyes what was missing in my words.

"All of it?" she asked, her eyes studying me.

"All I've experienced," I finally admitted.

"Experienced? You've been married for five months. Are you telling me…?"

"I told you in a letter that an angel appeared to Joseph…"

"Yes, telling him that he was to marry you. You didn't say he was told to abstain."

"How could I put that in a letter, Elizabeth?" I half cried, half laughed. "It has been a private matter we've discussed with no one else."

"And still, he married you, knowing he could never fully claim you as his wife," Elizabeth clucked her tongue, surprise evident in her eyes.

"Only until Jesus was born…"

"Ah, so you have…"

"It is custom to wait to resume marital relations after the cleansing period, is it not?" I looked down at my hands, not fully sure I wanted to be discussing this private topic.

"So tonight…"

"Shh." I placed my hand over her mouth. "They are right outside, probably hearing every word we speak." Right then, Zechariah's laughter echoed throughout the courtyard and through the small window in the kitchen.

"My husband is much too talkative to ever attempt eavesdropping on me," Elizabeth chuckled. "When you were here, he had lost his speech, and you unfortunately were unable to see Zechariah in his full glory. At times, I miss the quiet…"

"I thought you said supper was ready." Zechariah's loud voice echoed from the courtyard.

"Coming, dear," Elizabeth called back.

We returned to the courtyard, and I marveled at the two infants contentedly lying in their fathers' arms, both sound asleep. I suspected that their lives would be intertwined well beyond mere friendship.

We ate supper, conversation flowing freely amongst us. We filled them in on all that had taken place in the last few weeks since traveling to Bethlehem. Even Zechariah listened wide-eyed while Joseph shared the news of the shepherds following the star to our humble cave to worship the newborn King.

One hour turned into two, and two into three. I stifled a yawn, and felt Joseph's eyes on me. Elizabeth quickly stood to her feet. "You both must be exhausted!"

"Exhausted?" Zechariah questioned. "They just got here…"

"Come," Elizabeth said, a smile on her face. "Let me show you to your room." We followed her into the house, and she led us to the familiar room I had previously stayed in. "John's cradle is there in the corner. He outgrew it a few weeks back. Zechariah made a new one a good bit deeper, since John can nearly pull himself up. He is such a strong boy," Elizabeth said with pride. And then, with a parting smile, she left the room.

I watched as Joseph gently lay Jesus in the cradle. He turned then, his eyes finding mine. Suddenly, I felt self-conscious. My body had just recently endured a long pregnancy and an arduous delivery. Though forty days had passed, my body wasn't nearly what I had envisioned it to look like on this night. This very special night.

"Are you afraid, Mary?" Joseph quietly voiced as he made his way toward me.

I shook my head. Then nodded. And then shook my head again. The sun was quickly descending behind the hills, and I hoped it was enough to conceal my trembling hands. I looked up into his eyes and could read his concern.

"I'm not afraid…of you," I quickly assured him, but he looked doubtful. "I'm fearful of disappointing you." I closed my eyes. There. The truth lay out before us, my soul laid bare.

"Mary," he whispered. He took my hands in his and led me toward the sleeping mat. Gently, he took off my outer garment, and I watched as it softly fell to the floor. His finger traced my lips and then moved down my neck and stopped at my collarbone.

"Mary," he whispered again, this time his mouth hovering near my ear. "If I'm so callous a man that I could even remotely be disappointed in the woman God has given to me, then I am undeserving of you." He gently kissed the places his finger had just touched, his garment soon joining mine on the floor.

I lay in silence, listening to Joseph's deep even breathing, and marveled at his patience with me, even this night. This night, when I knew he had waited for so long and yet still cared more about me and my fulfillment than his own. I turned onto my side so I could see him better in the moonlight. How I loved him. I had loved him before this night, but now…now it was so much deeper. Now I felt connected to him in a way I hadn't before. In a way I didn't understand but could certainly feel.

Unable to sleep, I lay awake for some time, my mind pondering this day and all that had taken place. Hearing Jesus' soft whimper from across the room, I lay quiet and still, wondering if he'd fall back asleep on his own. His whimper grew louder.

Silently, I rose to my feet and made my way across the floor to retrieve him. And then I moved to the ladder that led to the roof. The full moon cast enough light to see my surroundings as I found my familiar spot from months before. It was odd how God was showing Himself, and I found myself wondering why God had chosen to speak to such a group of people.

First the shepherds, then Simeon and Anna. His love and devotion to the poor was obvious. Was He proving His concern for them? He seemed to be paying special attention to the longing of their hearts, hearts longing to know the Messiah. God was revealing His own heart in that He cares about all individuals, poor or rich.

Tears filled my eyes as I realized God's deep compassion. Today He had granted an old man's request and ministered to an old woman's heart. We were called to honor the aged.

Please, may I never forget.

I pulled Jesus closer to my heart. He was my child. It was instinct to nurture and protect him. At times, I forgot He was not just any normal human baby. He was God in human flesh. He was the Messiah. And he was my son.

Simeon's words of caution came back to me. I had tried to put them aside through much of the day, but now, in the still of night, they penetrated my heart. *Suffer. Like a dagger to the heart. A dagger?* Was such pain my destiny? And if this was the pain I was to suffer at the expense of my son, how much more would He be made to suffer?

The sob I had been holding in all day burst forth. As Jesus nursed at my breast, I wept for the affliction He would one day endure. *"I'm sorry, little one. I'm so sorry."*

I saw his shadow as he sat down beside me, his arm coming around me and drawing me near. "I'm sorry, Mary." Joseph kissed my forehead. "It's been on my mind too. And as much as it hurts, as much as it must cause uncertainty in your heart, I believe you need to focus on the beautiful moments you have with Jesus now. For if we approach the future with anxiety, we will miss the wonder of this moment. Each and every day is a miracle. It's a miracle, Mary."

I nodded my head against his shoulder. He was right. God had chosen me to be Jesus' mother. And I intended to make the most of every moment I had with him.

We stayed three nights with Zechariah and Elizabeth before returning to Bethlehem. Joseph was little by little finding enough work to provide for us. We contemplated returning to Nazareth, but as much as we desired to return to the familiarity of our home, we didn't feel released to do so. At least not yet. We didn't understand it but were willing to wait for God's guidance.

There was an intimacy between us now, an understanding we had never shared before. I had known Joseph was withholding a part of himself, but I hadn't realized how much. During the day, his eyes now followed me constantly, and I could read the desire in his eyes, his desire for me. And each evening, after Jesus was fed and sleeping soundly, Joseph would draw me close.

Sharing our bodies with one another brought more than just pleasure. It also brought a sense of comfort. A comfort deeper than words. And then we would lie beside one another in perfect peace, perfect harmony, knowing that what we shared with each other, we would never share with another.

Each morning I would work by Zada's side, aiding in the preparation of supper. Penina, Remiel and Zada's daughter, stopped by often. She was married to Joed, who was a stonemason. He and Joseph had just recently begun working on a project together. Penina reminded me so much of Zillah, so it didn't surprise me that we became fast friends. Her son Jeriah was only a few months older than Jesus. We often sat in the courtyard in the afternoons, nursing our sons and discussing the future.

"I believe I'm with child again," Penina whispered, a smile on her face.

"Already?" I glanced down at Jesus. He still seemed so small, although he was nearly six months old. How I loved his pudgy little legs. I reached down and gently tickled the bottom of one foot, enjoying the smile in his eyes as he gazed up at me in adoration. Not even Joseph could quite master that look.

"I began feeding Jeriah mashed sweet potato and squash a few weeks ago. He'll be a year old in six weeks' time."

Penina sat Jeriah on the dirt-packed ground. I watched as he quickly crawled toward the small cistern of water, Penina snatching him back up before he fell into it. "The disasters I save this child from each and every day!"

I laughed. As much as I looked forward to Jesus reaching that milestone, I dreaded it as well. Keeping up with his demand for milk was about all I could handle at the moment. I sat Jesus down near my feet and handed him a few wooden blocks Joseph had recently made for him.

"So, it seems you're staying? I'm glad. I hate the thought of you returning to Nazareth." Penina glanced over at me.

"I so look forward to introducing Jesus to my parents. But at the same time, I hate to leave. We've been here for so long and have met so many wonderful people. I hate the thought of leaving any of you behind."

"Perhaps Joed and I will be able to come visit you in Nazareth one day." But even as Penina said the words, I knew it wasn't very likely. At least not anytime soon. Joed's work was here. And Penina was now expecting their second child.

I smiled as Jeriah reached for a block out of Jesus' reach and handed it to my son. Jeriah had a sweet spirit about him. As inquisitive as he was, he also seemed to look out for others. He'd be a kind older brother one day.

"You don't have much time to become pregnant yourself, Mary. Not if we are going to continue having our children close together." Penina's laugh echoed throughout the courtyard.

"I may have to skip this pregnancy, Penina, and join you on the next one." This time, I joined her in her laughter.

"Unless you're abstaining, Mary, you'll soon be pregnant again as well. I see the smoldering glances Joseph sends your way whenever you two are in the same room as one another."

I looked down at my hands, a flush of red spreading across my cheeks. "I've told him he needs to temper those glances."

"Why? Are you not aware that every woman who witnesses his ardent love for you is intensely jealous and wishes her husband felt the same?"

"Well, you're the one who's pregnant again so soon," I noted with raised eyebrows. Only Penina didn't smile. For the first time, I realized she really was longing for Joed to feel the same about her.

"Joed loves you," I said. My words did not convince her, and I watched helplessly as her eyes filled with tears.

My mind raced back to all the evenings we had all shared the supper meal together. How we'd wait impatiently for our husbands to walk through the threshold of the door. How we'd wait for their eyes to meet ours. And never once had I noticed Joed look at Penina the way Joseph looked at me.

"I wasn't his first choice."

I sat in silence, knowing she wasn't waiting for me to respond. She was wanting me to understand.

"Her name is Talia. The families were very good friends, and it was thought they'd marry one another almost since the day they were born." Penina swallowed, her eyes on her son as he grasped a fistful of dirt in his hand. He brought it toward his mouth but resisted at the shake of her head. He instead watched delightfully as it sprinkled from his hand onto his chubby leg.

"Joed was offered work in Jerusalem doing some repair on the temple, and while he was away, Talia… She gave herself to another. When she found she was with child, she married the man. He's older. His wife had died. He could offer her more than Joeb ever could."

"But does he love her?" The words were spoken before I could retain them.

"I believe they're content enough. Will they share what you and Joseph share? Probably not. But she has a beautiful roof over her head and is a mother to his two sons."

"And Joeb? Has he let her go?"

"I knew when he began pursuing me in such earnest that it was too soon. But I've loved him for years, and when he suddenly turned his affections to me, I didn't even hesitate. Only I didn't realize then what I know now… Turning your affections to someone is not the same as turning your heart. I suppose I should count my blessings. He's a good man. He works hard. He provides for his family. But he doesn't look at me the way he looked at Talia. I try to ignore it. And most days I succeed. But some days…some days I feel so completely betrayed, I wonder if I can continue loving a man who doesn't love me back."

I pushed a wooden block back toward Jesus. "I also thought I was going to marry another man. He's the brother of my closest friend in Nazareth."

"What happened?" Penina sat rocking her tired son back and forth. "Did he marry another?"

I told her my story. How in spite of our well laid plans, God had a better plan in mind. How my pain and my sorrow actually brought me to feel more deeply than I've ever felt before. How learning to trust was a painful but necessary experience. And how God could transform any person. And how perhaps more importantly a spark could ignite and grow into something beautiful. Something we hadn't even imagined. Something miraculous.

Early one evening as I was helping Vada prepare supper, we heard voices coming from outside. The door had been propped open to let in some cool air. At first, I thought it was the shepherds coming to see Jesus. They periodically stopped by to see how he was doing. But although the voices I was overhearing were masculine, I didn't recognize them as belonging to the shepherds'.

I wiped my wet hands on my apron and walked toward the noise. Standing just outside the door stood three men, each one dressed handsomely in robes of exquisite colors and jewels.

"The star most definitely stopped here, Gaspar. Why are you so insistent on contradicting me?" The man talking had long white hair and a neatly trimmed beard of the same color. He wore a golden-colored cloak.

"Melchior," Gaspar said with frustration. "I am most certainly not contradicting you. I'm only stating the obvious." Gaspar's hair was brown. And his face carried a brown beard with some gray near the edges. He wore a green cloak with green sparkling jewels attached. "Balthazar, who do you think is correct?"

I looked over at the third man. Balthazar? He was darker skinned than the other two men. His black beard was trimmed very short, and he wore a purple cloak.

"Our journey has been long, brothers. There is no sense in arguing over the star. Let us…" Balthazar suddenly glanced over and noticed me standing there.

"May I help you?" I asked. The three men were so entirely misplaced in this small town of Bethlehem. It was obvious they were men of means by the way they were dressed.

Balthazar stepped forward. "My lady, we have traveled long and far. In search of what, you might ask? This is the question we've been trying to answer for several months; since the appearance of a star, a star that has been constant since its first appearance whether day or night, it does not seem to matter. So, after much contemplation and many sleepless nights, we decided amongst ourselves to follow this star to see if perhaps there was a certain destination…"

"Are you looking for lodging?" I asked. Who were these men? Following a star? Who did such a thing?

"Lodging?" Balthazar shook his head. "No. We have a tent set up on the outskirts of town. We've been here three days, you see. For the star has ceased moving. It is positioned…there," he said, pointing above his head.

I stepped outside the doorway and looked up into the sky. Indeed, there was a star, burning bright and becoming brighter with each passing second as the sun was making its decline behind the hills. "Where are you from?" I asked.

Melchior stepped forward. "Persia," he answered. "We are astrological advisors to the king of Persia."

Gaspar stepped forward, joining his friends. "Is there a reason why the star would be hovered above your esteemed home?" He looked doubtful, almost crestfallen, perhaps wondering if they had followed a star for days on end for absolutely no reason whatsoever.

"I think you should join me in the courtyard," I said. All three men looked at me in surprise and then anticipation.

"I told you, Melchior. Didn't I tell you?" Gaspar entered the home. The other two quickly followed.

Vada stood in the kitchen, flour on her hands, her eyes staring in confusion at the three wise men standing inside her simple dwelling. "We have company, Vada. Would you mind if I took them out to the courtyard. They would like to meet Jesus."

"Jesus?" Melchior clapped his hands together in expectancy. "Yes, we are indeed here to meet Jesus!"

"Of course," Vada said with curious eyes. "I will bring you refreshments as soon as the bread is in the oven.

As we entered the courtyard, Joseph and Remiel stood to their feet, surprised to see we had visitors. "I'd like to introduce you to Balthazar, Melchior and Gaspar."

Gaspar turned to me in surprise. "We didn't tell you our names. Have you supernatural powers?"

I laughed. "I was listening to you in the doorway for some time before you noticed me. It was there that I learned your names."

Gaspar's face reddened, and then he smiled sheepishly. "Well, you are observant nonetheless."

"Where is the One who has been born King of the Jews?" Melchior said to Joseph and Remiel.

I took the swaddled bundle from Joseph's arms and lifted back the top of the blanket, unveiling Jesus' face. "This is Jesus," I said.

"This babe?" Melchior said. He stepped forward and peered down into the face of my child. He stood speechless staring into the eyes of my son. "This is he." Melchior voice was no longer filled with question but with certainty. "This is he."

"Well, step aside then," Gaspar admonished. "I'd like to catch a glimpse of the child as well." Melchior inched to the side, allowing Gaspar to get a good look.

Finally, after some time, it seemed they remembered Balthazar, and they both moved aside so he also could get a good look. Smiling, Balthazar timidly reached out and touched Jesus' cheek. "We've traveled far to worship you," he whispered, his voice full of emotion.

Eventually we sat, and I listened intently to every word as the wise men shared their story. It had begun in Persia where these great astrologers had gathered in an effort to comprehend the significance of what was happening in the skies above them. An event of momentous importance was happening, of that much they were sure.

With the support of their king and much preparation, the three wise men began their journey in an attempt to bring answers to the many questions they had. It was a long, perilous journey of at least a thousand miles. A thousand miles! The mere eighty miles Joseph and I had traveled from

Nazareth to Bethlehem suddenly paled in comparison.

They had traveled by camel, and the trip had taken many months, with their only guide a star. A star! Such faith they had that the star would lead them to just the right place. Having visited many fascinating places along their journey, they had arrived in Jerusalem only a few days ago, where they had been received by King Herod himself. Herod supposedly had shown great interest in their story and had told the wise men to return to him once they found the newborn king so that he could come worship him too.

I looked across at Joseph. He didn't believe Herod any more than I did, but we didn't say anything to the wise men.

"All of the Jewish residents under Herod's rule seemed very interested in the birth of this King. They seemed well aware of the prediction of the birth of a Messiah written long ago in the ancient books of the Old Testament." Melchior shifted in his seat.

Gaspar added his own voice to the story. "Honestly, I got the impression that some of them seem relieved that the reign of King Herod might be nearing its end."

"Gaspar!" Melchior reprimanded him. "Are you determined to have us burned at the stake?

"Herod has long been despised," Joseph said as he tried not to smile at the horror in Gaspar's eyes and voice. "You have no need to fear offending us."

Gaspar humbly thanked Joseph. He slipped from his seat and knelt before me, taking out a wrapped item from within the folds of his cloak. "I bring this day in honor of our Lord and Savior the gift of frankincense, a symbol of your priestly role, for you are no typical king. You are indeed precious in both meaning and value." Gaspar bowed low and laid the bundle of frankincense at my feet.

Gaspar had barely returned to his seat when Melchior leaned forward and, bowing low before Jesus, he presented his item of gold. "I also bring this day in honor of our Lord and Savior the gift of gold. Just as gold signifies royalty, purity and long-lasting worth, so also are you to be treasured and adored."

Balthazar knelt before Jesus as soon as Melchior returned to his seat. The emotion on his face was my undoing. The tears I had long been holding back began streaming down both of my cheeks. "I bring this day in honor of our Lord and Savior the gift of myrrh. Just as myrrh signifies healing, so too will you bring healing to our world."

A tear slipped down Balthazar's cheek, and he closed his eyes. "You will make the ultimate sacrifice to save us from our sins."

The gifts these wise men had bestowed upon my son were both rare and valuable. They had offered him the best gifts they knew to give. They were gifts given to a king, the richest of gifts that could ever be offered to a newborn king. The gold signified my son's kingly status; the frankincense, his divinity; and the myrrh, perhaps an anointing revealing his eventual sacrificial death?

I felt my heart squeeze. Simeon's words months ago and now Balthazar's gift indicated something in my son's future I was not yet ready to face.

Joseph's hand clutched my arm in alarm. I struggled to open my eyes. As he tried to explain, Jesus' cry pierced the air. Jesus rarely cried, and when he did, it was usually a soft whimper. I scrambled from our bed and quickly picked him up, cradling him in my arms.

"Shh," I whispered against his cheek. "Mama's here."

Usually my words comforted him, but tonight was different. He continued to scream, and I felt anxiety begin to fill my being. I pressed my lips to his forehead, checking for a fever.

"Mary, I had a dream." Joseph had also risen from the bed and was now standing behind me.

"A dream?"

"I've told you of the dream when God told me to marry you. This was the same. Very much the same."

"I turned toward him, fear evident in my eyes. "Is he in danger?"

"Bring him to bed, Mary. Perhaps if you attempt to nurse him, he will quiet, and I can tell you what the Lord said to me."

It took several attempts, but Jesus finally latched on. I pulled him closer, praying within for peace, for guidance. Finally, my eyes found Joseph's.

"It was the same angel who appeared in the first dream. He said, 'Arise and take the Child and his mother, and flee to Egypt, and remain there until I tell you; for Herod's going to search for the Child…'" Suddenly Joseph grew quiet.

"And…what?"

"That's all I wish you to know, Mary."

For the first time ever, Joseph's eyes could not meet my own. I felt a chill go down my spine. "You want to protect me. I know that. But in order to protect our son, I need to know what I am protecting him from."

Joseph closed his eyes. "Herod is going to search for Jesus…and if he finds him, he will destroy him."

A sob escaped my lips. "How do we escape him? He's the king of Israel!"

Joseph drew me near, his lips softly caressing my forehead. "We escape him by going to Egypt. The angel told me we would be safe in Egypt."

Joseph arose from the bed and began packing simple necessities we might need. When I attempted to rise, he waved his hand. "Feed him well. When he is finished, we will leave."

I closed my eyes, attempting to find a small bit of respite myself before the long journey to Egypt. My flesh craved sleep, and I desperately wished we could wait until morning to depart. But my spirit sensed a deep urgency to leave at once.

I felt a soft nudge. Then another. Opening my eyes, I saw Joseph kneeling beside the bed. "I fell asleep." I felt my cheeks redden.

"You were snoring," he chuckled softly. How I loved the gentleness in his eyes. In this moment, I was once again reminded of how blessed I truly was, even in all the uncertainty. "I've delayed as much as possible. It's time to leave."

Joseph helped me from bed and waited silently as I wrapped Jesus tightly in an extra piece of linen so he would remain warm as we traveled. Joseph then assisted in wrapping Jesus close to my chest. Taking the belongings he had packed not long before, we quietly slipped out into the courtyard.

"Shouldn't we say goodbye?" I hesitated for a moment. It felt wrong to leave without bidding Remiel and Vada farewell, especially after all they had done for us. They had shared their home with us for months now. And Penina! How I hated leaving without letting her know how much she truly meant to me.

"I think it's best if we do not. For their safety and for ours. The odds of Herod finding us are slim if no one knows of our destination."

May they feel our love and our appreciation. I followed Joseph from the courtyard and down the dusty road to the outskirts of Bethlehem. From the appearance of the moon, it would be a couple of hours before we received any light from the rising sun.

I clung to Joseph's arm as we made our way from town. I knew the journey to Egypt would be four times as far as our journey from Nazareth to Bethlehem had been. At least two weeks of traveling. But I found comfort in the fact that I was no longer pregnant. And even though I was carrying Jesus, I could at least give him to his father when my arms and legs grew tired.

"We'll go along the coast of the Mediterranean Sea," Joseph said. "And then through Gaza across the Sinai Desert. From there, we'll enter into Egypt to the Pyramids along the Nile. If it were not for the circumstances surrounding us, Mary, I would consider this a dream come true."

"Really?" I asked. "I picked you out as the stable, secure fellow whose only desire was to build beautiful items from wood and eat supper with his family every evening."

"And after the children are put to bed, lay down beside his wife…"

I nudged him as I put a finger to my lips. "Shh, Jesus is listening."

Joseph laughed.

"Why would this be a dream come true?" I asked.

"I saw an Egyptian when I was at the market with my mother one day. When I learned where he was from, I was instantly intrigued. From then on, I began mapping out various ways of traveling there if ever given the chance."

I looked up at him, surprise written in my eyes. "It can't be coincidence that the angel told us to take Jesus there."

Joseph's fingers squeezed mine. "God intricately weaves our lives, although we often do not see the reason behind the details until later."

There were two main roads to Egypt. The easier road was also the more traveled one; it passed through Gaza and then ran south along the Mediterranean coast. The other road, less used and therefore the more prudent one, passed through Hebron and Bersabee before crossing the Idumean desert and entering the Sinai peninsula. In either case, it would be a long trip.

We had walked for quite a while when Joseph turned to me, a stunned look in his eyes. "Mary…in Hosea, towards the end, there is a scripture that says, 'When Israel was a child, I loved him, and out of Egypt I called My Son.'

Out of Egypt. Using that scripture, the rabbi had always spoken of the relationship the Lord had with the nation of Israel. The love the Lord had for Israel and how He had rescued His people from slavery. God representing the father, and Israel the child. Clearly though, the meaning went deeper.

"What do you think it means?"

"Jesus is God's Son. One day soon, we will be traveling with Jesus from Egypt to the land of Israel. The Messiah…Jesus…God's Son is an extension of the Lord's love to His people."

We walked in silence then. A peaceful silence. Even though we were running from Herod, I felt at peace—because we were running in the direction God had planned all along. This was His plan. We needed only to follow it.

Our first stop was Hebron, which was about forty miles from Bethlehem. There, we secured provisions for our trip across the desert. We joined a small caravan of travelers because travel across the desert alone was almost impossible due to the oppressive heat, lack of water, and increased danger of bandits. It was said that the Roman soldiers who made the same trip would rather face battle than face the desert.

I held tightly to Jesus while seated on a donkey that Joseph had acquired just that morning. We traveled for hours that first day, and by evening I was drenched in sweat. I had allowed Jesus to nurse more often than normal in an attempt to keep him from getting dehydrated.

Halting for the night, Joseph took Jesus from my arms and, using his other free hand, he aided me as I slid down to the sandy ground. I felt my legs give way from beneath me. And then all went black.

"Mary."

I heard voices, but my mind was not making sense of their words.

Where was I? I struggled to open my eyes. "Mary." Joseph's voice finally registered.

I found I was lying under a canopy of sorts. Jesus was sleeping soundly, his warm body snuggled next to mine. I turned to look at Joseph, the concern evident in his eyes.

"Are you well?" he asked.

"Just hot and tired."

"Did you drink enough water?" Joseph was already standing and walking toward the donkey where he had tied my leather pouch of water earlier that morning, reminding me two…possibly three times before our departure to take sips often throughout the day even if I didn't feel thirsty. I felt my face redden. Had I even taken one drink? The frown upon Joseph's face as he returned with my leather pouch was evidence that I had not.

"It's full, Mary." Joseph handed me the pouch with raised brows. "You're lucky you didn't fall off the donkey with Jesus several miles back."

"I forgot it was there."

"Forgot?" Joseph tried to look stern, but when it came to me, he rarely succeeded. "I wish I had known you didn't need it because I ran out a long time ago." The twinkle in his eyes returned.

A smile formed on my face as I reached out to touch his cheek. "Tomorrow you can have some of mine." I laughed as Joseph stood to his feet, shaking his head with mock disgust.

"Tomorrow you will drink yours," Joseph said as he turned and walked toward the caravan of men.

We continued on our journey the next morning. Plants with inch-long barbs sprung up from the parched land. And Joseph warned me to stay away from any living animal, for it was sure to be poisonous, clawed and fanged. Here we were, out in the desert, doing our best to dodge thieves, lions, even feral dogs while carrying liquids in wineskins, solids in sackcloth, and whatever utensils we needed for cooking.

Once we reached Rhinocolura, a feeling of safety could be felt among us. From now on, there was little threat of being overtaken by thieves. Noticing a few sheep off in the distance, I shifted Jesus to my other hip and made my way down the dusty path to get a better look. I could almost smell the aroma of my mother's mutton stew.

I saw the cloud of dust before I could actually see them. Three feral dogs, their teeth bared, warning me to come no closer. I quickly turned back toward camp, wishing I hadn't ventured out on my own. Glancing back, I quickened my pace. One of the dogs was still following me, most likely hoping I would give him some food. I sighed with relief when I entered the camp.

I noticed Joseph then across the way, watching me, shaking his head partly in amusement and partly in admonishment. He had been watching me for some time then. He was always watching me. Always there to protect me.

Over supper that evening, Joseph leaned near. "Your friend doesn't seem to have any intentions in leaving."

"My friend?" I followed his finger to the edge of the camp, my confusion increasing as I surveyed the surrounding area. *My friend?* And then the dog lifted his head. The lone animal that had followed me back. I had forgotten all about him. He seemed to be studying me.

"He seems lonely. Do you think he's lost?"

"Most likely, he's never known a human's touch. Dogs who have known human companionship are usually friendly."

"He's frightened."

"Which is why they usually form a pack. They instinctively know it is the only way they can survive."

"May I give him these scraps of food?"

"I wouldn't," Joseph whispered, his warm eyes connecting briefly with my own before he stood to his feet.

He wouldn't. But he knew I was different, and he never once since the day I had met him expected me to react as he would or as anyone else, for that matter.

Assuring myself that Jesus was still asleep, I then made my way toward the dog with our scraps of food. Feral dogs were often infected with fleas, so I intended to keep my distance. When the dog stood to his feet, I knew I had advanced far enough. I scraped the food onto the ground and slowly backed away. He timidly stepped toward the food, hesitating only for a moment before scarfing down every morsel. I found myself wishing I had more to give him.

As we retired for the night, I wondered briefly before falling asleep if my *friend* would still be there in the morning. Why it should matter so much, I didn't know. Perhaps because I had left so many loved ones behind. The further into Egypt we came, the more alone I felt.

When I awoke in the morning, the first place I looked was the edge of camp. A smile crept across my face upon seeing the mangy mutt lying in the same spot from the night before. His eyes still watched me.

When we departed that morning in pursuit of Heliopolis, I looked behind me several times, hoping my *friend* had decided to join us. For three days he trailed us, and each evening I left our scraps of food where he could easily find them.

Finally, we reached our destination. We found a small dwelling and took up residence. This part of the Nile was said to shelter many Jewish communities. It was my hope that we would not be the only ones among them.

I wish I could say I always felt God's peace. Some days were more difficult than others. Some days, fear would attempt to steal my peace. Some days it won.

After many days of travel, we had found safe refuge in Egypt. There was so much to be thankful for. We had traveled much of the journey alone and tried to stay out of sight as much as possible in an effort to stay hidden from Herod, so it wasn't until our arrival to Egypt that we learned the details of Herod's rage. Word traveled that when Herod saw that he had been tricked, he became enraged and ordered every male child of Bethlehem two years and under to be killed.

I thought of Penina and of baby Jeriah. And my heart knew in an instant what this meant. I waded through so many emotions. Grief. Guilt. My heart was in such deep anguish for my friend. Would she even look me in the eyes should our lives cross paths again? I had fled with my own son in an attempt to save him. And now her son was dead.

A voice was heard in Ramah, lamentation, weeping, and great mourning, Rachel weeping for her children, refusing to be comforted, because they are no more.

I found myself wrestling with so many questions. Mainly, how could God permit the suffering of the innocent, especially babies?

Joseph explained it best, as he usually did. "God has given all men freedom, and in that freedom some choose to do evil," he said. "But even then, God can draw good from evil. God writes straight with the crooked lines men have twisted for their own purposes."

I found myself wondering how God could ever draw good from the murder of these innocent children. But I knew if anyone could, it would be Him.

Never had I felt so displaced, so alone. We were refugees. We were strangers in this land. I didn't understand their language. Trying to barter at the market for food was confusing. I often returned to our dwelling without the necessary ingredients needed to prepare a meal. Yet Joseph never complained. I could feel his own internal struggle.

Days turned into weeks—weeks of quiet work and hardship. Weeks of yearning for our homeland. All around us, we saw numerous signs of idolatry. So many strange gods with the faces of beasts.

But even amidst all the strangeness, there was joy. Joy of seeing Jesus growing and changing daily. He was so healthy. So strong. And this was made possible only by living so far from the danger we had left behind.

And so I relentlessly reminded myself that God had a plan so much bigger than my own comfort. So much bigger than my wants. And His plan was worth it. One day I would understand, even if right now I did not.

As Jesus' first birthday approached, I found myself missing my parents more than ever. How had an entire year passed without them meeting their grandson? When I had left Nazareth, I had only thought I'd be gone a month at the most. And now over a year later, I wondered if I'd ever see my father alive again.

At least in Bethlehem, I had their letters to look forward to. And while I was sure by now they knew we had escaped Bethlehem before Herod's horrible massacre, they had to be wondering where we had gone. I had begun several letters to them, but in the end had burned each one. While it seemed Herod believed he had gotten rid of Jesus with his scheme in Bethlehem, I found myself wondering if it were only a ploy. Some nights I'd awake from a deep sleep, afraid he knew exactly who we were and was just waiting for the day of our return. Perhaps he had someone watching my parents' house even now.

"Why are you awake?" Joseph's eyes were closed, his voice sleepy. He turned onto his side and pulled me near, tucking my head beneath his chin.

"I can't sleep."

"Why?" he persisted.

"I'm afraid."

"What are you afraid of?"

"What if Herod knows who we are?"

"He doesn't."

"How can you be so sure?" I closed my eyes.

"He's a madman. He reacts. If he were a rational man, then I'd wonder myself. But he's not rational."

I asked the next question that was bothering me. "When can we go home?"

"Soon."

"How soon?"

"I'm not God, *Agapi mou*." *My love.* "Only He can answer that."

"I've been wondering why He speaks to you more than He speaks to me." I squeezed his side and smiled when he grimaced.

"Isn't it enough He chose you to be the mother of His child?" Joseph pulled me near and nuzzled my earlobe with his lips. "Perhaps He thought you'd trust me more if He allowed me to hear His voice. Or perhaps He knew I'd listen." He grabbed both my hands and locked them in his own.

"Listen?" I struggled to free myself in vain. "You don't think I would have listened?" I lay still, pretending to pout. Finally, his arms relaxed. Still, I waited until he relaxed even more. And then I turned, grabbing both his sides with my hands.

"Mary," he groaned. "I should have never given in when you asked me where I was most sensitive."

"I'm glad you did." I kissed one bristly cheek and then the other. Finally, my face hovered over his, my lips nearly touching his. "I love you," I whispered.

His eyes looked tenderly into my own. "How much?"

"More than all the stars in the sky."

"There's a whole lot of stars."

"More than we could ever count."

"So you love me immeasurably?"

I laughed. "My love for you is immeasurable." And then he rolled me onto my back and kissed me until I was breathless. The love I felt for him scared me at times. The thought of ever having to live this life without him was too much for me to even contemplate.

I named the dog Nile. Joseph laughed when I told him the name I had chosen for him. Nile had been with us for weeks now. I was thankful that our home was on the edge of town. He was too timid to have ever ventured any further into the village. He still wouldn't let me close enough to touch him, but he seemed to accept me just as I had accepted him. He watched for me just as I watched for him. Even Jesus was growing attached and often pointed to the spot Nile usually lay, just beneath an olive tree on the side of the house. He came and went as he pleased. It wasn't unusual for a day or two to pass by without seeing Nile, but he always would return, and he always seemed just as happy to see me as I was to see him.

I first saw Ahti at the market. She was the most beautiful woman I had ever seen. Dark copper colored skin. Black wavy hair. Bright, almond-shaped, hazel eyes. High cheekbones. I was trying unsuccessfully to ask the merchant for cinnamon. Apple cake was Joseph's favorite dessert, and I wanted to surprise him with it this evening. Frustrated and near tears, I turned away from the merchant. Nothing I said seemed to make him understand me. He waved his hand, shooing me away, and began bartering with the next person in line.

I looked down at the ingredients I had managed to find…eggs, apples, and flour. But it was useless. It wouldn't taste the same without cinnamon.

The tiny amount the recipe called for made all the difference in the world. Jesus' head grew heavy against my shoulder, and I knew he had fallen sleep. Once home, I laid him to down.

Hearing a rap on the door, I went to answer it. A woman stood there, her hand outstretched. I recognized her from the market, the woman standing behind me in line. I reached for the item she was offering to me. A small package. I couldn't see what was inside, but I could smell it. Tears quickly filled my eyes. Embarrassed, I quickly wiped away a tear from my cheek.

"You're welcome," she said with a smile. I could tell she was touched by my passionate response. "I have yet to acquire such a reaction to a spice used for cooking. Don't get me wrong; it is a popular spice even among us Egyptians, a very popular flavoring additive, even I must admit."

I began to laugh. Really laugh. Soon I was crying and laughing. If Ahti was offended by my childish ways, she certainly didn't show it. She just stood there in my doorway, her eyes full of life, her smile unjudging in any way.

"Would you like to come in?" I finally asked when I had calmed down enough to realize she was still standing within the doorway.

"Not today. I am late returning home. But I will stop again. Perhaps with some rosemary next time." She began to turn away.

I knew we'd be good friends. She was kind and personable. And she made me laugh. When was the last time I had laughed—really laughed—the kind of laughter that brought tears to one's eyes? I couldn't even re-member.

"Wait," I called out. "What is your name?"

"Ahti," she answered. "Do you know what it means?"

I shook my head. My Egyptian vocabulary was sorely lacking.

"Ahti means a hippo goddess." She smiled big at my laughter. "Encour-aging isn't it that the first thing my father thought of when he saw me was a hippo."

I felt more tears running down my cheeks, and this time I didn't care. It felt so good to feel so alive and carefree. "My name is Mary."

"A very pretty name. And what does it mean?"

"Wished-for. My parents endured several miscarriages before my birth."

"Very fitting. *Wished-for.* Much more impressive than hippo goddess."

"Do you live nearby?" I asked.

"On the other side of the village. My husband's name is Nassor." She watched for recognition in my eyes and seemed content that I was unaware of the name. She waved goodbye before turning and walking away.

The Nile River was by far Egypt's most precious life vein. The balance of the nation's prosperity rooted precariously on the Nile River. Too much water meant devastating floods, while too little water produced famines. Most of Egypt was desert, but along the Nile River the soil was rich and very good for growing crops. The longest river known at this time, it got its name from the Greek word Neilos, which means valley. There was a saying among the Egyptians: "May you always drink from the Nile." In this way, they spoke blessings over those they respected. From the Nile's cooling waters came large, plentiful fish. And from its loamy riverbanks came mud used for bricks and papyrus used for books and boats.

Every year, the Nile flooded and saturated the parched land in water and life-giving silt. Less than half a mile in width, it made up for it in length, reaching throughout many countries. Some days I'd venture down to the river and sit underneath my favorite tree. There, Jesus and I would sit and watch the wooden ships float by.

On this day, Ahti joined us. I knew little about water and ships, and it was interesting to hear her tell about them. Her husband, Nassor, owned several of the wooden ships that traveled up and down the Nile River. From this, I gathered that they were people of means. They probably lived in one of the larger homes.

"See that boat there?" Ahti signaled across the river. "That boat alone can carry up to five hundred tons. That is as much as one hundred twenty-five elephants."

"Or hippos," I couldn't help but add. We shared a smile. "What kind of bird is that?"

"It's a blue heron. And that over there is a white ibis. They're scoping out the shallow waters for small fish."

As impressive as the Nile River was, it also reminded me of the tree of good and evil. It was full of snakes. More than thirty different species lived among its waters, and more than half of them were poisonous. That information alone was enough to keep me from venturing too close to the water's edge. And if that wasn't enough, the Nile was also home to a grayish-colored beast that was said to weigh as much as ten men. Known as a crocodile, it made its nests along the Nile's banks. Ahti said they could lay as many as sixty eggs at a time.

The Egyptians relied on fish for animal protein. But they obtained most of their food from the earth. The rich topsoil of the Nile basin measured up to seventy feet deep. I often saw men digging irrigation canals from the river in order to water the fields.

"What kind of crops do you grow around here?" I swatted away a fly trying to land on Jesus' cheek.

"Barley for beer. Cotton for clothing. And then of course wheat, flax, and papyrus." Ahti lay back in the grass, her eyes now closed. I admired her long black eyelashes. "The wheat, we grind into flour for bread. The flax, we spin into linen. And the papyrus, we dry into paper."

I knew that the Egyptians believed in many deities…several thousand to be exact. Magic was a power they used frequently to protect the inno-cent and to ward off harm. Prayers and offerings were made in an effort to gain favor with the gods. The verse in Isaiah was continually on my mind. *I am the first and I am the last; besides Me there is no god.*

The closer Ahti and I became, the more I wished for her to know the truth. The false gods she spoke of had no substance. But I knew in attack-ing her gods, I'd be attacking her, so instead I prayed for guidance. For wisdom.

"Joseph and I are so thankful for the work your husband has provided him." I knew Ahti had recommended Joseph to Nassor. Had it taken a lot of persuasion on her part? She talked little of her husband. I often won-dered if he were a good man. He was obviously wealthy. Ahti was always dressed beautifully. Even now, she wore various kinds of cosmetics to enhance her facial features. Her left wrist was adorned with several gold bracelets. And her ears displayed matching earrings.

"It has been difficult for him to find work here with no reputation pre-siding him," I added.

"Your husband is very accomplished, Mary. I asked Nassor to consider him for one job. The second and third came because of his performance. I cannot take all the credit." Ahti reached out to tickle Jesus' bare foot. Jesus giggled, his brown eyes full of merriment. His small hand reached out and gently touched Ahti's. Her eyes filled with tears, and she quickly looked away, perhaps hoping I hadn't noticed.

We sat in silence. Her emotions in check, Ahti turned back toward us. "He's perfect. Absolutely perfect. I can hardly believe he's only one. He seems older than that. Sometimes I wonder if he understands what we are saying."

I smiled. How many times had Joseph and I said that very thing? Jesus was indeed wise beyond his age.

"I'm Nassor's second wife." Ahti left those words hanging. I patiently waited, allowing her the time she needed to continue. "Layla is his first wife. She's barren." Again, silence filled the air. A gentle breeze lifted some of the black silt from the ground, blowing it against our bare feet. "He waited twelve years for her to conceive. And then he married me."

Ahti brushed a strand of black hair out of her eye. "As I am the youngest of eight, I suppose he thought his chances were good in producing an heir. And yet here we are…three years later and still no children." A sad laugh escaped her lips. "He has poor choice in women, wouldn't you say?"

I remembered my mother once telling me how her barrenness made her feel homeless. Before my birth, her arms always felt empty. "He gives the barren woman a home, making her the joyous mother of children." The words from Psalms flowed out of my mouth.

"Who does?" Ahti asked, hope filling her eyes.

"God does."

"Nassor told me you would try to turn me to the Hebrew God." Ahti looked down at her hands. "How can you believe in only one god? How can one god possibly control everything?"

"Only God is all-powerful, all-knowing, and all-loving. And He is the God over everything."

"Yet you cannot see Him," Ahti said with doubt.

I looked down at my son stretched out and sound asleep next to me on the blanket. God was revealing Himself to us. In the person of His only Son, Jesus, God was showing us what He was really like. "Only the one true God can satisfy the deepest longings of our hearts," I answered.

"Why did you come here…to Egypt? You speak lovingly of your parents still in Nazareth. Even I sense your loneliness. It was one of the things that drew me to you. I felt you understood me."

I had resisted telling Ahti the danger we faced in Bethlehem. But for some reason, I felt she was ready to listen…ready to understand. "Herod wanted to kill Jesus."

Ahti looked at me in disbelief. "Herod? King Herod?" I nodded. "I don't understand. What difference could a tiny baby have made to someone as powerful as he is?"

"A group of wise men came to Jerusalem not long after Jesus was born. They stopped at the temple, and when Herod's advisors overheard them asking where they could find the newly-born king of the Jews, they alerted Herod. Herod called for the wise men. They told him that they had seen a star in the sky and had followed it. They wanted to worship this new king. Herod asked them to send word when they found the child so that he could worship him, too."

"So, did the wise men find this little king?"

Yes. And soon after, God warned the wise men of Herod's plot in a dream, and they took a different route home." Mary studied Ahti. Did she dare tell her the truth? "Not long later, Joseph also had a dream, and we left in the middle of the night. Supposedly when Herod realized that the wise men had evaded him, he ordered the death of every child in Bethlehem below the age of two. The murder of all the innocent babies happened only hours after our escape."

"Are you saying Jesus is the king the wise men were talking about?"

I nodded.

"Jesus?"

Again, I nodded.

Ahti's eyes studied my sleeping son. Hadn't she just said how perfect he was? Was accepting him as God's Son too much to ask of her?

"That day at the market when I stood behind you as you tried to find the right word for cinnamon, I was staring at him," she said. "You had him up on your shoulder, and he was staring back at me. And I know this sounds strange...but I felt something...something I hadn't felt in a very long time."

A tear dropped onto her cheek, and then another. "I felt like he understood me. But more than that...I felt as if he understood my pain."

That night, I lay next to Joseph. Ahti believed that Jesus was different, a god even. But she wasn't quite ready to say there was only one God. I couldn't fault her for that. After over twenty years of worshipping so many gods, how could I expect her to change her mind in just one afternoon?

"Joseph?"

"Mary." He lay beside me, his eyes closed. After a long day of work, he was ready for sleep.

"What is Nassor like?"

"Nassor?"

"Ahti's husband."

"He's like any Egyptian man. Thin, tan, and confident."

I nudged him. "A bit more detail than that, please."

"He owns several ships. He has two wives. But he doesn't have any children…yet."

"And is he kind?"

"Kind?"

"Is he like you?" I asked, snuggling up close to him and gently caressing his cheek with my lips.

Joseph finally opened his eyes, a curious gaze filling them. "Why all this sudden fascination with Nassor?"

"I want to know if he is good to Ahti."

"He is a good provider. A good leader." I sighed. "I've never seen him mistreat her or raise his voice toward her." I sighed again. "If you're asking if he loves her with the same amount of passion that I love you with…then no…I don't believe he does. It's rare to find a love like ours, Mary."

"How is it rare?"

"You don't feel it?"

"Of course I feel it. But I like the way you put it into words."

Joseph yawned. "Then perhaps tomorrow I'll write you a letter. To-night…I'll sleep."

"Just one phrase?"

"Being loved by you gives me strength, while loving you gives me courage."

My smile was short-lived as his mouth covered mine. Every day of marriage, we became more deeply intertwined. More deeply connected. More deeply devoted. I had found that love was a sacrifice. Sometimes love required one to bear the weakness of the other. Joseph had proven this to me on many occasions.

I understood Ahti's fear of being unable to have children. I felt it too. It had been two years since Jesus' birth. And for the last several months, my monthly menstruations came and went like clockwork. Barrenness ran in my family. On both sides. My mother had struggled to get pregnant, just as her mother had. And I couldn't help but think of Elizabeth and how many years she had waited for John's arrival.

I was afraid. Afraid I would be unable to conceive without the help of the Holy Spirit. It was children who assured a wife's position in her home. I thought of Layla, Nassor's first wife. Had she been able to provide him with children, he most likely would not have married Ahti. And now that Ahti was having trouble conceiving, would he now choose a third wife?

Rachel, Jacob's favorite wife, was said to have preferred death to child-lessness. She must have felt forgotten and alone when her sister Leah had given Jacob child after child while she waited and waited. Barrenness was thought to be a curse and a punishment. And yet I remember my father saying once that it would be better to die childless than to have children who were without the fear of the Lord.

"Will you marry another if I cannot give you a child?"

Joseph's hand halted midway to his mouth. He had just dipped his bread in the seasoned olive oil. Drip…drip…drip. I counted the drops of olive oil falling onto the floor where we sat. His brow lifted as he pondered my strange question. "You want to discuss this now…over dinner?"

"Yes."

Joseph took a bite of his bread. Dipped it again. And took another bite. "We have a child." He glanced over at Jesus, who sat between us eating small pieces of bread and cut up grapes.

"I know. And I know that God has a purpose for Him beyond what we can understand or perceive. I don't take lightly what God expects of me, and I know you don't either." I looked down at my hands. They were clenched in my lap. I unclenched them. "Wouldn't you like a son…a son to carry on your family name?"

He sat watching me. He could see my struggle. As perceptive as he was, he probably had sensed my inward battle for days now. "I would like a child. A son…a daughter…either would be just as wonderful as the other. But I want a son or daughter with you. Only you."

"So, you wouldn't marry another in order to garner a son to carry on your family name?"

"I have no need of a second wife. One is plenty."

"Plenty? You say that as if I've brought you nothing but trouble."

Joseph smiled. And then laughed. "I must admit, my life was much simpler before I laid eyes on you."

I knew he was teasing, but a part of me did wonder if we could go back in time, would he make the same decision? Would he marry me knowing what he knew now?

A loud rap sounded at the door, interrupting our discussion. Joseph rose to answer it. I didn't recognize the voice on the other side of the door.

It was unfamiliar…and very solemn. When I heard my name, I picked up Jesus and made my way toward them. It was an Egyptian man. He looked to be in his forties, and he wore a very grave expression.

Joseph took me aside, his expression full of sadness. "It's Ahti."

"Ahti? Is she all right?" I felt my hands begin to tremble. "Is she all right?" I repeated. But I feared the answer was not one I wished to hear.

The Egyptians followed an elaborate set of practices when they buried their loved ones. They believed these practices were necessary to ensure immortality. They did not believe in cremation. Some feared the dead bodies would rise again if mistreated after death, which was why preserving the body was so important to them. Before embalming the deceased body, mourners would cover their faces in mud and parade around town while beating their chests. Since Nassor was considered of high status in the community, Ahti's body was not embalmed right away. The process was postponed for three days in order to prevent abuse of the corpse.

On the third day, a funeral procession began. Two cattle pulled Ahti's body in a carrier, while friends and family followed close behind. During the procession, the priest burned incense and poured milk before her dead body.

Upon arrival at the tomb, the priest then performed what was known as the Opening of the Mouth ceremony. The deceased's head was turned south. This symbolized allowing the person to speak and defend themselves during the judgment process. Goods were then offered to the deceased. Although all coffins were made of wood, each was intricately painted and designed to suit the individual. Eyes were painted on so the deceased would be able to look through the coffin.

I felt numb. Completely numb. A week ago, Ahti and I had been sitting by the river. And today she was gone. I hadn't seen it coming. And because of that, I felt responsible in some way. Perhaps if I had cared more. Said more.

In just the short amount of time I had known Ahti, I knew that she hadn't wanted to die. She just wasn't able to bear living. Ahti had wanted to live just as much as anyone else, but sometimes living became too painful. The demands and pressures of life had finally overtaken her desire to live, at least in that moment. I couldn't help but wonder if she would have changed her mind if she'd just held on for one more hour...one more day.

I looked across the coffin at Nassor. For weeks, I had wondered about him. Wondered if he treated her right. Wondered if he loved her. Today he presented himself as strong. As resilient. But I knew better. The night he had come to our house to deliver the devastating news of Ahti's passing, I had seen his grief. His misery. Before he had left, he had given me a note Ahti had written. A note she had written to me.

I still hadn't read it. I couldn't. Not yet anyway.

For days, I questioned God. Why? Why was life so cruel? Why was it so difficult? I had never once felt deserving of the role He had asked me to play. And until recently, I had felt humbled...blessed that He had chosen me.

But now... Now I felt insufficient, as if He had made the wrong choice. There had to have been stronger women than I who could have carried out the vision He had for His Son. There had to have been a better alternative. Why had He chosen me? Why had He chosen one so weak? Why had He chosen one so fragile?

"It's not your fault," Joseph said one evening after dinner. "You can't blame yourself.

"I can't help but feel as if I let her down."

"How? By being her friend? By loving her?"

"I should have heard her cry for help."

"Ahti knew you'd come in an instant if she asked you to. She knew you loved her, Mary. She knew you'd try to stop her. She knew you'd try to keep her here. She left us because she wanted more. She was searching for a better life."

Part of me knew Joseph was right. Ahti had no longer been able to see a future without pain or despair. No matter how much I wished she had been honest with me, she hadn't. I couldn't change that.

"You should read her letter."

"I can't."

"You choose not to." Joseph stood to his feet. Retrieving the note from behind the vase, he handed it to me. Then he picked up Jesus and left the house.

I watched from the window as Joseph threw Jesus in the air, Jesus giggling uncontrollably until he landed safely back in his father's arms. Joseph did it a few more times, and then finally they turned toward the path. Whistling, Joseph invited Nile to join them. Picking up his head from where he was lying beneath the olive tree, Nile studied them before turning his head toward the house. He knew I was still inside. He lay back down, content to stay and watch over me while they took an evening stroll.

Joseph was right. It was time for me to read Ahti's letter. I held my breath and slowly opened it.

Dear Mary,

Do you know what I see when I see you? Strength. Vulnerability. Hope. Courage. Confidence. And the list goes on. I don't doubt for a moment why your God chose you for such an amazing task as raising His son. And don't you doubt it, either. Take all you've been given and nurture it. Let it grow. Trust Him even when you are unsure of the destination. Jesus. Jesus is going to change the world.

I love you.

Ahti.

I fell to my knees, deep sobs wracking my entire body. Even in her most frail moment, Ahti had fought to encourage me one last time.

I felt hope arise when my time of bleeding didn't come. Four days…five days…a full week. Then two. With each and every day, it seemed more and more probable that I was with child.

I waited to tell Joseph. Even when I began to feel some of the symptoms I had first felt with Jesus, still I waited. My heart yearned for my friend. *Oh, Ahti, how I miss you.*

One morning after Joseph had already left for the day, I began the daily preparation of making bread. Looking toward the mantle where Ahti's letter lay, I noticed a second letter perched behind it. How long had it been there? I honestly had no idea.

I paused what I was doing and made my way toward the mantle. The letter was tucked behind Ahti's but was taller. I reached up and grasped it in my hand. It was Joseph's handwriting. And it hadn't been written in the last few days. I could tell because the ink wasn't new. I reached for Ahti's letter and examined them both. They seemed to have been written around the same time. I sat Ahti's letter back on the mantle.

Moving toward the mat where Jesus lay sleeping, I slowly lowered myself into a sitting position. Finally, I opened it, my eyes taking in the page of words. Words written just for me. I smiled. And then I began reading.

Mary, Mother of Jesus,

I have no doubt that you will go down in history as Mary, Mother of Jesus. It will be your greatest accomplishment.

But to me…to me you are known as Mary, the wife of Joseph, my dream come true, my love, my everything.

Your smile, it has captivated my heart. You were made for me, Mary. I've never been so sure of anything in all my life.

I'll journey to the ends of the earth for you, Mary, in an attempt to keep you safe from harm. I'll die for you.

My heart, it aches for Ahti. And so I cannot begin to imagine how much more your heart aches for her. I believe you reached her, Mary. She was battling between what she had always known and what now felt right. I don't doubt for a second that you'll see her again. You'll see her, Mary. You'll see Ahti, your hippo goddess.

Half laughing, half sobbing, I reached for the edge of my gown in order to wipe away the tears so I could see the words on the page.

I don't need a child to make me whole. You, Mary, are enough.

I promise to handle your heart with care and treasure it with love. You will always be the sole owner of my heart, and on this day, I vow to be completely yours forever,

Your husband, Joseph

I needed to read those words before I told Joseph the news of my pregnancy. My heart needed his confirmation that no matter which direction our lives went, he wouldn't be disappointed in me.

Feeling a small hand in my own, I looked to the side to see Jesus perched on his knees, his beautiful soulful eyes searching my own. I drew him near, kissing his forehead and then each of his chubby little cheeks. "How I love you, little one." Then I gathered him in my arms and rose to my feet.

I couldn't wait until Joseph returned in the evening. I needed to tell him now. I left the house and made my way toward the marketplace, where he had been commissioned to build a wooden platform and several benches.

We passed a oasis-like place of palm trees and olive groves before suddenly emerging out on the sands once again. Along the riverbanks lay stone cliffs and quarries which provided the Egyptians with the material needed for their great monuments. Finally, I began passing mud-brick houses which were alive with voices as women cleaned and made their dinner preparations. I was beginning to recognize some of the words. Not enough to carry on a conversation, but enough to get a general idea.

I passed a group of travelers who were from Al'Qasr, or at least that was the impression I got as I caught bits and pieces of their conversation. Ahti had told me it was a small medieval town built by the Ottomans deep in the Western Desert. It was part of what was known as the Dakhla Oasis, which was a series of small towns with over five hundred hot springs. Ahti had traveled there with Nassor on their honeymoon. Of all the towns, Al-Qasr was the most impressive. Its name meant the castle. Ahti had told me she would take me one day. How I wished we could go.

The market was bustling today, and it took me awhile to locate him. Once I did, I stepped back, content to watch him work for a while. He ran his hands over the smooth plank of wood he had obviously just sanded.

Wood was one of mankind's oldest building materials, and Joseph was skilled in his profession. I loved that he took great pride in his work. Each job he performed, he did to the best of his ability. Never in a hurry, always taking his time. Just as he was with me. He was a patient man. A solid man. A secure man.

A man I could depend on.

Joseph was Jesus' model of what a father should be. What an excellent model he was to his son and would be to this child I now carried. My eyes filled with tears at his fearless commitment to me. He had risked his own reputation and status for me. Just like our heavenly Father, who is always faithful and never deserts us.

Joseph glanced up then, as if suddenly aware that someone was watching him. His eyes were serious, as we were among so many unfamiliar people. I watched as he scanned the crowd, his eyes passing me by for a split second and then instantly returning. His eyes softened, and then he smiled. He beckoned me to him.

"Such a beautiful face to look upon this cool Egyptian morning," Joseph said, once I had managed to weave myself through the crowd of people. "I didn't know you were coming to market today?"

Usually I informed him of my comings and goings. We often shared lunch together if I traveled into the marketplace. But in my hurry to see him, I had not thought to prepare anything before I left the house. He seemed to realize it too.

"Is everything all right, Mary?"

"I read your letter." The words came out rather quickly. My eyes had filled with tears, and I didn't want to scare him.

"Ahh. My letter. I was wondering how long you were going to let it sit on that mantle."

"I'm with child."

I watched as his eyes changed from humor, to shock, to question, to surprise, to delight, to tenderness. Jesus reached out his arms for him, and Joseph reached across the table and took him from me.

"What do you think of that, Jesus?" Joseph kissed his little cheek. "A little brother or sister?" Then his eyes met mine again. "I love you," he whispered.

"I love you more," I whispered back. He raised his brows in mock denial. There were moments in life I knew I'd never forget. This was one of them.

I lay in the tall grass, Jesus sitting next to me. I came here often to the spot Ahti and I had so often confided in one another. Watching the ships pass by, I wondered as I often did if any of them belonged to Nassor. Joseph had heard a rumor that he was to take a new wife soon. I knew Joseph wouldn't have told me unless he believed it to be true.

My husband, always trying to soften the hurt.

I reached for Jesus' hand and brought it to my lips. He looked up at me in adoration. "How do I love thee, let me count the ways." It was a game we often played. He giggled and grabbed my hand, pushing it toward his right foot. I laughed with him.

Starting with his littlest toe, I began to count off all the ways I loved him. "I love thee freely. I love thee purely. I love thee in the morning. I love thee at noon. I love thee in the evening. I love thee by sun. I love thee by moon. I love thee by stars. I love thee every day. And even out of sight." By the time I had gently squeezed all of his toes, he was giggling uncontrollably.

It was in these moments I felt completely honored to have been chosen to be his mother. How had I, a girl from an isolated town, practically raised in poverty, stood out? And yet, God had called me by name. He hadn't cared that I had nothing to offer. Nothing of material value, that is. He had lifted me from obscurity to a position of blessing.

I now saw people differently. I valued them differently than I had before. I now realized God knows each and every person thoroughly and intimately. It didn't matter how old, or how broken, or how disabled, or if you were of a different culture. *Ahti.* Or even if you were the enemy. *Herod.* God was mindful of each and every person.

And He was prepared to redeem them. No matter the cost.

"Story?"

I looked down at Jesus, surprise evident on my face. "You want to hear a story?"

He nodded, a smile stretched across his beautiful face.

We spent so much time alone together that I often regaled him with stories from our past. Stories that my father used to tell me. But this was the first time Jesus had asked for one. I swallowed past the lump in my throat. Pulling him closer to me, I picked one of my favorites.

"This is a story of a King and three very brave men. Now, these men had very strange names. They were known as Shadrach, Meshach, and Abednego. They lived in a place called Babylon. And all three of them worked for a King named Nebuchadnezzar.

"One day King Nebuchadnezzar decided to build a huge image made of gold. It stood at least ninety feet high! It was so big, they say that fifteen men could have stood on top of the other to be that tall."

"The king decided he wanted all the people of any language to bow down and worship the statue of gold. And then he said if anyone didn't obey him, he was going to throw them into a fiery furnace."

It was getting late, and I knew we should begin our walk home, but Jesus was so enthralled with the story that I continued on.

"But you see, God doesn't want us to worship anything or anyone other than Him. And why would we even want to pray or worship something that isn't even real? Only God can answer our prayers. Only God can help us when we need help.

"The music began playing, and everyone stopped what they were doing and bowed down to worship the golden idol. Everyone, that is, except for Shadrach, Meshach, and Abednego. And some men who were jealous of their positions ran to the king to tell him.

"King Nebuchadnezzar was really angry when he heard the news. And he immediately ordered the three men to be brought in. 'Explain your-selves!' he said when they finally stood in front of him. 'Is it true...?'"

"Has dinner not been prepared?" A gruff masculine voice interrupted my story. I looked up into Joseph's kind eyes. "What is the meaning of this? I will give you one more chance to make my dinner. I've been hard at work all day, and I'm starving."

"Well, then, I'm afraid you'll have to starve, for I only make dinner for...Jesus." I started laughing and Joseph followed suit.

"Actually," Joseph said as he picked Jesus up and turned him to face him. "King Nebuchadnezzar gave them one more chance to worship the image of gold, but again the three men refused. 'We did not make a mistake the first time,' they said to the king. 'Nor will we apologize for not bowing down. Go ahead and throw us into the fiery furnace, for our God is able to save us. But even if He doesn't, we will never serve your gods or worship any golden image.' This made the king so mad that he ordered the furnace to be heated up several degrees hotter. And then the soldiers took the three men to the furnace. As the soldiers were pushing the men into the furnace, the flames of fire killed them because the fire was so hot."

Joseph indicated for me to continue.

"When Nebuchadnezzar looked into the fire, he saw four men walking around. And so he asked his advisors how many they saw. 'Four,' they said. The king was amazed that the three men were still alive. And he was sure the fourth man was an angel. He called Shadrach, Meshach, and Abednego out of the fire, and they walked out without any burns, nor had any hairs on their head been burned. In fact, they didn't smell of fire at all. And in that moment, Nebuchadnezzar knew that the three men worshiped the one true God. So, from that day on, the king made an announcement that nobody should speak badly about Shadrach, Meshach, and Abednego's

God, or they would be badly punished."

"And then they all went home and ate dinner," Joseph said. He smiled over his shoulder as he walked toward the path. Nile, who had been sleeping in the tall grass near us, also stood to his feet. He watched to see if I was going to follow Joseph.

"Had you been home first, you would have noticed there was lamb stew simmering by the fire. And baked bread resting on the table."

Joseph tossed Jesus in the air, smiling at his contagious giggle. "She's smart. Don't ever underestimate her." Joseph stopped and waited for me to catch up. "I heard your voice as I passed by."

"So inviting was it?" I teased.

"You have the most attractive, alluring, tempting, fascinating, enticing voice I've ever heard." Joseph reached for my hand and brought it to his lips. "It's my most favorite voice in the world."

We had been in Egypt for nearly a year when Joseph woke me in the middle of the night. He gathered me close and whispered into my ear. "Herod is dead."

"You had another dream?" I asked. I knew there could be no other explanation. Joseph said it with such certainty.

"Yes, another angel appeared to me while I was sleeping. He said, 'Arise and take the Child and His mother, and go into the land of Israel; for those who sought the Child's life are dead.'"

I began to cry. A cry of release. A cry of serenity. *Thank You, God.* Finally, we were free to go home.

Herod was very old and very ill at the time he had ordered all the baby boys to be killed in Bethlehem. Some say he was suffering from paranoia and was extremely delusional. He killed anyone who posed even the slightest threat.

Not long before he died, Herod ordered all of Israel's rich and powerful people to be shut in the great hall of Jerusalem. He then gave orders to have all the rich people killed after he died. Some believe he did it to prevent them from becoming king after him. And others believe he knew no one would grieve at his passing, so he wanted to make sure there was deep mourning when he died. Perhaps it was both.

Five days before Herod died, he killed the eldest of his remaining sons. He didn't want him to become king after him. He then named his son Archelaus as the next king. Herod was seventy years old when he died and had reigned for thirty-seven years.

The morning we were to depart for Israel, I remembered Nile. I had been so busy preparing for our journey, I couldn't exactly remember when I had last seen him.

"Nile," I called. "Come, Nile," I called again.

"Egypt is his home, Mary. Perhaps it is best this way."

"I just wanted to say goodbye." I called for him several more times. He didn't appear. I gathered Jesus in my arms and joined Joseph on the path that would take us home.

Jesus reached up and wiped away a tear on my cheek. He then pointed to the olive tree where Nile usually laid. "Come…Nile," he called, his tender, childlike voice echoing mine from earlier.

"Goodbye, Nile," I whispered. *Goodbye, Friend.*

Periodically during our travels that day and the next, Jesus would call out. "Come…Nile." And every time, it would take me back to the olive tree beside our little home in Egypt. Was he there? Was he wondering if we had abandoned him?

The evening of the second day, I heard Jesus' excited voice. "Nile!" he exclaimed. And I turned to see Nile standing in the trees, watching us.

"Nile!" I cried. "So you decided to join us after all." Tears of relief flowed down my cheeks. I looked over to find Joseph standing next to me, Jesus in his arms.

"I suppose he couldn't quite resist your invitation, little one," Joseph said as he kissed Jesus' cheek.

We traveled for several days and drew near to Judea. While Joseph knew we were to return to Israel, he wasn't entirely sure if it was Bethlehem or Nazareth we were to return to. That evening at an inn where we had stopped for our evening meal, we overheard some men speaking of how Archelaus was far worse than his father had ever been. I could sense Joseph's concern as we discussed whether to continue on to the next town. The family eating next to us asked us to join them as they traveled to Gaza before settling for the night. It was safer to travel in numbers, so we agreed to join them.

It was beautiful traveling along the eastern coast of the Mediterranean Sea. We had just barely left Egypt, and it felt good to be in familiar territory again. Joseph walked ahead with Pinchus, a man nearly as old as my father. Despite his age, he was in good health, and it was obvious he was still quite active.

I was content to walk behind with Pinchus's wife, Zara, who was also with child, her fourth in the last nine years. Three of their children ran back and forth between us; Ziva was eight and she resembled her mother. Hadar was six. He continually teased his older sister, pretending she was about to step on a poisonous snake or spider nearly at every turn. Rachil was three, not much older than Jesus. And she matched the meaning of her name, A Little Lamb.

And then there was Hanan, Pinchus's son from a previous marriage.

Hanan's mother had died during childbirth. My heart went out to him. He was twelve and so compassionate toward his siblings.

We had traveled nearly two miles when suddenly Joseph stopped and turned around. His eyes, normally calm and full of joy, were now wary... guarded. I stopped too. He felt something. Something wasn't right.

"You need to rest?" Pinchus asked. "I think it's best if we arrive before dark."

"I have a strong feeling...a warning almost..." Joseph's eyes scanned the territory around them. We were about to enter some rocky terrain.

"You want to turn back?" Pinchus looked surprised. "We've traveled this terrain on several occasions. We will be fine. Come along." Pinchus waved us all forward.

Joseph hesitated, his eyes staring into mine. *What do you think*? I shrugged my shoulders. Perhaps we were still troubled by the news we had heard earlier back at the inn. Joseph turned to follow after Pinchus.

"Why is he so worried?" Zara asked as we continued after them.

"He senses something isn't right." I began to pray. *Father, please guide us. If we are to turn back, give us another warning.*

"No," Jesus said. Joseph was holding him just a few feet ahead of me. Jesus' head was facing me, his eyes full of certainty. "No," he said again. Jesus comprehended much but said little. His vocabulary consisted of about twenty words. And he rarely said the word no.

Joseph turned and walked back to me. "I prayed for another warning."

"I did too. Let's go back."

Joseph turned toward Pinchus. "Both Mary and I feel ill at ease about continuing on. I can't say for sure why that is, but I wish you would all join us."

Pinchus warily studied us. "You do what is best for your family, and I'll do what is best for mine. Until we meet again." He waved before guiding his family up over a small hill and out of sight.

We traveled back to the inn where, just a few hours before, we had been eating dinner. Thankfully, there was a room left for us. Feeling overwhelmed and apprehensive, we readied ourselves for bed.

"Do you think Archelaus knows about Jesus?" I asked. I glanced over at Joseph, his eyes closed not in sleep but in prayer.

"I don't know. But he rules with tyranny and cruelty like his father. That can't be good. Even if he has forgotten of his father's murder of the innocent babies in Bethlehem, what if Jesus' name is brought up again during his childhood? Perhaps we were not to leave Egypt quite yet?"

My entire being cringed at the thought of returning to Egypt. "But the angel came in a dream relaying that it was safe to leave. Wouldn't God at least warn us if we were entering a trap?"

Joseph turned toward me, his hand gently caressing my now swollen belly. "With every child we add to our family, there is more at stake. Jesus is God's Son. I don't doubt for one second that He will do what is necessary to keep him safe. But I do struggle with trusting Him to do the same for you…for this one we have yet to meet."

I laid my hand on top of his. "God is more than able to take care of us all." I said it with such surety, I surprised even myself. Joseph turned his head but not before I saw the tear on his cheek. "You don't always have to be the strong one," I whispered as I bent over and kissed his tear with my lips.

"The first time He brought us on a long journey, you were big and pregnant, but it was of His doing. This time…it is of my doing." We lay facing each other, the full moon in the window allowing us to see each other fully.

"Big and pregnant?"

"You were pretty big," Joseph laughed. He grimaced when I grabbed his side.

"They say it's not unlikely to get even bigger with the second pregnancy."

"This time I will stay silent," Joseph said. He slid out of reach before my hand could touch him.

We lay there for some time before I finally fell asleep. I awoke later in the night, surprised to see Joseph standing by the window.

"What is it?" I asked. I stood to my feet and joined him.

Joseph took my hand and pulled me close. "God sent a warning."

"Another dream?"

Joseph nodded. "We are to continue northward toward Nazareth. Since it is a part of Galilee, we should be safe there."

"But doesn't Herod's son Antipas rule Galilee?"

"He does, but he is said to have a less violent disposition."

I was elated by the news of returning to my hometown. Jesus was nearly three years old, and my father and mother had never laid eyes on him. I took in every little thing as we traveled, looking forward to the day we would finally lay eyes on my simple, rural community nestled into the hills that surrounded it.

The next morning before we left the inn, we heard the news. An entire family had been attacked the night before by bandits hiding in the rocky cliffs near Gaza. All but one had lost their lives. The only survivor—a twelve-year-old boy named Hanan.

We could have continued on toward Bethlehem, but instead we turned east. Joseph led us along a route that stayed on the east side of the Jordan River for two main reasons. First, the river contained many springs and, consequently, more villages. As I was an expectant mother once again, he wanted to make sure I had aid should I need it.

And secondly, both Galilee and Perea had the same governor, which in turn offered us additional security. The alternative route would have saved us two days, but we would have had to go through Samaria, and it was a place we hoped to avoid at all costs since the inhabitants there were hostile to Jews.

Nazareth offered a quiet and solitary place for us to raise Jesus and the children God chose to bless us with. Its small size and lack of notoriety would help keep our family out of the eyes of anyone looking for Jesus. And yet it was also close enough to surrounding cities where we would feel like we understood what was going on around us.

Having grown up in Nazareth, I knew that it would offer us the protection we needed from the outside. And its simplicity would offer Jesus such peace during his boyhood.

Passing through many towns along the way, we then turned west and crossed back across the river when we drew near Pella. The familiarity of the terrain brought peace to my heart. As we grew near Mount Gilboa, my thoughts went back to nearly three years ago when Joseph and I had made our very first journey together, stopping there near the hot springs.

So much had changed since then. Instead of carrying Jesus inside my womb, Joseph now carried him on his back in a leather-bound carrier.

"Perhaps I could join you in that secluded pool this evening," Joseph said with irony.

I felt my face flush red, remembering back to the night I had invited him to join me in the pool. And how quickly he had declined. So much had indeed changed since then.

Joseph stopped and now looked at me, the humor I loved so much now evident in his brown eyes. "Did I embarrass you?"

I stopped too and reached for my pouch of water. "I had no idea how much restraint you exercised during that time."

"Believe me, it wasn't easy."

"What if God had asked you to remain celibate for a lifetime?"

"To not touch you for a lifetime?" Joseph stared at me. "Or what? Not have you at all?"

I nodded. "Or not have me at all."

"See… This is a topic that is off limits. I did what God required of me in that area. And now that requirement has lifted."

I laughed. "You're so weak!" I then turned, anxious to reach our stopping point for the night.

"I'm stronger than most men," Joseph called out after me, amusement evident in his voice.

He was. He was stronger than any man I knew. Strong in character. Strong in self-control. Strong in courage. Strong in fortitude. Strong in loyalty. And strong in love.

As we neared Nazareth, I began pointing out familiar sights to Jesus. This would be the place where Jesus would spend his childhood. I wanted him to know everything about it. I wanted him to love it as I did. To some, Nazareth was rather small and unimportant. But to me… To me, it was home. I had been born and raised here.

As we began to climb the hills of Galilee, I grew quiet. My thoughts turned to my parents. It had been so long since I had seen them. So long since I had heard from them. I wasn't sure if my heart could endure the loss of either one of them.

"Do you think…?"

"They are fine, Mary." Joseph slowed his pace and reached for my hand. "There is no way your father would depart this world without first laying eyes on his grandson."

I smiled. Joseph always seemed to find the words to lift my spirits. I stopped walking. Joseph tugged on my hand, but when I resisted, he turned toward me. Jesus lay sleeping, his chubby little red cheek pressed against Joseph's shoulder.

"Thank you." I hoped Joseph could read the gratitude I felt—how indebted I felt to him for all he had been to me, all he had done for me. How could I ever repay him?

"You're thanking me?" Joseph pulled me near. He leaned down and nuzzled my neck. "From the time I first laid eyes on you, I knew my life would never be the same." He kissed one cheek and then the other. And then his eyes studied my lips.

"Honestly, I feel privileged you chose me. I feel honored He picked me to help you raise His Son." Joseph kissed me once. Then again. "I mean, here we were just seeking to live ordinary lives of faith when the most extraordinary events completely overwhelmed our plan." He kissed me again. "How often does that happen?"

Not very often. Generation after generation had known of God's promise to send the Messiah. One who would rescue us and be our King. How could we have known He'd choose us?

We continued to the top and then began our descent to my little town of Nazareth, situated beautifully in the valley below. One day soon, I would make the climb with Jesus to the southern side. There, I would tell him all about the exploits of Josiah and Saul. Of Ahab and Gideon. Of Deborah and Barak. The southern view represented Israel's past, and there were so many stories to be told.

Then I saw him. My father. He was standing just beyond the well where

I had gathered water for our family throughout the years. His eyes were scanning the terrain, and I realized he hadn't seen me yet. How often did he come out to watch for us?

My eyes filled with tears. He looked older, and he still walked with a wooden rod, it seemed, as one was tightly grasped in his right hand. How blessed I had been to be raised by such an affectionate man. He had been my pillar of strength. My support when I needed it most.

"Father!" I called out to him, my pace quickening now that the terrain wasn't so steep. He saw me then and hobbled toward me, joy evident on his face.

"Mary," he cried as he gathered me into his arms. He held me close. "Mary," he whispered. "You're finally home safe where you belong." He held me while I wept. Tears of sorrow. Tears of hope. Tears of gladness. So many tears.

Then he stepped back and cupped my cheeks in his hands. "Where is this boy…this Messiah I've been waiting to meet?"

I turned to find Joseph waiting just a few steps back. I beckoned him to us and then reached up and withdrew Jesus from the leather carrier. He was awake. I shifted him on my hip so my father could see him better. "I'd like you to meet our son, Jesus." Jesus reached out his hand and caressed my father's left cheek.

"Jesus the Messiah," my father said as he took him from my arms. "My Messiah," he whispered as he gathered him close.

Seven Years Later

I sat beneath my favorite sycamore tree, watching my children play, just as I used to do on this very hill not so very long ago. I could still beat every one of them in a race. I watched as Jesus lined each of them up and once again discussed the rules so they'd each play fairly. How I wished that I could join them in the race, but my present condition presented me from doing so.

I gently caressed my pregnant belly, hoping Joseph was right and this time it would be a girl. Reaching out, I gently patted Nile's head. He opened his eyes briefly before closing them again in contentment.

"Now, what do you do when you get to mother?" Jesus asked.

"We tag mother's hand," Simon squealed with delight.

"And then what happens, James?" Jesus knew well that James was the mischievous one and would be the first to try an alternative way if he thought it would help him win.

"We round the tree… Can't we just start? We all know the rules, Jesus."

Jesus knelt down and cupped little Judas's chin in his hand. "And then what, Judas?"

"Run like the wind," Judas whispered, in his sweet yet serious little voice.

"I'd rather be on James' team, Jesus. Why can't I ever be on James' team?" Joseph knew James could run the fastest of the boys.

"Joseph, it wouldn't be fair to Simon and Judas if the two fastest runners were on the same team. This is the fairest way to divide you up." Jesus stepped back and looked at his siblings. "Now, is everyone ready?"

"Yes!" they all cried in unison.

"Get ready…get set…go!"

I watched with my arms outstretched as James and Simon ran toward me, their legs extended as far as they could stretch them. James tagged me first, but Simon wasn't too far behind. This just might be the time Joseph and Simon would win. I was hopeful, but of course sad for the disappointment Judas might soon face.

James reached Judas first, and Judas took off as fast as his three-year-old legs would carry him. He was nearly to me by the time Simon tagged Joseph, but I knew it wouldn't be enough of a gain. Joseph was extremely fast.

I felt Judas tag my hand and watched as he rounded the tree. A few seconds later, Joseph tagged my hand. Rounding the tree, he picked up his pace, knowing today would be a different outcome. And it was. Joseph tagged Simon's hand just before Judas reached James.

"He reminds me of his mother," a very familiar masculine voice said from directly behind me. I looked up. Joseph's head hovered just above mine. "Inquisitive. Excitement over all the world has to offer. Sees the best in everything. And competitive."

"I'm not competitive!" I looked up at Joseph. "I'm not."

"So, competitiveness isn't what made you run so fast and beat out every boy in our small town?"

"I was faster. I can't help that."

"Ahh, but that day… That day you took my breath away. Watching you race with all those boys, the look in your eyes as you passed the finish line. It's a memory I'll never forget."

"Yes, well, that's a memory I try to forget. It most assuredly goes down as the most embarrassing day of my life."

Joseph touched my cheek. "You're blushing…still…these many years later." He laughed.

"You can't even begin to imagine how mortified I was when I took your cloak off at home." I glanced over at the boys. Jesus was discussing how to have the right attitude whether you win or lose.

"It's not about winning or losing. It's about how you treat others," he said. "Your goal should be to encourage and push yourself and others to be better instead of winning at all costs." Jesus then began to tell them the story of Cain and Abel and how unhealthy competition often takes us places that we don't want to go.

"He's amazing, isn't he?" Joseph whispered. "The knowledge and wisdom that pours out of him." Joseph shook his head in amazement. "If they just took half of what he says to heart."

Jesus finished his speech and turned toward me. "How are you feeling, Mother?"

"I'm well. A bit uncomfortable, but well."

I watched as he sauntered over to me. This beautiful ten-year-old boy. "Will you tell us a story?"

"Which story?" I asked. He knew all the stories by heart now. He often told them to his brothers.

Jesus dropped down onto his knees beside me. "How about the one of God parting the Red Sea?" He motioned for his brothers to join us. "Mother's going to tell us a story," he called.

They ran to the tree and sat down. Jesus looked around at his brothers and then up at me. "I lived in Egypt, didn't I?"

"Yes," I assured him, even though he was well aware that he had. "You lived there for nearly a year." Jesus leaned back against the tree, closing his eyes in contentment. Judas leaned against him, no longer upset about losing the race.

"The Israelites had been slaves in Egypt for over four hundred years…" I began.

I felt Joseph's strong warm hand envelop mine. And I smiled.

Bibliography

http://www.womeninthebible.net/bible-people/mary-of-nazareth/

https://opusdei.org/en/article/life-of-mary-x-flight-into-egypt/amp/

https://www.ancient-egypt-online.com/ancient-egyptian-geography.html

https://www.ancient-egypt-online.com/river-nile-facts.html

https://billygraham.org/answer/how-do-you-know-there-is-only-one-god/

https://www.thejournal.ie/readme/column-suicide-isn%E2%80%99t-wanting-to-die-it%E2%80%99s-not-being-able-to-bear-living-519398-Jul2012/

https://www.whychristmas.com/story/cominghome.shtml

https://www.whychristmas.com/story/wisemen.shtml

http://www.biblestudy.org/maps/the-journeys-of-mary-and-joseph.html

http://www.dltk-bible.com/cv/three_faithful_men-cv.htm

https://truthbook.com/jesus/illustrated-stories/the-trip-to-bethlehem-for-the-census

https://www.neverthirsty.org/bible-studies/life-of-christ-early-years-of-jesus/jesus-dedication/

https://www.biblicalarchaeology.org/daily/people-cultures-in-the-bible/people-in-the-bible/anna-in-the-bible/

https://www.maristmessenger.co.nz/2014/09/30/mary-today-mary-gives-birth-jesus/

https://goodquestionblog.com/2014/07/10/how-long-did-jesus-live-in-egypt/

http://www.wordofgodtoday.com/jesus-born-in-bethlehem/

https://bible.org/article/daily-life-time-jesus

https://www.crosswalk.com/faith/women/3-things-you-didn-t-know-about-mary-mother-of-jesus-in-the-bible.html

http://www.jesus-story-.net/nazareth_houses.htm

http://www.jesus-story.net/nazareth_food.htm

https://bible.org/seriespage/lesson-10-mary-most-blessed-women

https://www.inspirationalchristians.org/biography/mary-the-mother-of-jesus